CLUNG

CLUNG

Max Brand®

GUNSMOKE

This hardback edition 2009
by BBC Audiobooks Ltd
by arrangement with
Golden West Literary Agency

ISBN 978 1 405 68273 2

British Library Cataloguing in Publication Data available.

Printed and bound in Great Britain by
CPI Antony Rowe, Chippenham and Eastbourne

Chapter 1

The Lord having made Clung and placed him where he did, the rest followed by the inevitable law of matter-of-course. Nobody understood this, Clung least of all. The whites said he was "just a plain, no good Chink, growing up for a rope necklace;" the Chinese said he was "possessed of a devil." Clung probably thought that both parties were right. He never said so, but then Clung was not given to words. The whites would probably have lynched the boy save for two things: first, Clung confined his attentions to the Mexicans; second, everyone had a warm spot in his heart for old Li Clung, the boy's father, who ran the laundry in that Arizona town.

In the Southwest they will tell you that when a Chinaman is good he's not too good to bear watching, and when a Chinaman is bad—well, he's awful. Clung was bad. He killed men. Everybody knew his record, or at least a part of it, but for the sake of old Li they postponed the inevitable hanging. Nevertheless, if Clung had been built in a different way, or had lived in a different place—

The lot of a weakly man in the Southwest is peculiarly unfortunate. There is no place for him; people wonder why he exists. He's a public encumbrance—an eyesore. Clung was weakly. For a Chinese he was tall; among whites he was of middle height; but he was exceedingly frail. His hands were like the hands of a woman, small, transparent almost. It was a graceful thing to watch that delicate hand against the ugly red-brown of a whiskey glass. His wrist was so slenderly made that if a strong man had grasped him there the bones would have crunched together.

Obviously he was a half-breed of some sort—perhaps his mother was Spanish, though old Li would never speak of that. She must have been white; otherwise there was no accounting for the fine, pale complexion of Clung. His eyes, too, were not slanted, but wide, gentle, brown. His hair was black and as smooth as silk.

Being weakly, Clung was early forced to find something which would take the place of physical strength, because without protection of some sort he was sure to perish early. For this was the Southwest, and the border was in a continual need of taming. Clung had not far to look before he found out what he must do. He became expert in the use of weapons.

Nothing is very really mastered unless it is first at least commenced in childhood. A man must begin to learn acrobatics before he's ten. The same thing is true of language study and other things—amongst them of guns. Clung began using revolvers when he was hardly more than an infant. His father, old Li, pampered the boy; he used to show off his accomplishments to his patrons. When he was eight years old, Clung had a little twenty-two rifle. And he practiced with the weapons continually. Li paid the bills and Clung banged off countless rounds of ammunition. The cowpunchers showed him many ways of carrying a gun and how to pull it, and whirl it, and shoot with a quick turn. Of course he could never have been great with a gun if he had not had the instinct for it; anyone in the Southwest will tell you that. A man may practice all his life, but unless he has an instinct for shooting quick and sure he will never be a startling success near the border.

Those early times were golden days for Clung. The patrons teased him and talked with him; old Li adored him. Little Clung, when he was not playing with his knives or his guns, sat crossed-legged on a table near the front door of the laundry, and kept his blank brown eyes fixed on the passers-by, and smiled the faint, faint smile of the Orient. He always wore his pig-tail twisted in a funny knot on top of his head, and Li kept it tied at the end with a ribbon of black silk. When he turned his head, with one of his catlike motions, the ribbon flounced foolishly from side to side. Then the golden days ended.

Clung had grown up; he possessed his full portion of slender, erect height; the cowpunchers were beginning to ask him when he would open a laundry of his own, and Clung, in place of answering, would wave those fragile hands unmeant for work, and smile that faint smile of the Orient. Then on a day a stranger came to town and entered the laundry. He was a Mexican of much importance; he had two followers in the street on horseback. The Mexican did not know Clung. How should he? Neither did he know that after the midday meal Clung loved to sit in the sun on the little table near the door, with his legs folded cat-wise under him, and sleep, and smile into the sun while he slept. Also, Clung did not like to be roused from that after-dinner siesta. Of all of this, however, the Mexican was ignorant. He came in with the sun flashing on his silver braid, and started to ask Clung a question.

It was not answered, so he snapped Clung on the end of the nose with his riding quirt. It must have hurt exceedingly, but Clung merely opened slowly those wide, brown, gentle eyes, and his smile never altered. He looked beyond the Mexican and into a thousand years of space. It angered the Mexican to see that impassive face. He reached out to grip Clung by the shoulder and shake him into complete wakefulness. Then it happened.

Before that hand touched the Chinese shoulder a knife appeared from under the silken tunic of Clung, and the knife blade passed in and out of the palm of the Mexican's hand. There is no place on the body more sensitive than the palm of the hand. Perhaps that's why school-mistresses whip refractory children there. Strong men have been known to weep when hurt in the palm of the hand. The Mexican screamed with pain, leaped back, and drew his revolver with his uninjured hand.

There was a white man in the laundry at the moment, and he swore in court afterwards that the gun of the Mexican was out of the holster before Clung made a move. Then a gun appeared, as if conjured out of thin air, and the Mexican dropped in a heap with a bullet fairly between the eyes. His followers started shooting from the road; Clung killed them neatly and with dispatch; a bullet through the head of each.

And he remained sitting on his table by the door. The marshal found him there, smiling into the sun. The judge cautioned him, declared it self-defense, and dismissed the case.

Chapter 2

In the Southwest any man can be excused for one shooting match, provided that the other party is Mexican; but a second affair causes people to frown, and a third is almost sure to bring down the heavy hand of the law. Now, within a week Clung killed his fourth man; within ten days he had killed his fifth.

Always he was apprehended sitting cross-legged on the little table at the door of the laundry, drowsing after dinner; always his excuses were allowable; always the Mexicans were the aggressors. They were avengers come to wipe out the blood-debt. They waylaid Clung and fell upon him at weird times and in strange places, and they were killed suddenly, neatly, with bullets through the head.

This caused his marksmanship to be more admired than ever, but the cowpunchers ceased to linger at the table of Clung and he was no longer asked to show his skill with the guns, shooting at fantastic targets. This caused Clung to wonder. Finally he went to Li with one of his rare questions, but Li merely raised his calloused hands to the witnessing gods and shook his head.

The silent feud went on. The Mexicans had marked Clung, and now and again they came in parties or one at a time, heated with mescal and eager to win a great name. They departed again the worse for wear, and Clung still sat cross-legged on the little table near the laundry door. This continued; men began to refer to Clung as a bad 'un.

In the end it was sure to result in tragedy to someone more important than a Mexican, but the fatal day delayed. Li grew older, more withered, more like a yellow mask of grinning comedy; Clung continued to bask every day in the sun.

And so it came to a spring day when the air was cool and a little crisp and gently fanned the cheek of Clung where he sat on the table. He raised his head and saw a triangle of wild geese winging north; their honking dropped to him, now a single cry, now a faintly jangled chorus, wind-blown; the smile went out on the lips of Clung.

He uncurled his slender legs and asked money of Li, and received it, for the old Chinese had forgotten how to refuse. So Clung went out and returned with a little Victrola. It played with a wheeze and a rattle, but nevertheless it kept a rhythm. Clung brought in an Indian girl and in the evenings he learned to dance.

He practiced diligently, silently, for hours and hours, un-

5

til the girl would drop to a chair, exhausted. Having mastered the steps, he wound his pig-tail in the most obscure of knots and put on store clothes—the clothes of the whites—and rode many miles to a country dance.

Now, as anyone from the Southwest will tell you, this was very rashly done. Men were loth to touch Clung, however. They would as soon have put hands on a rattler coiled to strike.

It seemed that tragedy would be averted again from the path of Clung and the day of reckoning postponed, for it chanced that there was in the crowd a marshal exceedingly wise in the ways of the border. He came to Clung and spoke softly—with his hand on the butt of his gun. He explained that Chinese were not welcome at dances of whites. The dreamy smile returned to the lips of Clung. He tried to shove his hands into the alternate sleeves, but was prevented by the unaccustomed cuffs of the white man.

He stared about the hall until he saw a girl laughing at him. She had pale yellow hair and the light burned like a fire in it, and her throat was white, and the bosom that curved out below it was as keen as snow. Clung turned very pale; he was whiter than the whitest man in that room. He managed to wriggle his fingers into the alternate cuffs; he bowed to the marshal, and turned on his heel.

According to all rules of man and the unwritten laws of the Southwest, the thing should have ended there, but where the laws of the Southwest leave off, John Barleycorn often begins. He stepped in here in the person of Josiah Boyce.

Now, Josiah wore guns because everyone else wore them, but he had never been known to use them on even a rabbit. He probably wouldn't have known what to do with them if they had been naked and loaded in his hands. Ordinarily Josiah was a sleepy fellow who sat in corners twisting his long moustaches and looking out upon the world from beneath shaggy brows with moist, pathetic eyes. But when he had a few drinks of whiskey under his belt Josiah became a noisy nuisance. He was always either extremely confidential, going about and assuring everyone that they knew him and that he was their friend; or else he waxed boisterous and insisted on telling greybearded jests. He was in his boisterous mood this night. Unfortunately he forgot for a single second about the record of Clung. The moment the marshal turned his back, Josiah rushed up, clapped his hand on the shoulder of Clung, and whirled him around as if he were a top. He started to bellow out that the damned Chink ought to be whipped, and that if no one else would do it, he'd take the job on his own hands.

Everyone laughed, except the marshal, who started on the run. Clung was smiling, and the marshal had seen that smile before. What Clung really saw was not Josiah at all, but the convulsed mirth of the girl with the yellow hair. The laughter, apparently, thrilled Josiah with joy. He saw himself at last in the role of a successful entertainer, and grasped Clung by his pig-tail, preparatory to dragging him out of the hall.

The marshal was only a step away when this happened—only a step away—one step too late. He arrived just in time to receive the toppling body of what had been Josiah Boyce in his arms. Clung vanished through the door.

They started a half-hearted pursuit, but Clung rode one of the best horses in Arizona and his weight was so light that the marshal knew he had no chance of wearing down the fugitive. He called off the ride and went back to town to have Clung outlawed. In the meantime Clung cut back by a sharp detour and went to the house of his father.

Li sat on a cushion on the floor with a taper-light rising high on either side of him. Across his knees a large volume was opened; he wore on his head a little black silk cap with a crimson tassel. Clung closed the door softly and stood very conscious of his store clothes—waiting.

When Li finally looked up, it was with a slow glance, starting at the boots of Clung, and the further the glance traveled up the person of Clung, the paler Li became until he looked like parchment which has first been yellowed with age and then bleached in the sun. Then he got up without a word and went to a little safe at the side of the room. He opened it and took out a bag of money—a canvas bag plumply filled.

"It is all I have, my son," said Li. "Go!"

Clung took it in his hand, weighed it, and slipped it into his pocket. He seemed very excited and his nostrils were quivering, so that he was not a pleasant sight to see.

"I have killed a white man," he said.

"It is true," nodded Li.

They talked much more perfect English than the whites around them, and Li, for some reason, would never talk their native tongue with his son.

"Father," said Clung, "I am not well about the stomach."

The old Chinese ran to him swiftly, making a little sound of dole, a sort of guttural whine.

"No," said Clung, "they have not hurt me, except here."

And he pressed both slender hands against his breast.

He said: "I have seen a white woman and I am hungry with a hunger that food will not fill up; and I am weak and sick here."

Old Li cried out in Chinese, a harsh wail.

"Mix herbs for me," said Clung rapidly. "Make me strong before I leave, for I have far to go. They will never leave my trail."

"Oh, my son," moaned Li, "there is no drink of herbs that will help you. No water will put out the fire of woman; it will burn you to ashes; it will make you hollow."

"You," said Clung in his soft voice, "are not like me. No woman could make you burn or make you hollow. Why am I different?"

"Your mother was white," said Li.

"I am neither white nor yellow," said Clung. "Father, I am

damned two ways. I go."

He stood stiff against the door, one hand raised high over his head; old Li stiffened in the same manner. Then Clung turned and caught the knob of the door. He swung it open and then closed it again. He turned on Li.

"Your eyes have told me one thing and your tongue another," he said. "Which lie shall I hold to, father?"

Now one does not need to live in the Southwest to know that the last crime for a Chinese is to turn against his father. Li grew green with horror; he could not speak.

"It is true," said Clung, smiling his own faint smile. "You have lied to me. Now tell me the truth."

Chapter 3

"You have doubted your father twice," said Li. "For each doubt you shall be tortured a hundred years hereafter."

"And for the third doubt," said Clung, "I shall be tortured terribly for a thousand years. I doubt you again. Why am I different?"

"It was the will of God that made you unlike your father. You are all your mother."

"It is true," said Clung. "You have been good to me, but if I were like you, father, I would take this knife, so! and cut my throat wide and die. As it is, I take it, so—and take you by the throat, so!—and hold this knife at your breast, so!—and say: 'The truth—tell me the truth!' "

Old Li was a brave man, as many a riotous cowpuncher had learned in his time, but now a tremor like the palsy of old age struck him. He stared fascinated up at the changed face of Clung.

"A ghost!" he whispered.

"Of whom?"

"Of your father."

The knife glimmered, twisting slowly in the hands of Clung.

"Devil," he said, "who was my father?"

"A white man—an American," said Li, "and your mother white also."

"But," said Li softly, "you are my son! See! the knife trembles in your hand—you are shaking with hunger to strike—but you cannot—you are my son."

"I," said Clung slowly, "am white?"

He stepped back; he uncoiled his pig-tail with a single movement, held the hair taut, and severed the sinuous, snaky length with a single slash of the knife. The black hair, springing back, fell wildly about his face.

"Why?" said Clung.

"A man wronged me," said Li. "He was not young; his wife could have no more children. I stole the baby. I made him my son."

"Who?" said Clung.

"He is dead; she is dead."

"And I am living," said Clung.

"As my son. Will the white men believe you are white? Will the yellow men believe you are yellow? No, you are nothing, but my son. In your mind you may know you are white; in your heart you know you are my son. It is done; it is perfect."

"You are not afraid?" asked Clung.

"Shall a father fear his son?"

"Yellow devil!"

"True. And there is a devil in my son; my people have seen it."

Clung took out the canvas bag of money and dropped it clinking on the floor.

"So," said Li, nodding. "But you will come back."

"Never."

"No man can live alone. It is written."

"It shall be unwritten again."

"The white women," said Li. "The hunger, my son."

"Damn you!" whispered Clung.

But he dropped to his knees; he folded his hands on his breast.

"I go," he said. "Give me the blessing of one who departs."

The calloused, yellowed hands touched the black, rough-shorn head, and Li uttered a sing-song incantation in the language of his fathers. Afterwards Clung rose and spurred out of the town of Mortimer, but because of the devil that was in him, he chose a way through the very heart of the place where men could not choose but see him pass. A crackle of firing rose on either side of him, and Clung fired four times in return. Spenser and Wilson fell with bullets in their legs; Jefferson was hit in the shoulder and spun like a top before he dropped; Marshal Clauson was not touched, but his best horse was shot under him. The tall dapple-grey which Clung rode flickered out into the night and the men of Mortimer rose in crowds and formed six different posses and combed the desert in every direction. For four days they stuck by the trail.

Nevertheless, they did not catch Clung. They sighted him several times sliding over the hills or down some hollow as swiftly as a cloud shadow on a windy March day, and as soundlessly. They tried to chase him in a circle, as men chase wild horses; Clung broke through that circle and left Sandy Matthews and young Glover badly shot up behind him. That put heart in the men of Mortimer, because it proved conclusively that Clung was not shooting to kill. If he had been —well, the men of Mortimer remembered sundry Mexicans shot neatly through the head. So they rode recklessly on the trail of Clung, but at the end of four days he had disappeared hopelessly into the desert; the purple hills which shroud men and their doings had swallowed him up. The posses went back to Mortimer and a fat price was placed on the head of Clung.

As for Clung, he was sorry when the posses went back. It had been good fun—much better than any game of tag; he even followed the posses to the outskirts of Clauson in the late afternoon of the fourth day, and he sat his horse on the brow of a hill and watched the lights grow out in the dusk of the evening, street by street, striping the broad heart of the night. Then he turned his horse about and rode towards the northern hills.

All was not well with Clung. He was thinking of those days when he sat cross-legged on the little table at the door of the laundry, with his eyes closed, smiling into the heat of the sun. Also, he thought of old Li, sitting with the tall taper on either side and the big volume spread across his knees; he thought, last of all, about the yellow-haired girl who had laughed at him. The hollowness returned to the heart of Clung.

He remembered now that he was white—he remembered it every time the edges of the rough-shorn hair flipped in the wind across his face; but what good was there in being white if no one would believe it? He hardly believed it himself, and hardly prized it, as yet, for the old precepts of Li swept through his brain: "The white man is a fool before whom one listens twice and speaks once." The chief new sense which came to Clung was one of freedom, of a power and a will to roam at ease through all the desert and the hills. He was an American; he felt a sense of ownership in three million square miles; the first spark of patriotism smouldered in him, the first sense of nationality.

As yet, it worked obscurely. He had lived with his thoughts harking back to the lives of his ancestors. Now those yellow ancestors were gone, but still his thoughts harked back. Newness overwhelmed him; his blood ran faster; the air drew keenly down in his lungs; there was a tang to life; there was a birth of pride of race.

It was this same thing that caused his loneliness, perhaps, for he was like a mariner who returns from a long voyage and meets all his old friends, and knows them, but they will not recognize him. On the very day that he became a white man, the whites commenced to hunt him.

He knew perfectly well the outcome of the chase. They had missed him today; they would miss him the next time and the next that they hunted him, but in the end he would be taken; his destiny was no less certain through being postponed. There is no outlaw who has not known, and there is none who has not thrown away, the thought of tomorrow and lost himself in today. The law of compensation worked in Clung; freedom was doubly sweet because it would not last forever.

He had led a strange, shut-in existence. Now he saw the world, since he was in danger of being lost from it, and behold! it was fair to see, and filled, now, with his white brothers. At this point in his reflections a gun banged close by and a bullet whizzed by his head; a group of the posse, returning late, had sighted him through the dusk. He raised his gun, poised it—and then spurred the grey off through the dark. At that moment he had no further taste for blood, but he carried away at that galloping pace the certainty that his white brothers who filled the world would be in no hurry to claim their relationship with him.

Chapter 4

There followed a month of comparative inactivity for Clung. On several occasions he descended upon stores and purchased what he needed in the way of supplies, but the most picturesque incident recorded of him during that period was the ride into San Marco, where he held up a barber's shop—backed the customers into one end of the room, and then took his seat, guns in hand, and forced the barber to trim his wild, black hair. He had the image of the barber in the glass before him and the latter could not make a suspicious move without being seen. When his hair was cut Clung ordered one of the men to drop a five dollar goldpiece in the hand of the barber, and before he left, he announced that if the stranger attempted to collect that five again he would have to reckon with Clung later on. The five was never collected; and the heart of the barber was softened towards Clung.

Rumor had not dealt too gently with the fugitive in the meantime. Crimes performed hundreds of miles away from Clung were saddled upon his luckless shoulders, and all men believed the tales. They could hardly accumulate fast enough; men taxed their inventions to create appropriate crimes for Clung. He was the only Chinese desperado known to Arizona, and much was expected of him. In the episode of the barber's shop, for instance, rumor made him kill everyone in the place before leaving, winding up his pleasant little party by cutting the throat of the barber with his own razor.

Meanwhile, Clung rode by night and slept during the day. He missed the long sun baths at the door of the laundry and moreover this continual life by night was beginning to dim his tan; once when he saw himself in the mirror behind a bar he hardly recognized the rapidly changing color of his face. He did not mind the loneliness—all his life he had had it, and it might be said that he was educated for the part of a lone rider of the mountain-desert. Only one vision returned to disturb him both by day and by night, and this was the picture of the girl with the pale yellow hair, laughing sometimes, sometimes merely smiling; but always with an air of mockery as if she had something to confide in him if he could only reach her and listen.

It was because of this troubling vision, perhaps, that he started riding one day before the dusk had set in. His goal was nameless; activity was his only end, until, in the slant light of the late sun, he caught a flash of color. He swung the grey to the left and raced for two miles up a gulley; then he dismounted and crept to the top of the ridge and sheltered himself behind a bush.

In due time the color reappeared—bright blue, with a splash of yellow, developing into a girl riding at a dog-trot. The blue was the color of her waist, and the yellow was the straw of her hat. She passed close, but not close enough for Clung to see her face. He followed her with his eyes until she had passed out of view around a winding of the trail; the moment the sun winked for the last time on the bright yellow of her hat, something went out in Clung. It was as if a light had been shining in him, and being puffed out, he was suddenly left all dark and cold inside.

He went back to the gulley, swung into the saddle, and pursued the blue and yellow vision, keeping always just out of her vision, lurking, and trailing her like a dangerous shadow until she came to the largest ranch-house that Clung had ever seen. It was rather more like some fine old Colonial house in the south, and around it, on every side, stretched a deep verandah, with a roof supported by white pillars. There were evidently artesian wells near the house, for green things grew around it—a stretch of lawn—a hedge of some unfamiliar plant—a number of spreading palms whose fringed limbs brushed together, like whispers in the wind of the evening.

The barn behind the house was almost as large as the residence itself, and up to this the girl rode, dismounted, tossed the reins to a man who came from the barn-door, and ran into the house carrying a small parcel. All this Clung witnessed from behind the brow of a hill, squinting his eyes to pierce the distance and it seemed to him that all the brightness and the happiness in the world was bounded there by the four walls. Truly, he was marvelously lonely.

He left his horse again, waited until the darkness formed a sufficient screen, and then approached the house, soft as one of those oncoming shadows of the night. It was completely dark, now, and he sat comfortably on the moist, cool sod under a palm, only a few yards from the front of the verandah.

A servant appeared—a Chinese—and Clung smiled to himself, tilting back his head with half-closed eyes; the yellow race were servants in his land—but he was one of the white brothers. There is no warmth like that of self-content. It stole over Clung now like a man from the Arctic warming himself before a pleasant fire and caressing the objects of comfort with his eyes. The servant lighted a row of square-framed Japanese lanterns, at once the verandah grew bright with the soft flames. Now the Chinese turned, his pig-tail flopping awkwardly, and the door clicked shut after him.

The doors opened again almost at once, held wide by a little old man in black clothes with a white vest, crossed by a golden chain. He was stooped from work at a desk, and age had bared his head as religion bares the head of a monk. Against the redness of that bald head the circle of silver hair made pleasant contrast. As he held the doors he was smiling and speaking back towards the hall within, which lay just out of range of Clung's vision. Next came an invalid chair wheeled by the girl he had seen riding. Her clothes were now filmy white, to be sure, and until this moment he had never seen her face; nevertheless, he knew that it was she. He closed his eyes. He felt that he could tell her presence as one tells the species of a flower in the night—by its peculiar fragrance.

Clung had the Oriental love of perfumes. He could construct the history of his life out of the smells he had known. The peculiar, steamy aroma of the ironing room in the laundry, to be sure, was the background out of which all else grew, but against that background other things were trebly precious. Old Li had some rare silks from China and there hung about them a faint lilac fragrance which had clothed Clung's boyhood as with an atmosphere of poesy. Then there was the garden of Marshal Clauson. Flowers were to Clung what wine is to others. He had loved to walk slowly past the garden of the marshal in the night, slowly, inch by inch, breathing deeply—his head back and his eyes half closed—distinguishing the various scents and naming each unseen flower in the dark. He thought of this now when the girl came out on the verandah, wheeling the invalid. He hardly knew whether she were beautiful or ugly, young or old; he merely wished suddenly to be close enough to have the wind blow a fragrance from her to him. He sat there on his heels in a sort of happy expectation until this thing should be.

It was a rather sad emotion, also. It reminded him of certain paintings of flowers upon silk—Chinese work which old Li also owned and brought forth on state occasions.

Clung had loved those paintings but they always made him sad. There were other flowers, to be sure, which he could have and enjoy, but these peculiar, beautiful ones which the artist had painted, they must have been dust a thousand years before. It was the same with the girl. She entered his life with the scents of the flowers of other years; she was apart from him, unpossessed, unpossessable—another age and another world. He wondered that the two men did not sit before her as he would have done—with his head tilting back and his eyes half closed, drinking in her presence. This thought made him lower his head with a frown and look more closely upon the two fortunate ones who sat so close to her—see! they could reach out their hands and touch her, if they wished!

Chapter 5

This rapturous possibility, strangely enough, left them quite unmoved. They were as impassive as old Li discussing with a customer the prospects of collecting an old bill. Age in the one and sickness in the other doubtless explained it. The old man had tilted back in his chair and lighted a cigar; now he was turning the cigar slowly in his lips with one hand and insulting the night with drifting clouds of stench. They reached Clung and made him curl his upper lip in that smile of which Marshal Clauson so strongly disapproved. Contempt unutterable filled the soul of Clung, and hatred for one who could so violate the sweetness of the night air. He turned his disgusted stare on the invalid, prepared to be displeased. His fullest expectations were surpassed.

The man was large—a gross and heavy largeness. His shoulders quite filled the chair from side to side. Even in the distance Clung could accurately measure the size of the man's hand on the cane arm of the chair—it was fearfully wasted—it had strength left only to meet the grip of death—but still it was appallingly vast; the knuckles thrust out as if they would break the skin. Such a hand, filled out with muscle, could have crushed the bones in the fingers of Clung. Indeed, as he stared he felt a pain there running up to his elbow. Disease had made the sufferer ugly. His eyes were sunken, his neck was a gruesome thing of cords and sinews, and about those mighty, wasted shoulders the faint wind shook the clothes.

It was at once apparent that the fellow had not even the strength to raise himself and sit up in the chair, but what energy remained to him he consumed in endless shifting about. No position pleased him long. He kept shrugging his shoulders, moving his feet, clasping and unclasping his hands, twisting his head suddenly. His lips were never still. Now he attempted to whistle, now he scowled, now he talked—the complaining tone drifted across to Clung.

Now, since it was apparent to all eyes that the man was to die, why did he not bear fate with inscrutable countenance, smiling most when pain wrung his vitals? Clung remembered when a devil entered the body of his uncle Chu Wee, and sat in Chu's stomach. It took Chu Wee six months to die, but all the time he sat impassive, smiling, amiable; when he was well he had been a snarling demon. Truly the way of the yellow man in meeting death was much more beautiful than the way of the white. Clung was very glad of his double inheritance; he would take the best from the yellow and the best from the white.

The old man, on one side of the invalid, and the girl on the other, were very patient. She, in especial, continually rose to shift the pillows behind his shoulders and rearrange the robe which covered his enormous, lanky legs. The sick man coughed violently, and made a furious gesture towards the old man, who at once threw away his cigar, but he did it with an ill-grace which Clung could very easily see. He caught their voices now. The invalid had stretched out a hand to the other man.

"Father," he said, "I'm a terrible weakling—but that whiff of smoke just then—it nearly strangled me!"

"Beast," thought Clung, "why did he not strangle and say nothing?"

"H-m-m," said the other, "it's all right, Will. I'm—I'm really through smoking, for a while."

"And you, my dear!" said the sick man, turning to the girl.

She reached out with a smile, and took his hand between both of hers. At that the world reeled before the eyes of

Clung. It was plain; it was written clear; she was the man's woman!

"You ought to be out in the world of action and pleasant things," said the man. His voice was bass, but sickness had raised it into a sort of nasal key. "But I keep you down here in my little hell, burdening you with my own small misery. Good heavens, Winifred, sometimes I hate myself. I wish to God I could die now and get the thing over with."

"My dear!" she cried. So beautiful a thing must have such a voice. It was not high, and yet its quality was light, and there was a vibrant quality about it—a tone that pierced like the muted G-string of a violin. Now the man laughed, harshly and briefly.

"But sometimes I'm sure," he said, "that you would have never told me you loved me if I had not been so sick."

"Will," said the old man, "sometimes you're just a plain damned fool! Excuse me, Winifred; I'm going inside."

He got up and stamped into the house. It was all very disgusting to Clung. He thought of the girl as of a rare blossom which grows out of a foul soil.

"I wouldn't say it like that," murmured the girl, "but you *are* foolish to think I don't love you, dear."

"I don't doubt it," said the sick man, "but you never showed much liking for me while I was on my feet. When I got down and out you discovered—well, Winifred, to put it frankly, you discovered a place where you could be of service, and you took the place."

"Hush!" she said, and laid a white finger across his lips. The man kissed that finger and then rolled up his eyes to her with a ghastly smile. Clung shuddered; it was as if she had touched flesh white with leprosy; it was as if he had stood idly by and watched a holy thing polluted, and now his lithe, slender fingers coiled about the hilt of his knife. Even at that distance he could have thrown it accurately. He could have struck the colorless gash of the man's mouth; better still, he could have buried the blade in the hollow of the gaunt throat. She spoke again, and lost in the pleasure of her voice his nerveless fingers uncoiled and fell away.

"Surely I have proved how dear you are to me, Will?"

"Don't think I complain," he said. "I thank God that I can have even the sight of you for a moment. I know I'm going to die; I know I'm never going to live to make you my wife. Die! and at my age; with all the world before me. I feel—oh, God!—sometimes I feel as if I were already buried alive— and everything beautiful fills me with horror because I have to give it up—Winifred—even you!"

The wan, bony, shaking hands twitched up and covered his face; he wept loudly, catching his breath between sobs with a groan. Every sound cut Clung to the heart with horror and rage; he whipped out the knife and poised it—but the girl had leaned close and gathered the man close to her, pillow- ing his face against her shoulder and her breast. Her head was raised, and Clung saw her smile of ineffable pity and tenderness. It shone out to him like a light that pierced him to the soul and withered the strength from his nervous arm. Once more the knife dropped idly to the ground. It was then that Clung knew he must be near her—even if she were the defiled thing of another man. Then it came to him as plainly as if a door had opened and he had seen another room: the man was sick, but chiefly sick in his mind. He was sure of his death, and therefore he was sure to die.

Clung went back to his horse and rode straight for the house, the hoofs clattering loudly on the beaten path. He had pulled to a halt and whipped from the saddle to the ground. There he stood with his hat off, staring blankly at the couple on the porch; the girl rose and shaded her eyes to peer into the dark and make out his form.

He said: "I am riding north; it is night. May I sleep here?"

He spoke slowly, as always, with a little pause between his sentences. It gave the effect of a man of much culture, who chose his words and was proud of his choice, and indeed, to Clung, words were not light things. They were not unlike arrows loosed from the string, as he remembered from one of his few books—they could not be recalled.

The sick man scowled at him, his upper lip lifting loosely; it was very ugly. But the girl smiled and beckoned towards the door.

"You are very welcome," she said.

"I thank you," said Clung, and led his horse around the house towards the barn.

Chapter 6

After he had put up his horse he entered the house by the back door which opened on the kitchen. There were two Chinese servants there, working at the cleaning of dishes and the pans. They hushed their shrill chatter at his coming and he stood a moment staring idly at them, enjoying the silence with which the yellow man acknowledges the presence of the white, a silence crammed with meanings, all of which Clung knew. Then he went on and passed an open door beyond which sat the old man in an air blue with smoke, reading. There were around him, lining the walls, more books than Clung had dreamed were in the world. The old man glanced up at him over his spectacles, wrinkling his forehead in a quizzical frown. Clung stood in the doorway, straight and slim, and hat in hand.

"I am John Ring," he said in his sombre way. "The lady on the verandah said I might stay in this house till the morning."

The other opened his lips to speak, but Clung had bowed

like an automaton and gone on towards the front of the house.

He passed across floors as smooth as glass and glimmering under the lights; he passed through rooms wide and lofty where one might breathe more freely than in most rooms. He sensed a pleasant order as of a place where many served and few were masters. The air of this place was choice as incense in the nostrils of Clung. He began to wish that he were clothed as he had once seen a traveling man who passed through Mortimer—in white trousers, sharply pressed, graceful, cool, always hanging straight; and in a thin white shirt with a white collar and a necktie of bright colors pinned down with a golden pin. In the midst of these wishes he came to the front verandah, opened the door noiselessly, and stood beside the couple.

They sat silent, the man moving ceaselessly, the woman staring out into the night, and Clung imagined himself sitting once more under the shadow of that tall, dark palm, watching another self step boldly out on the porch, boldly into the presence of the woman, into her fragrance, stealing the breath of it from the man who was its rightful owner. He was wronging the man; therefore he hated him.

It was the girl who looked up first and saw him. He was conscious of her eyes, shocking against his glance—a perceptible thing like a stone dropped into an unplumbed depth of water.

"My name," said Clung, "is John Ring."

"I am Winifred Sampson," answered the girl, "and this is William Kirk."

In China one bows to acknowledge an introduction; on Fifth Avenue, also, one bows in the same way, though not quite so low and not so gracefully. The girl stared at Clung.

"Will you sit down?" she asked.

The chair was the one which the old man had sat in; it faced the girl, but it was near the horror—the sick man.

"I have ridden all day," said Clung. "I like to stand."

So saying, he stepped back just a trifle towards the wall of the house so that all the breeze that blew passed across the girl and then to him. He caught the fragrance then—nothing he could name, but a fact which he would be able to recognize thereafter. The other two had forgotten him, and he was glad, for as the silence deepened his mind, his will began to reach out past the invalid chair, and towards the girl. He looked fixedly at her; she glanced up; he stared blankly off into the night. It was nothing, an accident, perhaps, but to Clung a proof of power. The sick man kept shifting and muttering.

At length he cried out, throwing his shaking hands before him: "Winifred, why can't I sleep? Can't I even sleep, and forget?"

"I," said Clung, "can make you sleep."

For he had made up his mind that he would be the shield between her and the violation of the sick man's breath, his touch. It was ugly work, but it was for her. Unquestionably it was the first piece of self-sacrifice in the life of Clung. The others had turned to him.

"I was taught many things by a Chinese doctor," he explained. "I can make a drink which will do you no harm and give you sleep."

"Whiskey?" snarled Kirk.

"Hush," said the girl, "I almost think he can. Will you try, Mr. Ring?"

Clung bowed and turned back into the house. He went out through the kitchen door and ran swiftly past the barn and to a clump of shrubbery—sage. The dark could not misguide him. He gathered a few leaves of several kinds and then hurried back to the kitchen, where he ordered the servants to prepare a pot of weak tea. While they made the tea he baked the leaves of his gathering in the oven—baked them thoroughly dry. They gave off a pleasant aroma like the desert at midday.

When the pot of tea was brought he dropped the dried leaves into the water. It changed the fragrance at once and blended with the savour a light, keen scent of spicery. He carried the tea out to the verandah, poured out a cup, and held it for Kirk. He took it in a hand that trembled so much that he threatened to spill every drop of it, and the girl would have taken it from his hand, had not Clung forestalled her. He held the cup to the colorless mouth; the purple shaddowed eyes rolled curiously up to him and held upon his inscrutable face like the eyes of a dog turning up to the master who feeds it. It was disgusting, this presence of ugly death, but Clung discovered, with deep wonder, that he no longer hated this man. The moment he performed a service for him the sting of the horror of the sickness was gone. Undoubtedly only the mind of the man was sick and was wasting the body. If he could cure that then the mighty frame would fill out with strength again.

"It seems to me," complained the invalid, "that that's just tea—tea with a funny taste to it. I don't like it—much."

"It is only tea," said Clung, "made from strange herbs which do not grow in this country. They were gathered in China many centuries ago. The Chinese doctor I know has a little box of them, and he gave me some—just a few sprays of dried leaves and a few pinches of powder."

"What effect does it have?" asked Kirk curiously.

"You will see in a minute. You have not slept well for a long time?"

"Years—yes, every day is a year. There's an ache of weariness that goes from my eyes to the back of my neck."

Clung made the supreme sacrifice; he touched the abomination, the unclean thing. He laid one hand on the forehead of Kirk; he placed the other at the base of the man's neck.

"From here to here?" he asked.

"Yes," sighed the other, "keep your hands there. They are

cool; the pain seems to go."

"It is the drink—the herbs," said Clung calmly. "With this drink, which seems so mild, I have seen the old Chinese stop the death struggle and bring men back to life."

"By the Lord, I almost believe you!"

"You will find it is true. You are not going to die. You have been fighting the sickness. You do not have to fight it any longer. It is not necessary. The herbs will fight it for you. Give up all care about it."

"There is a coolness like ether flowing out of your hands," said the other faintly. "My whole body seems to grow light."

"It is because the herbs are taking effect. They are undoing the knots in your brain which have come there from your struggles to live. You need struggle no more. Relax. Let your muscles grow limp. You can rest; the herbs will fight the disease."

"Rest!" whispered the sick man. "Rest!"

It was like the poet's invocation to the muse.

"It is the effect of the drink," said Clung. "It begins to loosen all the fibres that ache; it is the coming of sleep. See, you can hardly keep your eyes open. You will sleep long. You will be watched and cared for while you sleep; there will be nothing to fear; the herb is killing the disease. When you wake you will be better—much stronger."

"Sleep!" murmured Kirk, and his eyes fluttered to a close. The girl reached out her hands with a sudden, impulsive gesture of fostering, but Clung raised a lean, transparent hand and warned her away, studying the changes on the face of the sleeper, the gradually completing relaxation of his features.

"Now," said Clung, "you may call the servants from the kitchen and carry him to his bed. He will not waken. I would carry him, but—" he made a gesture of apology—"I am not strong!"

Chapter 7

The servants came, at her call from the doorway, and with them came her father. She explained briefly to him the miracle which had happened, and he, swearing softly in pleased astonishment, followed the little procession up the stairs—first Winifred, carrying a light, then the servants, carrying Kirk in the invalid chair—then old Sampson, and last Clung. When they had the sick man in his room, at Clung's directions they removed only his slippers and loosened his shirt at the throat; then they covered him lightly and left him—all except Clung and the girl.

"I will watch him," said Clung, "and you must go and sleep."

"I am not tired," she answered.

"There are shadows under your eyes," said Clung coldly, "as if they had been painted there with purple ink—on silk. There is not much color on your lips; your face is very pale; you must sleep—rest."

She was whispering, for fear of waking Kirk, but Clung spoke aloud, simply lowering his tone until it was even less audible than her whisper.

"If I'm as ghostly as that, I *must* sleep," she smiled, "and you don't mind watching him by yourself? You are very good to him!"

"It is all for you," said Clung frankly.

She frowned at that.

"You are this man's woman," said Clung, "but you are beautiful, and therefore you belong to all men, and to me. If a man wants a garden for himself he must make it ugly;

but if his garden is beautiful the other men will climb the wall and make it their own by looking at it. And if they see a rose on a slender stalk, wounded, and drooping, sometimes men will slip over the wall and bind up the rose in the night, and slip away again."

"It's pleasant to hear you talk," she said, "and different! I suppose you have really stolen in the night to take care of a flower like that?"

"Oh, many times," said Clung.

The moonlight fell through the open window, leaving all the corner where the bed stood dark, but the rest of the room was flooded with silver radiance and this fell across the face of the girl. And looking to Clung, she saw him standing with head tilted back, his eyes half closed, smiling faintly. She had seen musicians in that attitude listening to a fine symphony, and she knew that she was like music to him. It filled her with strange fear.

"Then I may go?" she said.

"Yes."

But when she reached the door the sick man stirred on his bed and moaned. She ran back and leaned over him; at once the faint struggling ceased; something like a smile changed his lips; he slept perfectly and deeply again.

"You see?" she said, turning to Clung with something of triumph and something of despair, "he will waken if I leave him! Sometimes I almost wish—"

But she stopped short. The look of quiet meditation had been supplanted on his face by such a cold vindictiveness that a thrill of terror went through her.

"I will take the invalid chair," she said suspiciously, "and sit here beside him."

"It is well," said Clung. "I will watch you both. You also shall sleep."

"No; I never sleep while I'm watching him."

He took a straight-backed chair and sat there erect. The

moonlight struck the back of his head and she could only guess at the hollows of the lean face; the wide eyes were pools of shadows sometimes vaguely lighted when his head moved. She gained an impression that although he was not old he had lived much. He seemed to have lived whole centuries, and had gained, perhaps, uncanny knowledge out of the very length of his life—not a length of years.

"Tonight," he said, "you shall sleep."

Out of those shadowy pools which were his eyes she felt the influence come. She struggled against it at first and smiled to herself; it was as if this queer fellow were trying to hypnotize her. But why should she struggle against sleep? There was no danger—no harm in it, surely, and she was very weary. She yawned; her head nodded; her last vague impression was that John Ring was rising slowly from his chair, coming towards her with something like a smile. Then she slept.

When she woke yellow sunlight was there in place of the silver shaft of moon, and the new light fell on John Ring just as it had struck him the night before. She turned her head, and saw that Kirk still slept. His face was less pinched and drawn, and in the cheeks was a hint of natural color. She herself was marvelously refreshed.

The struggle to save a life was over, and with the burden lifted she felt raised herself in strength and lightness. She smiled across to John Ring, the bringer of this deep content, but he was as impassive as a statue of Buddha. She wondered, then, why she should make that strange comparison. The all-night vigil seemed to have affected him not in the least, and he sat with his head back, his eyes half closed. He must have sat like that for hours like the critic drinking in strains of marvelously beautiful music.

It made her abash her eyes, and then she saw that the hands which had lain loosely clasped in her lap now held a yellow flower, and scattered about the chair there were other blossoms. She raised her hands to her hair—it was crowned with a coronal of bloom. The fragrance of it came to her now. She rose suddenly from her chair, and the flowers fell in a flashing shower to the floor about her.

At that Clung started from his dream and threw out his hands, as though to catch the blossoms. However, his eyes went back to her almost at once. She had flushed and a pleasant warmth filled up her eyes with friendliness.

"What a strange fellow you are, John Ring," she said.

"Hush!" said Clung, and he pointed to the sleeper.

"It was a beautiful picture," said Clung, "even if it lasted only one night, for you."

"For me?" she answered, whispering.

"For you," said Clung, "as for me, I never forget."

She knew a thousand men who might have said some such trifling thing, but the solemnity of this stranger stopped the smile even as it began on her lips. He did not seem to say it to flatter her. He was announcing an impersonal truth. She had happened to make part of a charming picture which John Ring arranged; that was all. Now that the morning had come she was no more to him than a design on the wall—a picture in a frame—a painted thing. She could not help a little twinge of irritation.

"Was he peaceful all night?" she asked coldly.

"He moved little," said Clung. "When the sun came up he sighed. That was all. He will sleep now until noon. You may go; he no longer needs you."

"I know him better," she said—for it seemed as if this was a calm negation of all the effects of her patient nursing. "Even when he's asleep he knows whether or not I'm near."

"That," said Clung, "was when he was very weak. It is different now. He is stronger. He does not need you."

"It's not true!" said the girl, angrily.

"Try," said Clung.

She frowned at him, and then moved towards the door, her glance behind her, willing with all her might that the sick man should stir and moan at her departure. But he did not move; she reached the door and glanced at Clung. He stood, as she had known he would stand, with his head back, his eyes half closed, his lips smiling faintly. She stamped, but lightly, for fear of waking the sleeper.

"I could hate you!" whispered the girl, and was gone.

It startled Clung out of his dream, and he stared blankly after her. But finally he shrugged the thought away and began to pick up the flowers which she had shaken to the floor. The petals of the blossoms were already fading, and here and there they were darkly bruised.

Chapter 8

On the fifth day thereafter, William Kirk was strong enough to dress himself; on the tenth day he stood up and walked about; at the end of two weeks he climbed into a saddle and rode about the place at a soft trot; the next day he told Winifred that the time was come for them to marry and go north again into the world of business.

It was a drowsy, late afternoon, and they sat on the verandah, dressed in cool white, watching the idle brushing of the palm branches across the sky—a blue-white sky which would soon be taking on colors, for the sun was dropping rapidly towards the western horizon and already the shadows were growing darker among the hills.

"Besides," concluded Kirk, "I'm on my feet completely and ready for harness; your father is getting nervous—everything is set for us to call in the minister and jog back north."

"Why," said the girl, "you're not nearly your old self, Will!"

"Near enough to marry you, dear," he answered, "and get

back to some man-sized work. I'm sick of this dreamy life, sitting about chattering. Not cut out for that sort of thing. Can't do it decoratively the way Ring can."

"Where is Ring now?" asked the girl.

"Where he always is during the bright part of the day—inside, sitting in a dark corner looking at pictures in some old fool book. But that isn't answering me, Winifred."

She said gravely: "I'll tell you frankly, Will, that I don't feel like answering today. I'm tired—somehow."

"Confound it!" he said, with some heat. "You've been this way ever since Ring appeared!"

She answered without smiling: "Now, that's the silliest thing you've said for a long time, isn't it?"

"It *is* foolish," he admitted, "but that chap—damn it!—I know he's not one of us—I know I owe him a lot—"

"Everything," she said coolly.

"Everything, I suppose, but at the same time he makes me uneasy. By the way, who the devil is he, where does he come from, where is he going? Do you know?"

"Yes."

"The deuce you do! Let's have it."

"I'll tell you just what he told me. He came from there"—she waved a hand towards half the points of the compass towards the south—"he is going there"—she waved the other hand at the other points of the compass to the north—"and he is just a man."

"Sounds like Ring, all right. I never knew the fellow to answer a question the way any other man would. Personally I have very grave doubts about him."

"What sort of doubts, Will?"

"But let's get back to the important thing: Winifred, I wish awfully that you'd shake off your weariness and tell me I can bring out a minister and have the thing finished up."

"Somehow," she answered, "I like to have it kept in suspense for a while."

"But we can't go on drifting like this—beside, my business will go smash if I don't get back into harness."

"I think the drifting," she said, "is rather pleasant. It's nice to sit here—and not talk—and not think—in the warmth."

"That," he said angrily, "is a transcript from Ring!"

"I suppose it is."

This startled him erect in his chair.

"Winifred," he said, "I don't want to make a complete ass of myself, but I'd like to know just what you think of Ring."

"Ask him," she said. "He can tell you better than I can."

"There you go again! There isn't the slightest emotion in your voice—you talk exactly the way Ring talks—damn it! I beg your pardon, Winifred."

"Don't; but go ahead. Tell me how Ring talks. I like to hear about him."

"You ought to know how he talks; he's with you enough."

"Altogether," she said thoughtfully, "I think he's averaged about twenty words a day since he came. Most of the time he simply sits and looks."

"I know. He looks as if he were listening to you talking hard and fast when you're saying nothing at all. Confound him; he worries me. I'll be frank. I wish you'd tell me exactly how you feel about him."

"I don't mind in the least."

She leaned back in the chair, half closing her eyes, and smiling. Kirk swore softly, for it was Ring's expression made delicately beautiful on her face.

"I think I know," he murmured, "but go ahead."

She said: "Most of us live rather ugly lives, don't we, Will? We're pretty much discontented with today, we despise yesterday, and we only drag ourselves along through a hope of what a brave tomorrow may bring. That's the way it has been with me, at least, and I'm sure that's the way it is with most of the people I know. Do you agree?"

"Yes, I suppose life is pretty rotten if you take it cold-bloodedly like this. But this isn't an age of romance, Winifred. People are looking for action—and they're finding it."

"They are. My life has been filled by people who are leading lives of action; I really began to think them the only people in the world who amounted to anything. I was like a person going down a straight and narrow corridor with monotonous walls on either side and no prospect except the same dull passage to the end, and then—darkness. Now suppose a door suddenly opens on the side of that corridor and I pass through the door and find a world of wonderful beauty—flowers—rare perfumes—a garden filled with exquisite things perfectly arranged. That is what Ring did for me—"

"As much as that—are you serious, Winifred?"

She went on as though she had not heard him: "He taught me how to enjoy living for its own sake—taught me how to revel in every day as it comes. He is still teaching, and I—well, he'll be out here in a moment, and then you'll see. He always comes when the color of the evening starts. Before that he has no interest in the day."

Kirk stood up. He seemed very large, outlined against the growing color of the west. Those strong hands, too, were filling out, hands that could have crushed the slender wrists of Clung with a single pressure.

"You're quite sure of all this, Winifred?" he asked tensely.

"What is there to be tragic about?"

"Don't you see that if you feel that way about him there is no room for me?"

"But I feel for you in such a different way—I—"

"How much do you feel?"

She frowned at the floor.

"Will," she said, "if you really care very much, don't press me for an answer just now."

"I was right about it. You cared for me only as long as I was sick; I was just something to mother, Winifred, wasn't that it?"

"Do you insist on an answer now?"

"No—for God's sake! Not a word!"

He slumped into a chair, breathing hard.

Then: "I'll tell you what I think Ring is—for various reasons. No, it would be easier to show you than to tell you. He's inside—in the front room. Go to the window and watch him. I'm going to enter that room and say something."

She obeyed him, wondering, smiling faintly in expectation of the game to follow. Kirk stole to the inner door of the front room, and she saw him press it cautiously ajar. It made not a sound, and John Ring, sitting with his back to the door, in a corner, slowly turned the pages of a large book, poring over the illustrations. There was not a sound from the entrance of Kirk, that she could have sworn, but suddenly Ring sat erect, stiffening in his chair—the pages lay unstirred before him.

"Hands up!" called Kirk.

It was as if a gun-shot precipitated John Ring from his chair. One instant he sat there motionless; the next he was prone on the floor behind the chair. By magic, as if conjured from the thin air, a revolver was in his hand and leveled at the form of Kirk.

Chapter 9

"Come, come," called Kirk cheerily, though he had shrunk back against the wall, "only a jest, my dear Ring. Gad! looks as if it nearly turned out serious for me, eh? Pardon!"

He retreated through the doorway and rejoined Winifred on the porch.

"You saw?"

"He is a Westerner," she answered, "born with a gun in his hand. It was only natural for him to draw a gun."

"Don't you see?" smiled Kirk. "The worst law-abiding Westerner knows the game is up when he hears that: 'Hands up!' and he puts his fists high over his head. But a man to whom arrest is the same as death will fight it out even if he's cornered."

"You mean that Ring is an outlaw?"

"That's plain."

"I wonder!"

"Seems to please you, Winifred."

"I think it does."

"Good heavens, my dear, why?"

"My only doubt of Ring has been that he's too nearly effeminate. If he's an outlaw—well, you've removed my only objection to him, Will."

"Winifred, did you see his face when he lay there on the floor with that gun pointed?"

"Yes. It looked like murder, didn't it?"

"And you can smile at such a thing?"

"Nonsense. Nothing happened."

"But suppose, to complete my jest, I had had a gun in my hand and leveled at him."

"Then I suppose, Will, that I would now be closing your eyes and bidding you a long goodnight. Something about our friend Ring makes me feel that he seldom misses."

The big man answered: "And I begin to think that it's time something were done—"

"About what, Will?"

"I'll tell you after it's happened. Here comes your outlaw."

He stood in the doorway, perfectly serene, smiling at them in his own peculiar way. They had provided him with white clothes and now he came with small, slow steps across the verandah, seeming to luxuriate in the straightness of the creases in his trousers, and revelling in the neat coolness of his costume. Kirk turned on his heel and strode into the house.

He went on through until he reached the barn behind. There he said to one of the men who cared for the horses: "How long will it take you to reach Mortimer?"

"About fifteen hours of ordinary riding. Make it in eleven on a hell of a rush."

"This," said Kirk, "is a hell of a rush. Ride for Mortimer and see that man you spend so much time talking about—the gunman—I mean Marshal Clauson. Tell him that on this ranch there is a man of medium height and of a very slender build, brown eyes—deep black hair—handsome—under thirty in age—hands as small as a woman's—and very quick with weapons. Ask him if that man is wanted in Arizona by the law. Now ride like the devil."

He waited until the messenger was out of sight on the southern trail. Then he went back to the house. The voice of conscience, which speaks so small and carries so far, was beginning to trouble him; but when he came again, softly, to the front of the house, and looked out on the verandah, he saw the man called John Ring sitting near Winifred with his head tilted back, his eyes half closed, and a faint smile as of mockery on his lips. Beyond them the western sky was a riot of deepening colors, and towards this the girl was looking, but John Ring gave it not a glance. His eyes were fixed steadily on his companion. Kirk turned away. The voice of conscience troubled him no more.

Early the next morning Winifred sent one of the servants to tell him that she wished to speak with him. He sent back a note:

"I think I know what you want to say. I'm asking you for your own sake, just as much as for mine, to wait until tomorrow noon at the least before you say it. Will you wait?"

She did not send a written answer to the note, but when she saw him later in the day she said: "Of course I'll wait—as long as you want me to. And I know you're not going to be foolish, Will?"

"I'm glad you're confident in me," he answered drily.

She said with a sudden concern: "What is it, Will? You act like a little boy with a surprise to spring on the family."

"To tell you the truth," he said, "I have a surprise, and a corker. That is, I think I have. I ought to know by tomorrow morning. Will you wait?"

"Of course. I'll ask John Ring. He ought to be good at riddles."

"At this riddle," said Kirk, "he ought to be very good."

"There's something nasty behind that, Will?"

"Only a riddle."

And so he left her, and spent the rest of the day by himself; but in the evening the man called John Ring came to his room. He spoke simply and to the point.

"We have been friends. We are friends no more. Is it because of the woman—your woman? Tell me, is it because of your woman?"

The face of William Kirk contorted with pain, and a perverse desire to torture himself made him spring to his feet and fairly shout: "Damn your eyes, don't you see that she's no longer 'my woman'? I don't know whose woman she is— maybe yours. And you and I? No, we're no longer friends. Now get to the devil out of my room!"

"A loud voice," answered Clung, "says foolish things."

But he was smiling as he left the room, and Kirk knew with a cold falling of the heart that the stranger had gone straight to the girl. What would happen he could not well guess, but he knew her to be honorable as a man. She had given her word to wait until the next day, and he felt fairly confident that not even John Ring and his silence could make her speak before that time. Yet it was a night of no sleep for him. He went to bed late and tossed about for a while. At length he rose and began to walk up and down in the dark room. A low, orange-colored moon caught his eye, and he went to the window to watch its setting. Just before it sank out of sight, two figures walked across its image, a man and a woman, close together. Right before that moon they paused. The woman was looking up, and now she threw up both her arms. The man stood with folded arms and his head was bent. The moon rolled down below the hill-top; the two figures melted again into the dark from which they had come; and Kirk kneeled by the window and buried his face in his hands.

He went down to a late breakfast the next morning, hollow-eyed, nervous, his hands twitching violently so that he could hardly eat. There was such a growing weakness that he began to fear a relapse. He had barely finished his grapefruit when the two entered—John Ring and the girl. They had been through the garden, gathering flowers, and now they spilled a rich tide of color across the table, and stood there on either side of him, the girl laughing. He knew that Ring stood with his head back, smiling faintly; but he dared not look up and make sure. If he had been right, he would have had to jump at the man's throat.

"Look!" cried the girl, "sunlight outside and sunlight inside!"

She raised a double handful of yellow blossoms and let them shower down upon the table.

"Clung!" called a voice from the kitchen.

He dropped to the floor, a gun in either hand.

"Clung!" called a voice from the other side of the room.

"Clung! Clung!" they were all around him.

"We've got you, my boy," called the voice of Marshal Clauson, "are you going to let us take you, or do we have to make a killing here?"

And Clung, thinking swiftly, thought of the fusillade of bullets—some of them going wild, perhaps—the girl—bloodshed—horror! He rose and tossed his guns upon the table. He pulled another six-shooter from the front of his white trousers; he threw a long knife after the rest. Then he folded his arms.

"I am ready," said Clung.

Marshal Clauson appeared at the door of the kitchen. His eyes were narrowed, like those of a man prepared to do a desperate deed. He held two revolvers poised.

"Get your hands over your head, Clung!" he ordered; "come in behind him, boys, and shoot if he bats an eye."

"I will not make trouble," said Clung.

The marshal, still white faced and narrow eyed, got between his victim and the table where Clung's weapons lay.

"I begin to think you won't—and I'm damned glad of it, Clung. For a Chink you show an amazing pile of sense."

There were six other men entering the room from various angles, each with leveled guns, yet even those who approached Clung from behind came softly, stealthily, as if each man was attempting a desperate deed alone.

"Get the irons on him," ordered Marshal Clauson.

They were produced, a new, glittering pair; Clung held his arms patiently in position, and the manacles snapped shut.

"It was you?" smiled Clung to Kirk.

Chapter 10

But Kirk turned from those eyes as if he found them difficult to bear. He ran to Clauson and touched him on the shoulder.

"What d'you mean by 'Chink'?" he asked

"What I say. This gent looks white, don't he? Well, he ain't. This, ladies and gents, is Clung of Mortimer. Half-breed Chinaman—son of old Li Clung—same town."

The hands of Winifred, as if frozen in place, had held the last of the yellow blossoms. Now the fingers curled over it, crushed it shapeless, colorless—a bruised, ugly mass, which dropped now unheeded to the floor.

"Who sent me word?" asked Clauson. "He gets half the reward."

"I don't want the—the blood money," said Kirk.

"Wash your hands of the business, eh?" grinned the marshal. "Well, if you know Clung's record, I don't blame you."

He passed a large silken bandana across his forehead.

"It's the cool of the mornin', all right, but I don't mind saying that I've been feeling some warm. Yep, even when we had the drop on this bird I wasn't particular happy. I tell you, I've seen this same Chink—well, why talk about what's done? We've got him. That's all. And he'll be hung nice and regular if I can keep the crowd from lynching him at Mortimer. What's the matter, lady, you look sick?"

A sickly pallor, indeed, had swept over her face, and now she moved for the door leading to the front part of the house. The course brought her unavoidably close to Clung, who stood with his head high, tilting back, eyes half closed, smiling faintly. One instant she paused, near him, and surveyed him from head to foot. Then an uncontrollable shudder swept over her; she covered her face with her hands and ran from the room.

"Makes her sick to know she's been in the same room with Clung, eh?" said the marshal easily—it was a great day for him. "But I tell you, gents, this Clung ain't so bad—for a Chink. Only one white notch in his record. And that was the fault of old Boyce, I guess. Lead him out, lads."

"One minute," said Kirk, and he approached Clung and touched him on the shoulder; the other writhed suddenly away.

"Listen," said Kirk, speaking so softly that no one else might hear, "I'm sorry, but I had to do it. I suspected something was wrong; I didn't dream it was as bad as this. For what you've done for me, I'm grateful. Tell me what I can do to make your last days happy, and—"

"Wash the thought of what I have done away," said Clung.

"Let me pay you for the medicine you used, at least."

"The medicine was common leaves dipped in tea. Half a cent would more than pay the cost. I healed your mind, not your body."

"Making a fool out of me from the first, eh? Still, I feel like a dog about this—er—Clung."

"It was not you," said the other. "It was fate. I have forgotten you already."

"Damned if I don't think you have. Cool devil you are, Clung. It was the girl; the thought of her drove me on, Clung."

"You have lost her," said the prisoner. "She is gone from you."

"Nonsense! The moment you are gone she'll come and cry her shame away on my shoulder. A Chinaman! Gad, poor Winifred will be under the whip!"

"The flowers," said Clung faintly, "they will save her from you."

"Damn your yellow hide!" muttered Kirk, "I wonder if I understand you?"

"No, you can never understand. Marshal Clauson; will you take me?"

They led him outside and helped him to the saddle of his own grey horse.

"Now," said the marshal, "there's something about you —damned if I know why, Clung, that makes me start sympathizin' with you. Foolish, I know, but I can't help it. Listen here. If you'll give me your word, I'll let you ride back to Mortimer, with your hands free and no rope around you to suggest a lynching to the crowd. Gimme your word?"

"The marshal is kind to Clung," said the other. "He has a

garden of flowers—"

"Best in Mortimer, eh, lad? First I remember of you, Clung, is seeing you snook around that same garden. Here, Johnson, unlock those irons."

And so it came to pass that Clung rode like a free man into Mortimer. A crowd gathered at the first appearance of the cavalcade and there were murmurs and some threatening shouts.

"But they won't do nothing," said the marshal to Clung, "partly because they know me, and partly because they see you got your hands free—and because you look so damned—well, white, Clung!"

The marshal himself turned the key on Clung's cell. He said through the bars: "If there's anything I can do to make you easy, lad, speak out."

"The marshal has a garden of flowers," said Clung.

"Well?"

"Clung has often passed by the garden, slowly, in the cool of the evening."

"Damn my soul! You want flowers? Clung, I'll bring 'em up myself; yep, me and the old woman'll pick 'em for you together."

And he went away swearing reverently. A love for flowers is like a love for little children; it brings men together through strange distances. The marshal that evening sat in his house, in his office, sorting the flowers for Clung, when Mrs. Clauson appeared with word that old Li Clung was at the front door.

"But you better let him stay there," said Mrs. Clauson, "unless you want a lot of Chinese tears on the rug."

"Tears?" snorted the marshal. "There won't be no tears; more likely a knife. Show the old scoundrel in."

But the visit of Li was both short and silent. He came to the door, nodded, grinned, produced a little canvas bag which he left on the edge of the marshal's desk, nodded, and was gone, silent-footed. The marshal, as soon as he recovered from the first astonishment, opened the bag, with some fear lest it be an infernal machine. What he found was a neat lit tle pile of ten-dollar gold pieces, with some twenties to crown the lot. Old Li had arranged the bag like a basket of fruit, putting the best on top.

Clauson started to tell his wife of the marvel, but he changed his mind and went instead to the laundry of old Li. There he called the proprietor to one side, cursed him softly and fluently in the languages of both sides of the border, and then returned to his home. He was much moved; gold has a singular power of touching the emotions, and the gold which is earned through the sweat and labor of a Chinese laundry—Marshal Clauson was forced to loosen his collar. He swore his way through his supper and would not speak to his wife; so she knew that he was moved by some gentle emotion and watched him with a gleaming eye. They had no children; he was the beginning and the end to her.

Old Li, however, evidently had heard the legend that constant dropping of water wears through the stoutest stone. In the morning he appeared again and placed another canvas bag on the edge of the marshal's desk. Clauson seized a large ledger and hurled it after the disappearing form of Li, but he dodged through the front door and was gone.

Left to his leisure, Clauson, wiping perspiration from his forehead, examined the contents. It was more; it was double the size of the first bag. Marshal Clauson weighed the bag, sighed, closed it, and then rode in a fury to the laundry of old Li Clung. He hurled the bag at the head of Li and followed it with a tremendous tirade. He informed the Oriental that bribery was a prison offense, and that any more damned monkeyshines would land Li behind the bars. Moreover, it was hopeless for him to attempt to save his son. The boy was done for—too bad—but impossible to change the law. Life had to pay for life.

But there was not much peace in store for the marshal. He had scarcely installed himself in his office again and eaten an orange to cool the thirst of his rage, when the door opened once more, and Li, nodding, smiling, was once more in the doorway. He was dressed in robes of state, a black silk cap with a crimson tassel, long sleeved tunic braided with gold, a pig-tail of prodigious length. He produced from the mysterious depths of one of his sleeves the third bag of money and deposited it with a bow on the edge of the desk. The marshal reared himself up slowly from his chair. He seized first on a massive book, and then on the butt of a gun, but still old Li did not move; Marshal Clauson delivered himself of his favorite curse, famous through the length and breadth of Arizona.

"Thunderin' hell!" he roared, "am I a fool or jest plain crazy?"

Chapter 11

The Chinese drew himself erect; dignity fell about him as visibly as the toga of a Roman senator carrying an appeal to the leader of plundering barbarians at the gates of the imperial city.

"It is all that Li Clung has," he said in his faultless English. "And his money is not stolen."

He opened the bag and spilled the contents across the desk. There was gold of three denominations and there was an intermixture of silver.

"Li Clung," he said, "has gone to his friends. Li Clung has borrowed what they would give. Li Clung makes a gift to the marshal; a little present."

The marshal, with wildly staring eyes, gathered the money and poured it back into the bag.

Li Clung held out his calloused hands.

"Li Clung will work," he said, "he will be the slave of the marshal Clauson, if this money is not enough."

"You damn fool," said the marshal hoarsely, "it's gettin' too near my price. Take your fool money away!"

"Li Clung," said the unmoved Chinese, "is a poor man, but he will bring much money. He will sell his house. He has silks and pictures. He will sell them and bring the money to the marshal. He will eat stale bread and drink only water and bring to the marshal all that he makes. Every month he will bring money—a little money. A present to the marshal from Li Clung. Li Clung will bow to his gods, who are very strong, every day. He will beg them to bring a long life to the marshal and much happiness. They are strong gods. They will bring children to the wife of the marshal. They will fill his house with peace and happiness and many voices of his friends."

"My God!" whispered the marshal, staring as if he saw a ghost.

He rubbed his knuckles across his eyes, which were dim.

"Can a Chink be like this? Li Clung, you hear me swear to God that if there was a chance for your boy he'd get it, but he ain't got a chance. The law won't give him no look in. If it would, I'd see that he got out, and it wouldn't cost you no money. But it can't be done, Li. The boys want blood for the death of old Boyce. A Chink can't get away with a white man's death. You ought to know that."

A pallor fell on the face of Li Clung; it was like a shower of ashes.

"Li Clung will tell the marshal a little story," he said, "if he will be heard."

"Li," said the marshal, "there's something inside me that's aching as if I had a son of my own. Sit down and talk, Li."

"It is not a good story," said Li, overlooking the proffered chair. "Li Clung has been a strong man and a bad man. Li Clung was in Cripple Creek."

"The hell you were!"

"And there was a man called John Pemberton."

"I knew John well. He was a hard one, was old John."

"Li Clung had a young wife, and Li Clung had two little sons. Li Clung loved them all. Sometimes it seemed to Li that his heart would break, there was so much love in it for his wife, and for his two sons. He had room for them all, but it swelled the heart of Li Clung. And every morning and every evening Li Clung bowed before his gods and made himself humble for fear his gods should be jealous, Li Clung was so happy.

"But the gods of Li Clung are fierce gods and strong gods. They grew angry with him. They took all his happiness—see! they took it as suddenly as Li Clung takes the stalk of this flower and bends it and breaks it—there are three flowers gone because that stalk is broken. So it was with the gods of Li Clung.

"They sent John Pemberton to the house of Li for money, for John Pemberton needed gold. He came to find money and he came very drunk. He found no money but he found my wife and my sons. She made crying out, being a woman. He struck her in the face and she fell and struck her head against a stone, and died so—being a woman. And the two sons, when they saw their mother die, they made much noise, screaming together, so that John Pemberton, he feared that they would bring in many men upon him, so he took them by the heels—"

"God!" whispered the marshal, and tore the bandana from his throat.

"Li Clung came home that night and his heart was singing with happiness. He found his two little buds dead, and he found his flower faded and dying. But there was a small voice

47

left in her no bigger than the humming of a fly, and with that voice she told Li Clung how all that had filled his heart had been poured out again and thrown away like water on the sand.

"Then Li Clung buried his dead.

"He waited. John Pemberton took a woman to his house. The woman bore him a son and died. Then Li Clung was ready. He went in the middle of the night and tied the mouth of John Pemberton with clothes so that he could not cry out."

"But Pemberton was a big, strong man, Li."

"Li Clung was not weak," said the Chinaman. "He tied the mouth of John Pemberton so that he could not cry out, and then he made him know by signs that Li Clung would take his son and go away.

"And Li Clung went away with the boy; afterwards John Pemberton died."

"By God," cried the marshal, "then your boy is young Pemberton!"

"My boy is Clung," said Li solemnly.

"I begin to see. Yet you've got a yellow skin, Li. Well, my eyes are getting wide open."

"Li Clung hated the little boy he had stolen, but after a while he came to love him. The hands of a baby are strong hands."

He made a gesture which the marshal did not see, for his face was buried in his hands.

"Li Clung loved the boy and took him into his heart, which was empty. He gave him all things that he could give him. Then he saw that Clung carried the blood of a white father in him and that he was a destroyer, and sometimes Li was glad, because he did not wish well for white people and Clung would be like a plague of locusts, consuming. But now the son of Li Clung is about to die, and Li Clung is very weary. He has no strength, and he is sick about the heart. He has brought gold to the marshal. Is it worth this life?"

"Li, if this yarn would be believed—we'd get off Clung. He's only killed one white man, and that was in self-defense, more or less. But d'you think you could convince the boys that Clung is all white? Nope; they're out for blood. I'd take a chance and let him go, but there's another appointment due for this job, and if I let Clung go another man is pretty sure to get my place, and—"

But Li Clung was already disappearing through the doorway.

Marshal Clauson sent his wife to the jail with fresh flowers for Clung, and took a long, hard ride through the country to shake off the thought of Clung. But when he came back the same case attacked him again.

This time it was in the person of the girl whom he had seen in the room at the time of Clung's capture. She was all in white, and she seemed to Marshal Clauson the most beautiful woman he had ever seen.

Chapter 12

"I suppose," said the marshal, after he had seen her seated, "that you've come about the Clung case? Want to make sure that he will get his? Well, he will. There ain't no reasonable doubt about that."

She winced deeper in the big chair, and then raised her head in the way she had caught from Clung.

"I have come to find out if money will be of any use to him in securing a good lawyer," she said steadily.

"That's the way of it, eh?" queried the marshal, and he shifted the lamp so that the light fell more directly on her face. "Well, lady, I'll tell you now that it would be simply throwing away good coin. There's only one verdict a jury would bring in a case like this, an Arizona jury, anyway. Josiah Boyce wasn't much account, but then he wasn't no harm to anybody neither. He's dead and there's a life owing somewhere to the law—a Chink's life at that."

Every time he used the word, carelessly—he noted that the girl winced. He went on: "Boyce ain't the only one. There might be a ghost of a chance if he was. There's others. Clung has left a trail behind him a mile long, and it's thick with dead Mexicans. He's a nacheral born killer, Miss Sampson, and that's the shortest way to the truth of the thing. He shoots too straight not to kill."

And the girl, thinking back to the keen picture of Clung, saw how he might be both a lover of all things beautiful and also a dealer of death. The marshal, watching, saw the hardening of her face. He was thinking many things.

She said, rising: "There are a great many twists in the law. Good counsel may save him, and if it may, I want him to have the chance."

"Ma'am," said the marshal, "there ain't many twists in Arizona law—not in a case like this. You can lay to that. Maybe I can ask why you're so interested in this—Chink?"

The blood stained her face at that.

She said with some dignity: "Why do you keep forcing the word down my throat? I know he's a—Chinaman, but he's a rare man, Marshal Clauson, no matter what his nationality. If he took a white man's life, he also saved a white man's life."

"Clung did?"

"The man who betrayed him to you," said the girl, whitening with scorn and anger. "He was sick, nearly dead. We had given him up. Then Clung came and healed him, sat by him day and night, would not leave him until the man was cured."

"H-m-m," murmured the marshal, and his hand moved automatically towards the butt of his gun. "May I ask if this William Kirk person is still at your house?"

"No," she said, "he has gone north."

"Speaking personal," said the marshal slowly, "he'd better stay in his north. He was a bit too far south for it to be healthy. That kind don't never prosper in Arizona. Clung saved him, eh?"

"If there's a law of compensation," said the girl, "it ought to appear. A life for a life; that's what Clung gives."

"You'd throw in the Mexicans he finished off, eh?" grinned the marshal, "and the white men he didn't kill but just shot up bad? Throw 'em in for good measure, eh? Well, I don't mind saying—but I got no right to say anything. Miss Sampson, I'll have to be saying good-evening to you. I got a pile of things to do this night."

"And you'll see that the very best counsel is retained for him? Can we make you our agent in that, Marshal Clauson? I know you'll keep the murdering cowpunchers away from him."

"Lady," said the marshal rising with her, "I've spread the news around among the boys that if they tackle the jail to get Clung, I'll turn him loose on 'em with two guns. There ain't no better way of keeping Mortimer quiet. They've all seen him in action and it makes a pile of 'em sick to remember. Good-night."

She went, with bowed head; but the moment she had gone the marshal set to work, cheerily, whistling as he proceeded. First he opened a door so cunningly set into the wall that the cunningest eye of suspicion would never have detected it, and he took from it a small saw, a lever of diminutive proportions, rope, and a stout knife. These things he bestowed about his person, adding to his load an extra cartridge belt and two long forty-fives. Thus equipped he started straight for the jail and went to the cell of Clung.

Clung, as usual, was slowly pacing up and down inside the

bars, utterly oblivious of all that passed in the corridor. He did not even turn when the door opened and then clanged shut; but when he discovered that it was Clauson his face softened to a smile of infinite gentleness.

"Flowers!" he said, and stretched out the delicate hands.

"Flowers be damned," murmured the marshal cautiously. "Something better than that, lad. Freedom!"

"For me? If I go—what will come of the marshal?"

"Shut up. Before I was a marshal I done my share of hell-raising. I know. Also I know another thing. I've heard the story of old Li Clung. You're young Pemberton, all white—whiter than your dad by a damn sight."

"No," said the other, "I am Clung. I am not ashamed."

"Neither would I be. Old Li is a rare one. And you'd never have a chance of making the world believe that you're not a half-breed. Let it go. Arizona ain't the only place. Hit out—let the wind take you, south or north. And here's a word in your ear. If you go north, on the right trail, you'll find a girl that hasn't forgotten you. I think she *might* believe you. Anyway, she'd try like hell to believe you."

"And her friends?" answered Clung.

"That's the stickler. Rumor would follow you; you'd still be the Chink to most of the world."

"I am Clung. I shall not change the name. It is my pride. I will be what I am. It is the better way."

"The girl, Clung?"

In another man the change of expression would have been almost negligible, but knowing Clung, the marshal moved a pace back, wondering.

"She knew me for what I am," said Clung, stiffening, "and when she heard that I was 'Clung, the Chink,' you saw her as she passed me in the room. The pain of it is still with me. If I had been all white, the pain was so great when she turned from me that I should have groaned and fallen on my knees and wept and begged her to come back to me. But I made no sound. I am Clung."

"Clung, she came tonight and wanted to know what her money could do in the hiring of a lawyer for you. And the other man—he has gone north. She hates him. I think in a way, Clung, that I wouldn't have come here tonight if I hadn't seen her. She loves you, lad; she almost loves you even while she thinks you're a Chinaman. Think of it!"

That smile which the marshal knew, that stern curling of the upper lip, changed the face of the other.

He said: "If she came to me crawling on her knees in the dust it would not change me. She could not repay the pain of that time when she first turned from me. Such a pain, sir, would burn her away to light ashes and dust—kill her like flame. She cannot repay me. I do not ask repayment. It was my pleasure; it is my pain. I am Clung."

"You go south?"

"First I go to see my father; then I ride south. And some day the time will come when you shall need me. I will come. You will not need to hunt far or call long. I shall come. Time will not change me; distance will not make me forget. I am Clung."

"Clung, and a devil of pride," said the marshal. "The lone trail is a long trail, but good luck go with you. Your killings are not ended, and you'll die hard yourself. But—there's the saw. Oil, too. You can cut through those western bars in a jiffy. Once started—well, here's two guns. I know you'll get loose. Don't shoot unless you have to. That's all I ask; and then don't shoot to kill."

As he closed the door behind him, he raised his lantern and looked back; Clung stood with folded arms, his head tilting back, his eyes half closed, faintly smiling.

The marshal went back to his house and sat in his room waiting. An hour, two hours, three hours passed. Then he heard three shots fired in quick succession. He ran to the window and threw it wide; the echo of the sounds still trembled through the air.

"The south trail sure enough," said the marshal, "and the lone trail."

Chapter 13

But if the escape of Clung was due to the kindliness of Marshal Clauson, certainly there was not a living soul in Mortimer or in any of the marshal's wide district who faintly dreamed the truth. The marshal was more widely famed for a hard fist and a nervous gun than for a gentle heart, and the reward which his own act of unadulterated goodness brought him was a general suspicion of growing inefficiency; for people could not but remember the length of time during which Clung ranged the desert, how he was at length brought to bay by force of chance and numbers; and now the desperado was set free to prey upon society through the carelessness of Mortimer's marshal. It was enough to irritate a much quieter town than Mortimer; the knowledge of it floated up to the higher circles of authority and brought a cold, brief telegram to Clauson.

He defied the higher authorities with a snarl, for he knew that he was too valuable to be dispensed with; but what spurred him every day were the side-glances of careless contempt with which the cowpunchers and miners of the town favored him. Within a week Marshal Clauson hated the entire population of the Orient, particularly the Chinese, and among the Chinese he selected Clung himself for peculiar anathema. With all his heart he regretted the escape of the outlaw. That Clung was really white made no difference to the marshal—he could not separate his prejudice into fact and theory. He sent deputies far and wide in a vain effort to reclaim the fugitive from justice; but Clung had vanished from the face of the earth and not even a rumor of him floated back to the ear of Mortimer. Yet still the town waited, strong in the consciousness that such men as Clung, whether white or yellow, return eventually to their earliest hunting-grounds and bring a not inconsiderable portion of hell with them. They had seen Clung in action, and the picture would not fade readily from their minds. In the meantime they cast a glance of angry suspicion upon Marshal Clauson and were fain to remark in his hearing that all men are apt to grow old.

Which explains the mood of Clauson himself when one day his deputy entered from the outer office, leaned against the door and said: "They's a Chink outside wants to talk t'you, Clauson."

The marshal looked up with a start.

"A Chink?" he growled suspiciously. "See me? T'hell with him. Tell him I'm busy."

"I already done it," said the deputy.

"Tell him I'm out of town."

"I already done it," said the deputy.

The marshal narrowed his eyes wistfully.

"Partner," he drawled with dangerous calm, "you ain't kidding me a little are you?"

"I'll tell a man I ain't," said the deputy hastily. " 'S a matter of fact, Clauson, I told the fool Chink he'd be takin' his life in his hands if he come in talkin' to you jest now, but all he does is stand there with his hands shoved up in his sleeves and bat his eyes at me and say: 'All same Yo Chai see Marsh' Clauson.' I never see such a fool!"

"H-m-m," said the marshal. "Yo Chai? Don't remember the name. What sort of a looking Chink is he?"

"Kind of tall," said the deputy, "for a Chink; skinny; round shouldered; wrinkled old yaller face; long pig-tail; got a moustache that—looks like a shadow of yours, marshal—just a few stragglin', long hairs on each side of his mouth."

"Tell the old ape to beat it," grunted the marshal. "I had enough of Chinks. Wait a minute. How's he dressed?"

"Like a swell. All silk—padded stuff like a quilt, y'know. Red hat with a tassel; fancy Chink shoes."

"Well," sighed the marshal, "let him in. I s'pose somebody's been swipin' his dope and he wants help."

The deputy nodded and disappeared. His place at the door was taken almost at once by Yo Chai, a slender, rather bowed figure, carrying about him that air of distinction which goes with any gentleman no matter what the color of his skin.

But the marshal was in no mood to appreciate fineness in a Chinese.

"I'm busy," he greeted his visitor. "Start talkin' and finish quick."

A soft voice answered: "Yo Chai wait till Marsh' Clauson got plenty time," and he turned back to the door.

But the marshal at the sound of that voice leaped from his chair and shouted: "Wait!"

Yo Chai turned, and at the sight of him Clauson lapsed back into his chair, staring in manifest bewilderment. The Chinaman bore this scrutiny without changing a muscle of his face.

"Close the door," said the marshal hoarsely at last, "and sit down."

Yo Chai obeyed, and as he sat down murmured: *"Ta hsi."* (Great happiness.)

Marshal Clauson let out a great breath which blew forth his moustaches, and the light of battle died slowly from his little eyes.

"I was thinkin' for a minute," he sighed, "that you was—well, it don't make no difference."

"The eyes of Yo Chai are old," said the Chinese, "but he sees clearly."

Again, at the sound of that voice, the marshal started,

leaned forward with a scowl, and then settled back into his chair.

"Go on," he said. "What d'you think you seen?"

"Marsh' Clauson thought Yo Chai much like Clung. Speak same."

"Ah," said the marshal with renewed eagerness. "You know Clung?"

"Little bit," said Yo Chai.

"If you can lead me to him," said Clauson, "I'll—I'll be your friend, Yo Chai—and a marshal's the sort of a friend that a Chink needs in Mortimer, eh?"

"Marsh' Clauson want Clung?"

"Do I? I'll tell a man I do!"

"Why?"

"Because he's a devil, Yo Chai."

"*T'ao Ch'i?*" nodded Yo Chai, which means mischievous, young devil, and several other things.

"Yep," said the marshal, who had a smattering of Chinese, "*t'ao ch'i* and a lot of other stuff. He'd got me in wrong with the boys. Yo Chai, can you lead me to him?"

"Yes."

"God!" cried the marshal, and leaped from his chair with a shout of joy. "Yo Chai, you ain't lyin' to me? Give me one crack at him and I'm your man. How much d'you want for actin' as a guide?"

"Nothing."

"Nothing?"

"It is not worth money. It is a little thing to lead Marsh' Clauson to Clung. Also, Clung once belong Marsh' Clauson."

"I had him once, so you don't want anything for bringin' me back my lost property, eh? Yo Chai, I see you're a good sort. Where is he, Yo?"

The Chinese withdrew from the sleeve of his silken makwa, or horse-coat, a slender, dark yellow hand and pointed to his breast.

"I," said Yo Chai calmly, "am Clung."

"You?" gasped Clauson, "but Clung—your skin—"

He broke down, stammering.

"With soap and water," said the other quietly, "I can make my skin white again."

"And you come back," roared Clauson, "to show me how clever you are, eh? You come back thinkin' you can slip out of my hands agin? Clung, no man can't do it!"

"Clung knew," said the other gravely, slipping at once into perfect and fluent English, "that Marshal Clauson hated Clung. So he has come to give himself back. Marshal Clauson gave him a gift not long ago, but his heart was not with the gift. Clung has heard, so he has come back."

The body of the marshal seemed turning to jelly. He filled his chair loosely from arm to arm, his chin falling on his breast and his mouth agape.

"Clung!" he said faintly at last.

"At least," said the other with the suggestion of a smile, "the voice of Clung was known."

He produced from the folds of his garments, with dexterous ease, a murderous knife and two revolvers, all of which he laid on the table. Then he held out his thin wrists side by side.

"Fire shots," said Clung, "and then bind my wrists with the irons. It will seem that Marshal Clauson took me by force and he will be greatly honored."

Chapter 14

Could a miser resist the gift of the touch of Midas? And to Clauson the temptation was greater than gold, for the recapture of Clung single-handed would raise his reputation to an eminence, silence his critics, make him, perhaps, at a single stroke the greatest and most feared officer of the law in the whole of the Southwest. All these thoughts burned themselves into his brain and seared his heart with the brightness of the things he saw. It was the steady resignation of the eyes of Clung which recalled him slowly to himself. But even then he was shaken like a man who has ridden for two days without rest, cramped and tortured by the saddle. Clung understood the outcome of that battle without a word. He dropped his arms to his side.

"Another time," he said in his gentle voice, "the marshal may regret that he has lost me twice. Then he shall know where to find me. I am going to Kirby Creek. Gold has been found. Hundreds and thousands of men have rushed to Kirby Creek. Even Clung will be lost among them; he will be lost among them and known as Yo Chai. If you need me, send for Yo Chai. Be sure that I will get up in the night from bed, even from sickness, and come to you. *Ch'u men chien hsi.* As you go out of the gate may you meet happiness."

He had straightened himself to the former youthful lines of Clung, the killer of men, now he dropped back into the middle-aged stoop of Yo Chai, a rich Chinese merchant. Marshal Clauson stumbled—for a mist was before his eyes —to the door, and blocked the way for a moment.

"Listen here to me, Clung," he said gravely. "You're white. After this there ain't no doubt you're white inside and out. For a minute back I was near to takin' you at your word and slinging you in the coop, but I couldn't do it. A Chink is one thing, but a white man is another. And you're white, Clung, damned white."

Clung made a deprecatory gesture with his lean hands. They returned instantly to his sleeves and his dull eyes blinked past the face of Clauson.

"Don't stand there sleepin' on your feet," said the marshal

angrily, "I know you ain't a hop-head so don't try to look like one. Cut out the Chink lingo and ways. Maybe you're a good actor, Clung, but this don't make no hit with me. Act like a man and a white man, like you are—inside and out!"

To this strenuous appeal Clung replied by merely blinking his eyes. To move him was like trying to wear granite with water. It irritated Clauson, who felt that his forbearance deserved a greater reward of confidence.

"Clung," he said, "talk out. I'm your friend. I like you; but don't stand there blinkin' at me like a damned dobe idol! What you mean by givin' up the ways of a white man? Is it all just a disguise? D'you need a disguise agin *me?*"

"There was a man named Clung," said the slender man, "and there came a time when he learned that he was white. He was very glad. He went among white men and they were brothers to him. They were very ugly in many ways, but they were his brothers. He loved them. But one of them stung him in the palm of his hand like a snake that he had warmed by his fire in winter, and others hunted him like a coyote up and down the hills, and there was a woman—"

He stopped short and his breast heaved once.

"Oh!" said Marshal Clauson, "I begin to follow you for the first time, Clung. Well, if it's the woman that rides your mind, Clung, you can be easy. She come in to me before you went free and asked what she could do for you. She was willing to do all you could ask a girl to do for a Chink, and if she knew you was white—well—"

He finished with a suggestive smile, but the face of Clung hardened. He was picking up his guns and his knife again from the table and replacing them under his coat, and the way he handled them was not pleasant to see—the knife went home with a little jar that made the marshal start.

"Does the color of the skin," he said, his voice evil and low, "change the color of a man's heart? If she knew me to be white would that change *me?* No, the white man sees only what his mind tells him to see. He follows stupid and ugly gods. Clung is dead, and Yo Chai remains. He has gone back to the gods of his fathers. He is happy with them."

The marshal moistened his lips and then went on with less assurance: "D'you mean to tell me, Clung, that you'd rather be a Chink than a white man—one of the salt of the earth?"

"Is a white man more honest?" asked Clung, with a ring like metal coming in his voice, and an uncanny brightening of his eyes. "Is he cleaner at heart? Does he talk less and more wisely? Does he know better what is beautiful and good? No! he chatters like a coyote over a dead beef—all noise and no meaning. He licks the hand that feeds him and then he bites it to the bone. He sees what his friends see but nothing for himself. He loves a horse because he pays a great price for it; he loves a woman because her body is beautiful. But the horse may stumble before it wins a race and the skin of a woman may be cheap under rich clothes."

The marshal stepped back a little abashed, and his eyes wandered while he hunted for another argument with which to meet this tide of words, but the other swept on: "Who was Clung? *K'e pu chih tao t'a shih shui!* (I do not know what he was.) He was half white and half yellow. To be all white is not good. I have seen and I know. So I have killed Clung. Now there is only Yo Chai. He is all yellow. He will sleep on a kang; he will pray to the gods of his fathers. Behind his front gate he will sit cross-legged on a mat of reeds and smoke (Pah! Clung hated the smell of tobacco smoke!). But now he will be all Chinese—all yellow. To be white is to be a fool; Clung was a fool."

"Clung," said the marshal, scowling, "some of what you say sounds kind of reasonable, and some of it I don't follow and some of it is Chink chatter that no white man wants to know, but I sort of gather from your drift that what you said towards the end was enough to make me fight, eh?"

"Ah," said the other and his voice and manner softened

instantly from harshness to a gentle dignity that came from the heart, "Marshal Clauson is my father and I am *ta shih fu* (your big servant). Yo Chai must go."

"And this is the end of Clung?" said the marshal, half sadly. "Well, lad, you done your bit while you was hanging around these parts—nobody ever done more. But if you go up to Kirby Creek you're going straight to trouble, Clung. They've got a tough lot up there. There's Dave Spenser that some calls the Night Hawk. A prime bad 'un he is, Clung, and no mistake. But he ain't all that's there. I been to Kirby Creek and I tell you straight from the shoulder that it's fuller of fights in the night than a big city. Every other shack is a saloon and dance hall, and the ones in between is gambling joints. And the men that go to a gold rush is chiefly crooks and fellers that ain't made a go of it in other places. They got nothing and they're ready to risk their hides for a dollar. Don't go to Kirby Creek, Clung."

"Yo Chai," said the other, with a swift glint of his dark eyes, "is not a dog. He will not run because men bark at him. If they bite, he has teeth."

And to prove it, his slow smile bared a row of white, perfect teeth.

"That's just what I mean," said the marshal anxiously, "before you been there a day you'll get in a fight, and when you get in a fight the devil'll turn loose in you—and no man that's ever seen you pull your guns once can ever make a mistake in you if he sees you work a second time. Clung, I *know!*"

"What does it matter?" said Clung solemnly. "I will not be a white man, and I cannot be all yellow even if I wish. There is only one thing left to Yo Chai, and that is to die. And if he dies, he hopes it will be with steel in his hand. So!"

And speaking, his head tilted back in that familiar way, and his eyes half closed, and his smile dreamed on the far distance. As if he once more sat on the table in his father's laundry and exulted in the yellow, hot sunlight against his face.

"I go," he said, and thrusting his hands back into the alternate sleeves, he bowed until the black tassel of his red cap almost brushed against the floor. "I go, Marsh' Clauson. Once more: *ch'u men chien hsi!*"

And with bent shoulders and jogging pig-tail, he strode through the door at a pace of grave and sober-footed dignity.

Chapter 15

To at least one person in Mortimer the passing of Clung from the town that day would have been a great joy had he but known of it. That person was John Sampson. For a fortnight he had trailed Winifred about the town while she strove vainly to discover clues of Clung. As a rule she hunted alone, escaping from him with any pretext, for when he was with her he would ejaculate at every other step: "All this for a damned Chink!"

"For a human being!" she would respond angrily

"Half human, maybe," John Sampson would answer.

"You mean, because he's half-white? As a matter of fact, Dad, it isn't the white in him that interests me, but the yellow blood. He's the most unusual mind I've ever met."

"Now, to be frank, Winifred, the whole point is that you want another person to take care of, just as you've been taking care of poor Billy Kirk. As soon as Bill was well you sent him away and you don't care if you ever lay eyes on him again. It'll be the same with this Clung—if you ever find him, which you won't."

"Won't I?" she would respond with that little touch of

mystery upon which a woman always falls back when she is thoroughly baffled. "I have some tricks left with which I'll catch him."

"But no trick as good as the one I have for scaring him away."

"Would you do that?"

"For heaven's sake, my dear, are we to throw away our lives simply because Billy Kirk called down the law on the head of an outlaw?"

"On the head of a man who saved his life," she would answer bitterly, and this, as a rule, ended the argument for the time being, until John Sampson recovered his wind and his bad temper. For he was a little plump man with short legs, and men of this build are not meant to withstand the heat of the Southwest.

So John Sampson, as a rule, persisted in following Winifred through the morning, but when the afternoon came his will power became a less vital factor than his irritation, and he retired in dudgeon to his room.

However, this routine could not go on forever. It was manifestly impossible that he should fry himself on the griddle of benevolence in the Southwest until doomsday. He decided to put an end to the tiresome quest; he would unearth a thorough history of the wild exploits of Clung, some of which he had already heard, and armed with this tale he would go to Winifred and relate it to her with some embellishments of his own. If this tale of violence did not revolt her, nothing would.

To do him justice, John Sampson was a thoroughly kindly man, and if he showed malevolence on this occasion, the shortness of his wind and of his legs must be remembered, and the tireless insistence of a woman bent on doing a good deed. A charitable woman, undoubtedly, is an angel to the evildoers, but she is designed by God to try the patience of respectable men who possess a surplus of everything except time.

It was something of this madness which possessed John Sampson on this day. He had trudged from one dusty end of Mortimer to the other pursued by a haunting mirage—a cool room in his club far, far to the north. Having made up his mind to unearth the whole gruesome story of the killings of the outlaw, he decided to start at the beginning and wheedle something from the mouth of Li Clung, the reputed father of the man-killer. And he went, accordingly, as fast as his pudgy legs would carry him, straight to the laundry of Li Clung.

Now, the smell of a laundry in any land and in any city and clime is not that of a garden, and the odor of a Chinese laundry on a hot day in the Southwest, with the scent of sweaty laborers and the sharp taint of desert sand all mingling, is thrilling, indeed, but not poetic. John Sampson stood at the door and stared down the row of bobbing heads that wagged steadily from side to side above the ironing-boards.

"Haloo!" called John Sampson, but not a head stirred. While he waited he observed a little table at his right hand, full in the glare of the sun. Interesting things might have been told him about that table, and at least one story that would have made the face of Winifred Sampson turn pale. Presently a little Chinese in white, loose trousers and a black cotton coat, the forward part of his head completely shaven, hobbled from the back of the room.

"Li Clung?" asked John Sampson.

"Li Clung," nodded the Chinese, and removed the long stem of his pipe from his mouth. John Sampson saw a death's head of leanness, the skin pulled so tightly across the forehead that it shone, and the cheeks sucked into little holes at the center. The head was supported by a marvelously lean neck on which the skin hung in withered folds. Yet there was about this old, tottering wreck of a Chinese a suggestion of strength and further capacity for labor that moved a sense of dim respect in John Sampson. He began to see that it was possible for this old grotesque to be the father of slender, handsome Clung, the killer of men.

He said: "You have a son?"

Instantly the countenance of the Chinaman lightened, and his hand made a little movement almost as if he were about to reach out and touch the white man. The expression changed almost at once, however, to one of suspicious grief.

"I have a son," he answered simply, and his moist old eyes fastened earnestly on John Sampson.

"And he is in trouble," went on the financier easily. "Of course we all know about that. Now, Li Clung, I am a friend of a man whose life Clung saved. Understand?"

He raised his forefinger to emphasize and point his question, careful lest his vocabulary should be too large for the brain of Li Clung, but the Chinese returned at once: "It is true: Clung saved many men; he saved even more men than he killed."

John Sampson could not refrain from a little frown of irritation. It was not an auspicious beginning.

"I don't doubt it," he went on, "but I saw him save the life of my friend Kirk, and I'm grateful to him for it. I want to do something to show that gratitude, understand? Now, of course I can't do anything for him down here where the law is hunting him, but if I could send word to him to go north and meet me somewhere, there is a good deal that I might do. Can you tell me where he is, Li Clung?"

It was only the shadow of a smile that touched the lips of Li Clung, but John Sampson knew at once that the old man would rather die a thousand times than give the location of his son.

"How should I know?" asked Li Clung, and he raised his calloused hands, palms out. "My son has gone. Can I follow the wind?"

John Sampson smiled—and there was a great deal of kindness in his smile. He could not help admiring the old man's faithfulness and liking him for it. Now, kindness is the one human light which all men recognize independent of color and breeding; this time it shone from the face of John Sampson and reflected dimly on the face of Li Clung.

"You are a good man, maybe," said the Chinese dubiously. "Li Clung knows in your house Clung was taken."

"But you also know it was not my fault."

"That is true," admitted Li Clung.

"Now, Li, I'm going to be straightforward with you. If I can get hold of Clung, I can do a great deal for him. You want your son to be a wise man, don't you? Well, I can see that he goes to the finest schools; I can see that he has clothes as good as any white man; in a word, I can set him up in life."

His first note was the key that unlocked the heart of Li Clung; for in China, old and new, the thing most highly prized is education. Now Li Clung laid his pipe by on the table and drew a little closer to John Sampson.

"Li Clung," he repeated, "thinks you are a good man, and perhaps he can tell you—"

"But first," said John Sampson, for the last thing he wished to know at that moment was the location of the outlaw, "first I must ask you some other questions."

"Come," said Li Clung readily enough, and led the way back to his own little rooms behind the laundry.

Chapter 16

"In the first place," went on John Sampson when they were settled in privacy, "I want to know something about the—er—parentage of Clung. You see, it isn't always easy to place a boy of—er—foreign birth in the best schools—"

But Li Clung broke in with a smile and a wave of his hand. "Clung is the son of a white mother—"

"Yes," nodded Sampson, "his skin shows that much."

"And a white father," added Li Clung.

"A what?" roared John Sampson, and bolted out of his chair.

"He is not of my blood," said the old Chinese sadly, "but he has lived in my house and eaten my food and learned my lessons."

The white man stared at him, transfixed with wonder and a touch of horror. For his daughter Winifred had seemed strangely interested in the outlaw, and had persisted even when she thought him to be a half-breed Chinese. If she learned that he was all white, John Sampson shuddered for the results. There flashed across his mind a picture of his fortune descending through his daughter to the hands of an unlettered whelp of the desert, a man hunted by the law.

"It's a lie," he groaned.

"Li Clung," frowned the Chinaman, drawing up to the full of his withered height, "does not lie."

And the white man knew it was the truth; his own anguish of spirit confirmed it. A grim resolve came to him to save his girl from the possible horror of the future through the hand of the law. He shrank from it, but he had done harder things than this in his day, and for lesser reasons.

"Where is Clung?" he asked at length.

Li Clung observed him with steady eyes.

"Swear to Li Clung," he said, "that John Sampson means only good to Clung, that he means to give him schooling and make him a man among men."

The other set his teeth and swallowed before he could reply: "I swear."

But Li Clung hobbled at his burden-bearer's gait to a corner of the room and took down a dusty book from the shelf.

"The yellow man has his gods and the white man has other gods," said Li Clung, and returning he placed an open Bible before John Sampson. "Swear again on this book that you mean only good to Clung."

John Sampson laid his hand on the crinkling page of the open book and scowled at the Chinese. The word came up in his throat, up to his very teeth; and there it stuck. His tongue was so dry that he could not have spoken if he wished, and it seemed as if the heat which dried his tongue rose from the book he touched and ran along his arm and up to his heart.

"It is a little thing to do," urged Li Clung gently. "Swear on the book of the white god. My son is hunted; I must know if you are one of the hunters."

But John Sampson suddenly raised the book and hurled it across the room. It crashed against the wall and dropped to the floor again with a rush and rattle of the leaves; then he turned on his heel and strode heavily and quickly from the room and out past the swaying line of ironers on to the white-hot street.

Suppose a man buys a lead mine and finds that it produces gold; and suppose this gold threatens, like the touch of Midas, to divide the purchaser from all that he holds dear in the world. From these suppositions one might strike fairly close to the heart of John Sampson's mood. He loved his daughter as a vigorous, worldly man can love an only child; he loved her energy—so like his own—her beauty, her frankness; the charm and grace of spirit which illumined her to his eyes. Her charity, doubtless, went hand in hand with her other virtues, but it was the quality which he admired least and the force which now threatened to debase her to the level of an unlettered man-killer. For the same instinct which enabled him to read the purposes of speculators in the stock market gave him insight into the impulses of the girl. She followed the trail of Clung partly because he had received bad for good in a single instance, but mostly because of the very fact that he was an outlaw, hopeless, beleaguered by the hostility of thousands. To her he held the charm of a lost cause, something to be saved and therefore something to be cherished. Only his Chinese blood had kept her from regarding him as a young girl might regard a desirable man; now this single barrier was removed and John Sampson sweated with fear as he guessed at consequences. He went straight back to the little house they had rented, to rest and to think; he had a grave need of thought and planning.

But as he set foot on the lowest of the steps leading to the front porch there rose from the depths of the house a voice of thrilling sweetness; to John Sampson it was like the bugle call which announces the charge of the enemy's horse. He drew in a great breath and puffed it out noisily as a diver snorts when he comes up for air; and the singing of Winifred rose and rang in the slow cadence of the old song:

> What made the ball so fine?
> Robin Adair.
> What made the assembly shine?
> Robin Adair.

The favorite song of Winifred, and he knew that she only sang it when her heart was at rest; he leaped up the steps with the agility of a youth and stamped into the house. At the banging of the front door she came running to him, caught both his hands.

"Dad!" she cried gaily. "Can you guess the good news?"

His heart stood still; perhaps from some other source she had learned the true identity of Clung.

"Clung?" he managed to articulate in spite of his dry throat.

"Yes, yes—of course. And I've found him!"

"You!"

"Why, Dad, you look sick!"

"The damned heat," he muttered. "Enough to kill a horse.

Where's Clung?"

"In Kirby Creek. We start for it tomorrow."

He ejaculated: "*We* start? For Kirby Creek?"

"We do."

"Winifred, d'you know that's the hardest, roughest mining camp in the Southwest? D'you know that that's the haunt of Dave Spenser and a hundred other scoundrels who'd as soon kill you as ask you for a match? What fool suggested that you go to Kirby Creek?"

She sighed, and then fixed her eyes gravely on him like one prepared for a long debate.

"No one has suggested it, but it was Marshal Clauson who told me that Clung might be in Kirby Creek."

"Might?" cried John Sampson, seizing on the straw.

But it would not bear his weight.

"The marshal is almost sure that Clung is there, but he made me promise not to spread the news about. There's something quite mysterious about it, Dad. You see, he would say nothing to me about Clung and seemed furious when I mentioned the name of Clung. In fact, he called him a blankety blank Chink."

"Quite right," growled John Sampson.

"But," went on the girl, "when I convinced him that I meant nothing but good by Clung and told him my reasons he seemed a bit shaken and listened to me pretty closely. At last he told me, in his gruff way, that if I was really anxious to find Clung the best way would be to go to the worst bit of hell in the Southwest—Kirby Creek. I asked him how he knew that Clung was there. He answered, of course, that he knew nothing, and that if he were sure he'd go to the Creek and take Clung in the name of the law. Then I wanted to know why he gave me the hint, but he only winked and then refused to say another word. It was very queer, but I'm sure that he had some grounds for giving me the advice, and I'm also sure that he doesn't wish any real harm to befall Clung.

Isn't this enough reason why we should go to Kirby Creek and at least make the trial to find Clung there?"

John Sampson frowned, thinking hard.

He said at last: "Give me until next Monday before we start. In the meantime we'll hunt for more clues in Mortimer."

"But if we don't find 'em you *will* go, Dad?"

He looked at her in whimsical despair.

"Don't I understand perfectly, my dear," he answered, "that if I didn't go with you, you'd go alone?"

"Poor Dad!" she smiled.

"Poor Winifred," he responded, and his seriousness silenced her and set her thinking.

Chapter 17

Sampson went to his room at once and sat for a time with his hot face buried in his hands, then he took pen and paper and wrote to William Kirk, far in the north. No pleasant task, for his wet hand stuck to the surface of the paper; and his thoughts came haltingly.

Dear Billy (he wrote),

Hell has broke loose at last.

I wrote you that we were still on the trail of the scoundrel Clung; and here in this miserable little oven of Mortimer we have stayed all these days, walking these infernal, dusty streets; you know this alkali dust that stings your nose and throat like pepper. Here we've remained, but today the devil, as if he were tired of my rest, rose up and, in the language of the streets, hit me where I live. He hit me twice.

And both punches, Billy, are as hard on you as they

are on me.

First I went to see Li Clung, reputed father of our outlaw. I found a withered mummy of an Oriental, and began to pump him, but after the first draw I wanted to seal the well. For I learned right off the bat, Billy, that Clung is pure white.

It stunned me. Then I thought of trying to find out where Clung is hiding and warn the officers of the law—such law as they have in the sand-wilderness. But the old Chinaman grew suspicious. He wouldn't tell me another word.

So I went back to the house and the first thing that greeted me was the voice of Winifred singing "Robin Adair." You know how she sings that little song when she's happy?

And she told me that she had received a hint that Clung is in Kirby Creek. She wanted to start for the place at once. If she follows the trail of a half-breed Chinaman with this enthusiasm, what will she do when she learns that the man is white? God knows!

And what am *I* to do? I can't keep up with that long-legged girl of mine, and she's as tireless as a little devil —or angel. An angel when she does what I wish and a devil when she crosses me. Take a little of the coolest blue of heaven and salt it with some of the fire of hell and you have an idea of Winifred's stubbornness. What will happen if that fire touches the powder of Clung, the white man? But does Clung know that he's white? Isn't it possible that his father has never told him? Does anyone beside old Li Clung know that the outlaw is white? I think not; pray God that no one does.

For I tell you, Billy, in all seriousness, if Winifred learns that Clung is white she's going to do something that will make the rest of her life one long torment. She *must* not know. And I must have help to keep the knowledge from her. Billy, you must come down here and work with me.

Winifred has recovered from her first anger against you because you turned Clung over to the law; now I'm sure she'd accept you on the basis of a friend, at least. And as for you, if I can believe the letters you write, two fevers possess you: one is for Winifred and the other is for another sight of the desert. In fact, there is a thing they commonly refer to down here as desert-fever. The Lord knows it will never get me, but I'm afraid you're a victim. Perhaps you can't forget that you recovered your health down here in the wilderness.

At any rate you ought to be willing for a double reason to come back to me. We'll find reasons to give Winifred. Perhaps you can say that you regret what you did to Clung—inadvertently, at that—and that you want to redeem yourself in her eyes by helping her to find the outlaw. She'll believe you. On the subject of Clung, I assure you, she's blind and unreasonable and would question the help of no man. Perhaps this same quest for Clung will be the lever by which you pry your way back into the affections of Winifred. Oh, lad, it will be a happy day for me when that happens.

Whatever you do, do it quickly. I have secured a moment of grace. Until Monday we stay here, and by that time you can surely be with us, make your peace with Winifred, and start for Kirby Creek.

Kirby Creek! The dumping ground of half the desperadoes of the country—gun fights and killings every day —what a place for a woman to go! But a sheriff's posse could not keep Winifred back and I shall not make the effort.

Speed is the thing, Billy. If you want to save your game, play now!

Yours most miserably,
John Sampson.

He scrawled his signature and mailed the letter. It was hardly in the box before he wished it were out again. He should have made it stronger, more emphatic by far; but he walked back gloomily to the house.

He found Winifred surrounded with purchases. She had spent the afternoon in a dry goods store preparing herself for the life in the rough mining camp and laying in a stock of khaki clothes, short riding-skirts, broad brimmed hats, boots, spurs, and every necessity. She had thought of her father's comfort and in his room lay his own requirements neatly stacked upon his bed. He looked on them with a feeling that fate was upon him.

Also, she had learned all the details of the ways to Kirby Creek and had decided in favor of the stage which wound through the hills up and down a hundred miles to Kirby Creek. She became insistent that they take the stage on the morrow. There was apparently only one way to hold her in the town, and John Sampson took it. Before night he was in bed with a fever.

It was not all assumed, for his nervous anticipations had set his nerves on edge, and like the ringing of a bell the name Clung echoed through his head by day and night. Sometimes he recalled, bitterly, with how soft a step the fellow had stepped on to the verandah and into the lives of the three of them. How soft a step! Indeed, the strength of Clung was like the strength of silences. It would have been safer to guess at the mind and will of a lone wolf than to try to unravel the inner being of Clung.

Not the mental problem alone, but the physical labor of the quest and its danger occupied his mind. He regretted now that he had flung the Bible away from him in the shop of old Li Clung. Surely the father was in communication with his son and would warn him that John Sampson meant no good to Clung. And if that warning was carried to the strange fellow, what would be the outcome of it? Perhaps an approach in the middle of the night, silent as the slipping of a snake's belly over a polished floor, the gleam of a knife blade in the dark, and then the thud of the handle striking home, and horrible death; or the fellow might stalk up to him with his easy step in the middle of the day, shoot him down and ride off again into the heart of the desert. These fancies grew upon John Sampson, for though he now knew that Clung was white, he still attributed to Clung all the cold and subtle cruelty and remorselessness with which the Occident generally dresses its conception of the East.

In the meantime the long tenure of his bed began to irk him and the hours dragged slowly through Sunday. On Monday, the doctor had assured Winifred, her father would be able to travel over even a hard road. So Sampson waited for Monday nervously, thinking of Clung on the one hand and of William Kirk on the other; for Kirk might come on that day if he started from the north as soon as he received the letter of appeal.

So he delayed the hour for his rising on Monday morning, delayed it until the prime of the day; and he had hardly finished his dressing when he heard a very heavy footfall ascend the front steps, and then the excited cry of Winifred in greeting.

"Billy Kirk!"

"Winifred, by the Lord, it's good to see you!"

That heavy bass voice was like the trumpet of a rescuing angel to John Sampson.

Chapter 18

He hurried to his door, set it a little ajar, and shamelessly played the eavesdropper.

"And it's mighty pleasant to see you, Will."

"Honestly, Winifred?"

"Of course!"

A great note of relief came in the voice of Kirk.

"Then you've forgiven me, eh?"

"At least, I'm trying to forget about it, Will. I was pretty bitter about it for a while, but now I realize that you had no idea just what John Ring's status might be. It was two-thirds curiosity, wasn't it? You simply wanted to see if you had guessed right, and if Ring was really an outlaw."

There was a little pause, and even in his hiding place John Sampson winced, for he knew that the searching eyes of the girl were passing up and down the face of William Kirk. Then the voice of Kirk replied, growing hard as he nerved himself to an ordeal.

"I'll be straight with you, Winifred. I might wriggle out of it in that way, but I won't. The plain, dirty truth is that I was jealous of Clung."

"Jealous?"

"No, no! Of course I don't mean in that way. But I was jealous of his influence over you, and jealous of the way in which the fellow seemed able to make me out a coarse and stupid fool whenever the three of us were together. I always felt, you see, that he was the silk and I was the rough-surfaced wool. Is that clear?"

"Perfectly."

"What a little aristocrat you are, Winifred! Well, now your eyes are scorning me again and you're commencing to be formally polite."

"Not a bit. But I want to think it over. That's all. You have to expect that, don't you, Billy?"

"I suppose so. Take this into consideration, too. I was just back from a close call with death and my nerves weren't very strong. I was hardly myself when I made that very rotten move, Winifred."

"But I have to remember who brought you back from that

close call with death, Billy."

"Exactly, but ingratitude, now and then, is a mighty human failing."

"A very black one, Billy."

"If it's persisted in."

"Well?"

"I haven't persisted in mine. I'm going to try to undo in a way what I've already done."

"I'm perfectly ready to believe you."

"When you see me do it, eh? That's a man to man, straight from the shoulder way to look at it. If I can manage to help Clung, will that restore us to something of the old footing?"

"I hope so—in a way."

"This is straight stuff. Three things brought me back to the Southwest. Now, I know I might make a pretty speech and say that I came only for your sake."

"Please don't."

"My dear girl, I know you much too well for that. Well, there are two things beside you. The first after you, to be frank, is that I haven't gotten the feel of this dry, keen air out of my lungs. I've been hungry for this country. It's the desert fever. I've been dreaming about the open stretches, the wide skies, and I've smelled the sweat of hot horses in my dreams. Tried the outdoor life up north but it hasn't the same tang."

"You look wonderfully fit."

"Don't I! Hard as a brick, too. You'd laugh if you knew how I've been spending half my time. Rigged up a little target range at my country place and I've spent two or three hours a day there practicing with guns. Guns have a new meaning after one has seen a fellow like Clung make a draw. Gad! d'you remember how he dropped from his chair to the floor and how those guns of his simply jumped into his hands?"

She laughed, excited.

"I'll never forget it, Billy."

"So the first reason I wanted to come south was to live the life again. The last reason is that I want to redeem myself with Clung. In a word, Winifred, I want to help you hunt for him and find him and put him back on his feet."

"Billy, this is real man's talk!"

"If you can use me, tell me where."

"We start for a wild mining camp today. By stage. It'll be a Godsend to have you. Poor Dad is worn out with tagging about after me."

"Where is he? I'll pay my respects."

"Just knock at that door. He's dressing now."

And a moment later John Sampson found himself staring into the eyes of William Kirk.

He was singularly changed. He looked, as he had said, perfectly fit and hard as nails. The frame which had been wasted to pitiful gauntness by disease was now filled and a mighty bulk of muscles swelled the coat at each shoulder. More important still was a certain strong self-confidence in the man's bearing which went hand in hand with his bulk; of still greater significance was the brightness and steadiness of the eyes.

"Gad!" breathed John Sampson. "How you've changed, lad, how you've changed!"

He clapped a hand on either broad shoulder of the giant, reaching to the level of his own head to do so; and he conjured up, in contrast, the image of Clung, frail, delicate handed, nervous of gesture and gentle of eye. This was such an ally as he needed.

"I have."

"Chiefly—inside?"

"Chiefly inside."

"And Clung?" queried Sampson cautiously.

"Well?"

"I heard what you said to Winifred."

"John Sampson, you old fox!"

"And you Billy?"

"I suppose," said the other, and shrugged his heavy shoulders, "that I'll have to play the fox too."

"For whose sake, Billy?"

"Damned if I know."

"Not your own?"

"To tell you the truth—" began Kirk.

"You seem," cut in the financier dryly, "to be bothered a good deal by the truth these days, Will."

"H-m-m!" growled the big man. "And what if I am? Don't you think it's a fairly decent thing to be bothered by?"

"Excellent!" sneered Sampson. "Excellent! It will be of great benefit to you, my boy—in the hereafter!"

"What an infernal old cynic you are!"

"Not a cynic. Practical, my lad."

"That sort of practice—"

"Sends men to hell. Come, come, Billy. Between your gun practice up north you've been going to Sunday school, eh?"

And he laughed softly.

A young man is not apt to insist upon morals when he finds them scoffed at by his elders.

"I'm not lying to you, Sampson," he protested, reddening.

"Not a bit," said the other instantly, "you're merely telling me what you think you think. And I suppose that you're going to do exactly what you said you'd do when you were talking with Winifred. You're going to help her to find Clung."

"I am," said the other, and squared his shoulders resolutely, "I owe Clung more than that—more than—"

"Not so loud! Well, after you bring the two together you'll send them a wedding present and then step gracefully out of the picture—and back to your Sunday school?"

"Sampson, you'd anger a saint."

"I hope so."

"D'you really think that Winifred—"

"When she finds he's white, lad, the novelty of the thing

will knock her off her feet. Afterwards she'll have a good many years for repentance, but that won't help me—or you. You're still fond of her, Billy?"

"Hopelessly."

"Not entirely. Patience, Billy, accomplishes strange things with both stock markets and women. Besides, do I have to draw you a picture of what the girl's life would be with Clung? His blood may be white but his mind is Oriental, Billy. You know that."

"Listen," said the tall man and frowning he shook off the hands of Sampson, "if I listen to you any longer I may be hypnotized. I won't listen. I *want* to do the right thing."

"Of course. So you're going to begin by running to Winifred and telling her that you know Clung is white."

Kirk was silent.

"There's the door. She's in the other room."

Still silence from Kirk.

"She'll be glad to hear it; very glad!"

Kirk seized the knob with sudden resolution, hesitated, and finally slumped into a chair that creaked under the impact of his great weight; he sat regarding Sampson with an ominous and steady scowl.

"I suppose," he muttered at last, "that you win."

"I knew," nodded the other, "that you had not entirely lost your wits; they've been merely frostbitten in the north. Wait until your blood circulates and you'll be reasonable. I'm in no hurry. In the meantime, the thing of importance is to find Clung—yes—and then call the law on him before Winifred reaches him."

"A pretty little plan—very pleasant," sneered Kirk.

"By which you are the winner. If Clung is gone, she'll turn to you at last."

"What'll make her?"

"The habit of having you around. Habit, my dear boy, is usually several points stronger than what the poets call love."

And he teetered complacently back and forth, from heel to toe, and grinned upon William Kirk. The big man sighed.

"I came down here to have a good time," he said, as if to himself. "To enjoy a long vacation, and incidentally to set myself right in the matter of Clung. I seem to be on the way—"

"To just the same sort of a vacation, my lad," broke in the older man, "except that instead of putting yourself right with Clung, you'll put yourself right with Winifred. In the meantime you can play as much as you like—ride your sweating horse—swing your guns—drink this abominable bar whiskey—and in general, be a happy young fool."

"There's acid on your tongue," grumbled Kirk.

"And reason," nodded Sampson.

"After all," murmured the other, and he frowned into a corner of the room, "why not?"

Chapter 19

As if by mutual consent of horses, driver, and passengers, the stage, as it topped the last ascent above the hollow of Kirby Creek, came to a halt on the little plateau of the hill-crest. Below, clambering up in a rude swarm like soldiers to an assault, stretched the huts of the town, mere lean-tos propped against the steep hillsides. They were pitched like tents wherever the will of the owner decided, and decided hastily. Indeed, there were four tents to every cabin in that little host.

On the veritable verge of the town men labored at holes in the ground, and down the ravines on every side pick and shovel winked in the keen sunshine as the laborers burrowed at the soil. From this distance the utter silence made the stir the more impressive. Then the wind, which had been blowing down the main valley, swerved and blew directly in the face of the stage. Slowly up the wind came the voice of the labor, a clicking of metal in it, and the rumble of men's voices, and now and then the sharper note of a braying burro, or the whinny of a horse, but all subdued and blended by the distance into a murmur no louder than the hum of a bee—an angered bee, heavily laden and struggling against the wind. The men in the stage sat forward in their seats, and their hands gripped and relaxed automatically as if they were already in spirit attacking the earth and hunting for treasure.

Not an eye turned to right or left. They were thinking, each man of himself—visions of the "strike." And they were silent and awed. Gold! it banished the reality of burned, brown hillsides and the muddy creek far beneath. It raised visions of columned entrances, stately ships, beautiful women with jewelled hands and throats. All this of beauty and grace, but the light that it kindled in the eyes of the treasure hunters was a hard, keen fire. Not one of the passengers, not John Sampson in spite of his great wealth already accumulated, nor William Kirk with the desert-fever upon him, nor Winifred with her mission of charity, but found himself drawn at a single step to the edge of hate and murder and bitter battle for gold.

Down the slope and into the city of gold the stage passed. It rolled on unheeded, for every man on the rude streets was like the men in the stage; he was looking straight before him with keen, hard eyes, thinking only of himself, the strike he had made, or was to make, or had missed.

But already the receivers of gold were mixed with the finders and the spenders. Their presence was made known in a hundred places. Here came a woman with vast, red, bare arms—bare to the elbow. She carried a flimsy parasol of blue silk, and twirled it constantly. At every motion of her hand a score of great diamonds flashed in the sun; and around her throat was a yellow, glimmering chain supporting a glorious ruby. The jeweller was there on the heels of gold.

And another woman, sauntering. A man, passing, changed glances with her, stopped, and turned to walk on at her side. She and her kind who follow men over the world, they were here also on the heels of gold.

Here came two men, arm in arm, reeling. Alternately they cursed and laughed, then broke into a song of reeking vulgarity. The saloon was there on the heels of gold.

And now a large man in dapper clothes with a heavy gold watch-chain across the vast expanse of his stomach and a bright neck-tie at his throat. He walked leisurely, and his small, bright eyes picked out face after face and lingered on them a moment like the hawk searching the field below for mice. The confidence man was there on the heels of gold.

Passing him, another type—pale, slender, stoop-shouldered, with white hands exceeding agile and forever busied with the lapel of his coat or in pulling out his handkerchief. White hands and strangely agile and swift and sure, the sign of his trade. The gambler is here on the heels of gold.

The very air was changed in Kirby Creek. To breathe it was to breathe hope, chance, danger. It set the blood tingling.

William Kirk turned to Winifred.

"Do we stay here?" he asked.

"He is here," she answered.

"Can you trust yourself here among these men?"

"They're Southwesterners, Will. I'm safer among them than I would be walking the streets at home with an escort. Besides—"

"Well?"

"I like it!"

He looked at her in amazement. She seemed to have awakened; her face flushed, her eyes shining with excitement.

"Like it?" he repeated, breathless with his surprise.

"All of it!" she answered, and made an all-embracing gesture. "The dirt, the vulgarity, the cheating, the danger. They're men—all men—and all in action, Will!"

"But such an impossible gang of swine—" he began, and then he stopped short and some of her own fire lighted his eyes.

His blood ran with a thrill, warm and then cold. As she had said, here were men, real men, and all in action. It was the old lure of the desert, stronger, wilder, sharper, but the same. The chances bigger than in the north, the danger greater, and also the reward. And, somewhere among those men, he felt he should find a place for himself. It was the New World, the undiscovered country—himself and these. Three centuries of culture surrounded William Kirk, three generations of gentlemanly traditions. At this moment the first century of these traditions dropped away and he tossed it aside as a man might toss off an encumbering cloak when he is about to enter a fight for his life.

Chapter 20

By luck, they found a place to live in within an hour after they reached the town of Kirby Creek. It was on the outskirts of the town and the most commodious dwelling in the place. It had been inhabited by a prospector and his family, but a few days before his eldest son had been killed by a blow with a pick handle in a drunken brawl, and the prospector, in consequence, was leaving the camp. He sold his rights at an outrageous price and the three spent the rest of the day purchasing household furniture at prices running up to ten times that of the real value. Also they secured an old crippled Texan, Hugh Williams, for the housework and by nightfall they were eating their first meal in their new residence.

The house had been thrown together rather than built. Nevertheless it was a shelter and gave them privacy. Furthermore, it was on the extreme outskirts of the town, up the ravine, and the noise of the brawling, drunken miners would disturb them less in this spot.

Hugh Williams cooked amazingly well considering the rickety tin stove with which he had to work; and after supper, when it was decided that they should venture forth into the night life of the wild camp, they asked Hugh Williams to direct them to the best place. His answer was prompt and decisive.

"The only fit place," said Hugh Williams, "is that gambling house Yo Chai, the Chinaman, runs. Nobody ever called his games crooked, but such luck I've never seen. I was there when he won the house from Skinny Wallace."

"Won the whole place gambling?" asked Sampson.

"Draw poker," said Hugh Williams, and drew in a reverent breath. "The gold it was stacked all over that table, and the Chink, he wins one hand and then loses one, but the ones he lose don't amount to nothin', and the ones he win just bring in the gold in heaps. Nobody played much that night but just stood round and watched them two; and old Skinny Wallace, he kept right on drinkin' and playin' and losin'. Till finally he went bust!

"Then Yo Chai took the place and the next day he asked all the folks to come in and look at Skinny Wallace's machines, and they was all crooked—a brake on the roulette wheel and down to loaded dice. And Yo Chai he asked two men to watch while he had all the games put back on the level. Since then we can all see every bit of every machine. But still Yo Chai keeps winnin'."

"Much rough stuff around Yo Chai's house?" asked Kirk.

"Rough stuff? No sir, there's no rough house around Yo Chai. It don't pay to fool with that Chinaman. But Chapman tried to shoot up Yo Chai's place, and Yo Chai threw a knife and nailed Bud's hand plumb up agin the bar. Nobody fools around Yo Chai since then."

The recommendation was too strong to pass unfollowed. They wound down the hill, following Hugh's directions, and reached in due time the gambling house of Yo Chai. It looked like a stable except that the roof at no point rose to more than twelve or fourteen feet above the ground, but it was finished as rudely as any stable, and as the lumber had given out long before the place was finished, the roof was chiefly formed of tarred canvas stretched across the rafters. even this was lacking in one wide corner, and the gamblers played under the roof of the white, distant stars.

Through this gap, also, there came an occasional gust of wind which billowed the blue clouds of cigarette smoke in choking masses across the room—and sometimes it poured in such masses through the door that the building seemed to be on fire. The smoke in itself was enough to obscure the brightest of lights, and such illumination as there was consisted of lanterns of great size swinging from posts here and there in the wide structure. They made not a general glow of light but a number of distinct halos of brilliancy through the mist of tobacco smoke. Each halo embraced a table at which some game ran in full blast—crap, faro, chuck-a-luck, poker, every favorite of the Southwestern gambler; but beyond these halos, faces were continually passing to and fro and withdrawing into the twilight confusion like ships moving through a fog.

At one end of the room stretched a bar at which half a dozen men labored steadily to supply the demands of the customers, for drinks were served free at every table. However, since these did not come fast enough to suit many of the players at games which did not demand undivided attention, there was a continual stream of men running from tables to the bar, drinking hastily, and then turning to run back to their places. These, very often, collided with one of the Chinese servants who bore trays of drinks to the seated and more patient gamblers; each collision was announced by a shiver of glassware, a shrill clatter of Oriental rage, and the deep, booming laugh of a white man.

These were only high points in the general clamor, for the calls of the "men-on-the-sticks" and of the dealers and of the players kept up a continual monotone broken sharply here and there by a snarl of fury, a shout of delight, or the deep groan which announced that one of the players was broke. A tawdry, dim, drunken confusion, but here, as over the entire town, there was the glamor of chance which shot the smoky gloom full of rays of gold.

Winifred heard the voice of a stranger beside her saying: "Life! By God, here's raw life!"

And she turned to look up into the face of William Kirk. It was so changed by the shadows and by the hardening of the mouth and the brightening of the eyes that for the moment she hardly recognized him any more than she had known the sound of his voice. But she laughed, and throwing up her arms answered: "Life, Billy!"

The sound of her own voice startled her; it was rougher and more strained than she had ever heard it. And she knew, all at once, that the same fierce light which transfigured the eyes of Kirk was also in her own. She turned to her father, to see if he also had caught the fierce fever of the place, awe-stricken, amused, and more than half delighted.

But her father was not beside her any longer. It sobered her to coldness to miss him, and she cried out to Kirk in her alarm.

"There he is," answered the big man, and then laughed deeply, a boom and roar of sound, exultant. "There he is; he's in the fire, Winifred!"

The comfortably plump back of her father, indeed, was at that moment settling into a chair at the central table.

Chapter 21

This central table stood apart from the rest of the gambling hall; no matter how high the riot rang through the rest of the place, in this central space voices hushed, and it was surrounded by an atmosphere of comparative quiet dignity. Whereas the rest of the floor was thickly strewn with sawdust which served the double purpose of cleanliness and of muffling the fall of heels, the central table was supported by a dais spread with Indian blankets of price and rising a foot higher than the common boards. On the dais was a round table capable of accommodating five people in comfort, and no more were ever allowed to sit there. Moreover, a man had to show at least a thousand dollars in gold currency or in dust before he was allowed to sit in on the game, which was always draw poker. One of these chairs had been recently vacated by a disgruntled loser, and into his place stepped John Sampson.

The glance of Winifred passed from her father to the loser who had just left the chair. He was a Mexican, and she saw his face was darkened by a black malevolent scowl which shifted back towards the table and then returned darkly to the front. The Mexican joined a compatriot who leaned against one of the posts. The lantern overhead cast a sombre shadow which swallowed up the pair immediately, but when they moved on towards the bar she made out that the second Mexican was wrapped to the ears in a gray blanket. The loser made many gestures as they walked, speaking with his lips close to the ear of his companion. Winifred turned to William Kirk.

"See those two?" she asked.

"The Mexicans?"

"Yes. They mean mischief. One of them has lost a good deal of money, I take it, and he means to try to get some of it back. I want to get Dad out of here before any shooting starts."

At that Kirk stiffened, his big shoulders going back, and his face altered to a singular ugliness. At the best he was not a handsome man, with his heavily defined features, but now, at the mention of shooting, his lips twisted back into a mirthless laugh, like the silent grin of a wolf-hound, and his eyes lighted evilly. She remembered what he had said of practicing with his guns every day when he had been at his home in the north. She believed it now, for he made her think of the boy who has learned to box and goes about among his companions looking for trouble. His glance swept around the room, lingering an instant on the more marked faces, and then it returned to the two Mexicans, who by this time were leaning against the bar, drinking and talking earnestly, their heads close together.

"Leave this to me," said William Kirk, and his voice was dry with a peculiarly harsh command. "If there's trouble there's no reason why I can't take care of your father. In the meantime, he's robbing the robbers. Look!"

It was the end of a hand, and John Sampson was methodically raking from the center of the table a great heap of chips—a big winning. Other faces at the table turned enviously towards the new, successful player, but the dealer remained unmoved. She noticed first the yellow, slender fingers flying over the cards as he shuffled, and then the small, round wrists twisting as he dealt the next hand. She had never seen greater suppleness and grace. Looking up

90

above the hands she encountered the face of a middle-aged Chinaman wearing a crimson skull cap with a black tassel. For the first moment she concentrated on the dress of the man—a loose robe of a color somewhere between violet and purple, and heavily brocaded with gold: the wide, trailing sleeves making the slender grace of the wrists more apparent. Here, certainly, was Yo Chai, the owner, and now she studied his face carefully. The eyebrows were highly and plaintively arched, and a purple shadow on both the upper and lower lids made his eyes seem deeply sunken. From the upper lip straggled sparse black hairs but the mouth itself was finely and thoughtfully formed and the other features delicately chiselled. His expression was so devoid of life that he seemed rather a Buddhist rapt in mystic contemplation than a Chinese gambler concentrating on a game.

It seemed that Kirk had followed the steady direction of her glance, for he muttered now: "Rum old bird, isn't he? Seems to me I've seen him before. I suppose it's Yo Chai?"

As if to answer him, a miner dressed like a cowboy at that moment mounted the dais and stood beside the dealer shifting his hat awkwardly on his head. The Chinese turned and the miner leaned down to whisper in his ear. At that the dealer nodded, pulled out a long purse of wire net, embroidered with the figure of a flashing dragon, and handed the other several coins. The miner shook hands enthusiastically and departed.

"Yep," nodded William Kirk, "that's Yo Chai. A white man wouldn't talk as respectfully as that to anyone but the boss of a place like this. Watch the play; they don't lose any time in that game; ha! there goes your father's winnings!"

For John Sampson had pushed forward a large pile of chips which were matched by the Chinese; the hands were laid down, and Yo Chai raked in the chips. John Sampson shook his head and settled a little forward in his chair like one prepared for a long session.

"After all," chuckled Kirk, "this is better than playing myself. First time I've ever seen your father lose, and I've watched him play a good many times!"

So they stood leaning against the pillar near by and watching the progress of the game. It fluctuated here and there, but on the whole there was a steady drift of chips from the other four players to Yo Chai; even during the few moments of their observance they could readily perceive this movement. It seemed to exasperate John Sampson, and repeatedly he pushed out large stacks of chips; he was beginning to lose at a rate which enriched every player at the table. He was fighting rather than gambling, and Kirk began to chuckle steadily with enjoyment.

"For," he explained to Winifred, "your father ranks himself with the best of 'em at poker, and this will be a story I can tell a thousand times. Ha, ha, ha!"

For what followed, the exact situation of the dais and the players at the table must be borne in mind. Yo Chai sat with his back towards the bar and three-quarters towards Kirk and Winifred. Directly opposite him was John Sampson, his back, therefore, being three-quarters towards the same observers. The eyes of the two witnesses, in the meantime, were fluctuating chiefly from Sampson to the Chinese, for they seemed to be chief opponents in the game, and it was while they were watching Sampson rake in one of his rare winnings that Winifred saw her father stiffen quickly in his chair, his hand still among the chips before him. At the same instant a hubbub broke out at a neighboring table and William Kirk turned to watch it; Winifred's eyes remained fastened on her father. All that followed filled not more than one second at the most.

At the same time that John Sampson stiffened in his chair, Yo Chai, opposite, allowed his head to tilt back lazily, and a half smile stirred his lips; he seemed like a man blinking contentedly into a warm sun on a spring day. Also, he was shoving his chair back from the table with his feet. So the eyes of Winifred, following the apparent direction of her father's stare, plunged past Yo Chai and into the semi-gloom in the direction of the bar. There she saw the two Mexicans side by side. One of them was pointing towards Yo Chai, and as his arm fell, steel gleamed in the hands of both, the guns rising almost leisurely to the safe kill from behind.

It was then that the movement of Yo Chai changed from leisureliness to action as sudden as the winking of light. It should be borne in mind that all occurred so suddenly that John Sampson had not even time to cry out a warning; but the Chinese acted as if the eyes of the white man opposite him were two large, clear mirrors, in which he read the stalking danger: he swirled from the chair swifter than a dead leaf twisted by a gust of wind. The four guns of the Mexicans roared; and then there were two sharp, quick, barking reports in answer. The Mexicans sank out of Winifred's sight beyond the table.

Chapter 22

It was not a great commotion. John Sampson and another player at the table stood bolt upright, but rather as if in curiosity than in alarm. The other two turned in their chairs but did not rise. From the rest of the great gambling hall men swarmed to the point of action like water towards a whirlpool; and then Yo Chai rose from beyond the table and waved his frail hands apologetically towards his fellow players. The gun he had fired had already disappeared into the folds of his robe. His face was unchanged; he might have been rising to bid them a calm goodnight. But Winifred, watching him closely, started as though someone had shouted at her ear.

What she saw, indeed, was not so much the middle-aged face, and the rather shrunken, bowed shoulders, but the exceeding grace of the narrow wrists of the Chinaman and the transparent frailty of the hands. Already the crowd was leaving the scene of the firing and drifting back towards their original tables; William Kirk, who had run towards the spot, now returned, bringing John Sampson with him. She ran a few paces to meet them and caught her father by the arm with both her excited hands.

"Do you know who that was?" she cried. "Do you know who that was?"

Then she stopped the full tide of speech that was tumbling to her lips; a suspicion froze up her utterance.

"Who?" asked the two men at the same time.

"I don't know. I'm asking you," she answered.

"Sounded to me," said William Kirk, "as if you were about to tell us something. Who do you want to know about?"

And she lied deliberately, for she knew all at once that she must not tell either of these men her suspicion about Yo Chai.

"I think one of those Mexicans was a fellow I've seen in Mortimer."

"Really?" grunted her father. "Well, he's a dead one now."

"Not a bit of it," said Kirk. "That was a nice bit of gun play on the part of the Chinaman. D'you know where he shot those two fellows?"

"Where?"

"Drilled 'em squarely through the right hip—each one. They'll both live, and they'll both be cripples for life. When you come down to it, Sampson, that's better revenge than killing the beggars, eh?"

"Maybe," said the other man, "but let's get out of here."

"Why?" said Kirk, frowning. "This place just begins to look good to me."

And: "Why?" asked Winifred. "I agree with Billy!"

"Because," said her father, "if I stay I've got to go back to that game, and this is a good excuse for me to get away from the cards. That Yo Chai has bewitched 'em, Billy!"

It was strange to see how the environment of the mining camp had gained upon these three. Each was the inheritor of centuries of pacific culture, but half a day had moved them back a thousand years towards the primitive. In their nostrils was still the scent of powder; in their minds was still the picture of the falling men through whose flesh and bones the bullets had driven: yet they had already closed their senses to the nearness of death. A tale which in the telling would have kept them agape in their drawing-rooms, in the actuality was a chance event to be seen and forgotten. Ten centuries of refinement, of polish, were brushed away, and the brute with slope forehead and fanglike teeth rose in each of them.

In the older man it held the longest and moved him to leave the place as soon as possible. In the two younger it was merely a stimulus; but though they heard and felt the call of the wild, they were not yet of the wilderness. They followed John Sampson slowly from the gambling house of Yo Chai. At the door, when they looked back, they saw Yo Chai settling back into his chair with the extra man already in the chair of Sampson.

"By the Lord," growled the financier, "I've left like the Mexican before me, beaten and sulky; and there's my successor ready for the bait."

And then he led the way, grinning, from the house, for to be beaten was so great a novelty to him that it was not altogether displeasing. They took the course for their shack and Hugh Williams; they walked in such silence that finally John Sampson asked: "What are you thinking of?"

"Yo Chai," they answered in one voice, and then laughed

at their unanimity. "Yo Chai," chimed in Sampson, "but it's the first time in a month, Winifred, that you've got your thoughts away from the—half-breed."

And he glanced at William Kirk through the dim night.

"His blood," said the girl calmly, "is nothing against him. It's not of his choosing. Besides, he's whiter than most."

A remark which left the other two strangely silent, and in that silence they reached their cabin, and went to their rooms at once, for it had been a hard day. But when the voices of her father and Kirk died away in the next room and the bunks creaked for the last time as they turned and twisted about finding comfortable sleeping positions, Winifred remained awake, sitting on the edge of her bed. For her mind was haunted by a picture of singular vividness—the face of Yo Chai as he shoved back his chair, slowly, his head tilted, his eyes half closed like one who basks in the sun, a smile of mysterious meaning touching his lips. It grew out on her with astounding vigor and made another name grow up in her memory—Clung! She had been on the verge of imparting her thought to Kirk back there in the gaming house, but some strange impulse of caution had held her back.

Now the overmastering curiosity was too great for her. The impulse to go back to the gaming house, confront the impassive face of Yo Chai, and tax him with being Clung disguised, swelled in freshening pulses in her blood. The deciding force, oddly enough, was a sudden creaking of a bunk in the next room.

At once she knew that she must go, alone, and at once. It would be a great adventure; she felt that she could trust herself implicitly with the roughest of those Southwesterners; if it was a cold trail she would escape the ridicule of her father if she dragged him back to the gaming house; if it was the true trail she would have all the glory of the discovery in the morning. Besides, while Clung might reveal himself to her, it was very doubtful if he would acknowledge his identity in front of her father.

And so, at the creaking of the bunk in the next room, she rose straight from the bed and went to the window. It was close to the ground and already open. Through it blew the night wind softly, inviting her out; and beyond glowed the confiding stars and the lower, redder lights of the town. She slipped at once through the window, went to the shack which served as a stable, saddled her horse hastily, and rode down the trail towards Kirby Creek.

The creaking of the bunk was caused by one who, like Winifred, had not been able to sleep because of something he had seen that night in the house of Yo Chai. It was Kirk, and the vision which haunted him had nothing to do with the yellow face of Yo Chai, but with the roulette wheel, spinning brightly, clicking with a rapid whir to a stop, and then the droning voice which called the number and the color, "eleven on the red," "black five," "eleven red," "black two," "eleven on the red." It suddenly recurred to him that eleven had come many times on the red—four times as often as any other figure. He sat up sweating with excited eagerness. What a dolt he had been not to venture a few dollars on the wheel! Not that he needed money, but the excitement—the great chance—he might—

But by this time he was sitting bolt upright on the edge of his bunk, grinding his teeth and cursing softly in the dark. The heavy snore of John Sampson broke in upon him and he felt a great impulse to take the older man by the throat and choke off the noise. He began dressing hastily. The gaming house ran all night and he might as well take a whirl at the roulette wheel as lie awake and think about it until morning. His hands began to tremble so that he found it difficult to tie his shoes. Then he tiptoed cautiously across the floor. There was little need of such silence, for John Sampson was a redoubtable sleeper.

As Kirk opened the front door he heard the clatter of a

galloping horse speed away over the soft sod, and looking quickly to the side he saw what seemed the phantom of Winifred speeding through the night. He almost cried out to her, but an instant of thought made him check the sound as a foolish impulse. Yet the figure had seemed so familiar that he could not help walking to the side of the house and peering into the room of the girl. It was faintly lighted—very faintly, but he made out with perfect certainty that the covers of the narrow bed were too straight to conceal any sleeper. His breath went from him, and he turned and stared down the valley towards Kirby Creek. Then he ran to the stable, saddled, and made at a full gallop for the town.

Chapter 23

The first thing the eyes of Winifred sought when she re-entered the gaming house was the high central table, but at it the form of Yo Chai no longer appeared; a white dealer sat in his place. The beating of her heart decreased by a dozen strokes to the minute. She stopped one of the Chinese waiters: "Where catchum Yo Chai, John?"

"Yo Chai catchum home," said the waiter. "Catchum sleep."

"How long?"

"Maybe fi' minute."

"Where?"

" 'Loun' corner. Li'l square house. Maybe John show?"

His eyebrows raised in inquisition, and the girl slipped a fifty-cent piece into his hand.

"Sure," said the waiter, "plenty quick."

And he led her to a side door, from which he pointed to a

low, square building at the back of the large gaming house. Even as she looked lights appeared in two little windows. It was as if the place had awakened and were staring at her with ominous, red eyes through the darkness. The waiter disappeared and she felt a great need of reinforcement; to face Yo Chai in the public gaming house was one thing; to beard the lion in his secret, Oriental den was an affair of quite another color. She forced her fear back with a use of simple reason. Through the walls of any of these shacks her voice would ring out for a hundred feet, and the first murmur of a white woman's voice would bring a score of men to her help. She felt suddenly tender and sisterly towards all the wild men in that hall.

Before her courage cooled she went straight to the door of the little house and seized the knocker and rapped. While her fingers still clung to it, she saw that it was of brass, hanging from the mouth of a brazen dragon that writhed down the face of the door, his scales glinting here and there as if with inherent light. Not a pleasant sight. She regretted sharply that she had touched the knocker, and had already withdrawn a step when the door opened. It swung a foot or so wide and no one appeared at the opening. Then as if the opener decided that he might safely show himself, a Chinese, tall and of prodigious bulk, evidently a Manchurian, stepped out before her and stood with his hands shoved into his capacious sleeves—sleeves that might have contained a whole armory of knives and revolvers.

He frowned upon her, so that her knees shook. And because she knew her knees were shaking nothing in the world could have induced her now to draw back from her purpose.

"White girl lose plenty money," boomed the big Oriental. "Yo Chai not help. Yo Chai lose plenty money too. Too bad. Catch bad-luck devil."

He stepped back through the door.

"Wait," called Winifred eagerly, and she stepped close to the guardian. "White girl got plenty money. Want see Yo Chai. Maybe pay Yo Chai much money."

But the guard was not to be moved by eyes that would have shaken the firmness of any ruffian in Kirby Creek.

"Yo Chai maybe sleep. No can see."

And he began to close the door when a sing-song current of Chinese began from the deeps of the house. Chinese, but it made Winifred rise almost on tiptoe with eagerness. She thought that she recognized that voice. The doorkeeper turned his head and answered over his shoulder the speaker from within. He turned back, regarded the girl with a keen scrutiny, and then added something more to the inquirer—evidently a description. There came a sharp voice of command and the guard stepped surlily back from the door, motioning her mutely to enter. She slipped past him at once and found herself in a little box-like hall. On the wall opposite her hung a tapestry of shimmering blue silk run with a pattern of golden brocade, cunningly, so that while she guessed at dragon figures she could find neither head nor tail to the design. She only knew that it was beautiful and extraordinarily expensive. From the tapestry depended three scrolls of parchment covered with Chinese written in even columns, the central one much larger than the neighboring ones. This she saw by the light of two lanterns, one at either end of a rather long, narrow table directly before the tapestry and scrolls. They were unusual lamps, made in the form of two conventionalized forearms. The whole was so grotesque and interesting that it needed little imagining for Winifred to feel that two unbodied arms were there supporting their lanterns so that she could read on the scrolls something which it imported her to know—something of a fatal significance, perhaps. And the sight quelled her so that she could not help a timorous and regretful glance back at the door.

It was completely blocked by the bulky form of the Chinese

who stood with his arms folded, and his eyes gleaming ominously down at her. Panic caught at her.

"I have changed my mind," she said. "I'm going to wait until tomorrow before I see your master. Tell Yo Chai I'm sorry to disappoint him."

And she advanced towards the door with a hand outstretched towards the knob; but the guard did not move, and it seemed to her that he was setting his teeth to keep back a meaning grin. She was armed with a small revolver, and now, in her rush of cold terror, her hand moved down to the handle of the weapon. She checked herself in time, for she knew enough about the Southwest to understand that one must not draw a weapon until one intends to kill, and the shot must immediately follow the draw. She would reserve the weapon for an emergency. So she mastered herself again with a great effort.

"Where?" she queried.

The guard extended an arm of prodigious bulk and length and pointed to a door standing open at the left, with the view of the room beyond blocked by a tall screen. She hesitated a single instant and then stepped boldly through the doorway. Even as she did so, there was a click behind her. When she whirled she found that the door through which she had just stepped was closed. The Chinese must have followed her closely with noiseless, slippered feet. And the fear she felt was greater than if a gun had been held under her chin with an ominous face behind it. She seized the handle of the door; she could not even turn the knob, and as she strove to do so, it seemed to her that she caught a faint bass chuckling from beyond the door. Then came a whisper behind her.

She whirled and set her back against the honest wall, but nothing threatened her, apparently, from behind. Only the pleasant screen rose before her. And then, in midst of her panic she realized why that door had been closed. Until that time her voice would have struck through the walls of the house to the street. Now she was in the interior of the house and even if she screamed at the top of her lungs she would not be heard, probably. She thought of William Kirk, the bull strength of those shoulders and hands which would have torn that door down and felled the huge Chinese with a blow; and tears of helplessness welled up in her eyes.

Only for a moment. She knew, all at once, that her fear had not paralyzed her, for though her heart thundered fast it beat steadily. She was able to fight to the end, and she had the means for the battle. She drew the revolver; set her teeth; and stepped from behind the screen, crouching, ready to fire in any direction.

What she saw was Yo Chai himself. He sat among a heap of cushions, cross-legged, a crimson skull-cap with a black tassel on his head, his eyes half shut, and his frail fingers supported a long-stemmed pipe from which he puffed a slowly forming cloud of pungent, pale-blue smoke. Loathing, a desire to murder, filled the heart of the girl; and she drew the revolver close to her.

"Who locked the door on me?" she cried. "Who dared to lock the door on me?"

She pointed behind the screen.

Yo Chai removed the pipe slowly, slowly from his lips, blew forth another delicate tinted cloud of smoke, and answered in the softest of voices: *"K'e pu chih tao t'a shi shui."*

"English," said the girl fiercely. "Don't sit there jabbering your Chinese nonsense at me. Speak English!"

The eyes under their whimsically high arches did not vary by the stir of a lash as the gambler stared at her wearily, not in anger.

He repeated: *"K'e pu chih tao t'a shi shui.* I do not know who he was."

"You don't know?" she whispered, for terror had taken the strength from her voice. "You don't know? In your own house? Yo Chai, I'm not alone. Men wait for me in the street.

Open that door and let me go. Or if you won't, this gun is levelled on you—and I don't miss at this distance."

The head of Yo Chai tilted ever so slightly back and the dreamy smile she had known so well somewhere in the past crossed his lips.

Chapter 24

She did not connect it with Clung this time, but rather it seemed to her a characteristic of the entire Chinese race, a smile of devilish cunning and subtlety.

"You dog of a Chinaman," she said, her voice returning, a warmth of rage filling her now that she faced a crisis, "the white men will burn you—inch by inch. Call your servant; make him open those doors!"

Yo Chai arose, laying down the pipe on a little ebony table. He bowed till the long, black pig-tail slipped over his shoulder and tapped the floor.

"Yo Chai," said that softest of voices, "will open the door." And he stepped past her beyond the screen. That complaisance scattered her fears as a wind scatters the morning mist.

"Wait a minute, Yo Chai," she said hastily. "Maybe I've spoken too quickly."

The other turned and stood with his arms thrust into his flowing sleeves and his eyes looking past her. Seen at this close range his face seemed at least ten years younger than when she had first glanced at him in the gaming house. Moreover, his throat was more smoothly rounded than should be in a man of his age. The shadows about the eyes appeared now rather a coloring of the skin than the sunken pouches of debauched middle-age. The features, too, showed with extreme delicacy of chiselling. Altogether she had never seen a Chinese like this, and her first suspicion came back over her.

"Sit down again," she said with perfect calm. "I want to talk with you."

He bowed again, this time not so low, and turned back towards his cushion; but as he was in the very act of stooping she spoke, changing her voice, making it rough, hoarse, like the voice of a man, and bringing out the word with a sharp, aspirate force: "Clung!"

As a horse starts when the spur is buried in tender flesh, so Yo Chai started, whirled with a movement swifter than the eye could follow, and Winifred found herself staring into a face drawn and terrible with fighting eagerness; and below it, the yawning muzzle of a forty-five Colt.

"Clung!" she repeated faintly, and her lips remained parted on the word.

The revolver disappeared somewhere into the folds of his clothes. He drew himself up until the artificial stoop of middle-age disappeared suddenly from his shoulders; and his eyes went again past her, past her and into infinity.

"Call your men," said Clung. "I am weary of living. I will not fight."

She did not answer.

"Call them," he repeated, "or else I will go with you alone. Be quick before the mind of Clung changes. Quick! There is a reward on the head of Clung!"

"Oh, Clung!" she said at last, and she threw out her hands towards him. "Do you think I have come to betray you?"

"Who will call it that?" he answered in his soft, flawless English. "Clung is a dog of a Chinaman."

"I said it when I was afraid," she pleaded. "I thought—the door closed behind me—the big man acted as if he were making a prisoner of me. Clung, forgive me!"

"Clung has forgotten," he said quietly.

"But he will not forgive?" she asked wistfully. "No more than you would ever forgive that day when Marshal Clauson came to my father's house and took you. Clung, do you know that I had no part in that?"

"Clung has forgotten," he repeated with the same calm.

She sighed. Then, eagerly: "But we don't ask you to forgive us so easily. Do you know that Kirk has come from the north to help me find you and make some amends for what he did?"

"It is good," said Clung

And he smiled.

"And when I passed you in the room that day," she went on hurriedly, "it wasn't because I was not sorry for you, but—I had been thinking of you in another way, and—and—"

"It is very clear," he said. "A child could understand. You thought Clung was a man, and you found he was only a Chinaman."

"I see," she said sadly. "You will never forgive me, Clung?"

"Clung has forgotten," he repeated.

She bent her head.

"After all," she said, "what can we offer you? My father has wanted to send you north and put you in some fine school. But I see how foolish all that is. You could never go to such a place."

"My father is Li Clung," he said.

She winced, seeing that his head went back in the old familiar way and the lazy smile touched his lips.

"My father is Li Clung, and he has taught Clung what a Chinese should know: the prayers of Heaven and Earth and the teachings of Confucius. It is well; it is ended. Clung has learned a little. He shall learn more hereafter."

She began to speak, but finding his eyes fixed once more on the infinity behind her the words died at her lips.

"There is nothing I can do," she said. "I see that, and all

my hunt has been foolish. But if you should ever be taken again, I want you to send for us and we will get everything for you that money can buy—the best of lawyers and the influence of white men."

He bowed until the pig-tail once more tapped on the floor, and it was the sight of that shining, silken length of hair that convinced her of the unsurpassable barrier between them.

"When a white man wishes to show that he bears no ill-feelings for another man," she said, "he shakes hands when he departs. Will you shake hands with me, Clung?"

"It is good," said Clung, and held out his hand. The fingers were cold and lifeless to her touch; she withdrew her hand hastily and turned to the door. But there an overwhelming sadness stopped her. She went back to him with quick steps.

"I know now why I have hunted so hard for you, Clung," she said. "It isn't because I can give you anything, but because you can give me so much. Tonight we are parting. I shall never see you again. Can't we have one talk like the ones we used to have?"

He said: "Many words have little meanings."

And she laughed: "That is just like the old times. If you don't want to talk, let's have one of our old silences, Clung."

He bowed, and pointed on the floor to a comfortable heap of cushions facing his own. They took their places, and for a time the silence went on like a river. At length he picked up a little stick and struck a musically tingling note on the gong beside him—once, and then rapidly two more strokes. The shivering notes had scarcely sunk away before a little, bent Chinese, so hollow-cheeked and narrow of throat that it seemed as if every ounce of living blood were dried from his body by age, shuffled into the room bearing a tray. From this he produced two little tea sets which he placed on the small tables near them. Besides the tea there were little cakes, thin, and with a delicate, aromatic taste that gave added flavor to the tea.

She drank the tea; she tasted the cakes, the silence held. Once more Clung smoked his pipe in solemn-eyed, meaningless peace. The faint, blue drifts tangled before his face so that he was removed as if to a great distance, and looking up through the higher streaks of smoke she found herself staring into the face of a great, ugly image, squat, misshapen, grinning with the same heavy, unbroken, meaningless peace. It was a place for endless meditation, and the world which she knew slipped away from her like a cloak, and around her fell the silken influence of the world of Clung.

"Speak to me," he said at last.

"What shall I talk of, Clung?"

"It makes no difference. Clung wishes to hear your voice."

Once more he was smiling into dim distance, but his eyes dwelt finally upon her, more and more steadily, drawing his face closer to her through the wraith of smoke. It had seemed impossible that she could have any meaning to him. Now she thrilled mightily and her lips parted as she listened.

"The voices of men—the white men—are like the braying of donkeys; the voices of Chinese are like snarling dogs; the voices of white women are like scolding parrots. But once Clung rode for his life over the hills and he came about sunset time within sight of a mission church and all the bells were pealing. Then Clung heard you speak; and it seemed to Clung that he was once more riding over the hills, and the hills went up closer to the sky, and the red sky came closer to the hills, and in between there was the voice of the bells, sometimes deep and humming, and sometimes quick and high, but always music. If Clung were a rich white man, he would buy a woman with such a voice and she should speak to him every night just before he slept."

"But white men can't buy women, Clung."

"It is true," said Clung calmly, "they have no pleasure in life. In all things they are clumsy. They buy a horse and when it is old they sell it; they buy clothes and when they are old they give them away; but they take a woman for nothing. She is a gift. See, because she is a gift when she is old and withered the white man cannot sell her and he cannot give her away, for what man would take her?"

"Then you would sell the woman you bought—the woman with the musical voice, Clung?"

He pondered the question a moment.

He said at length: "When the bell in the temple is old and broken, do they throw it away? No, because the rich metal is good. Do they sell it, then, for the price of the metal? No, because it has made much music and it is a holy thing. Who can find the price of a holy thing?"

"But if you would not throw the woman away or sell her, why not take her as the white man takes a white woman—as a gift from the first, Clung."

"Because a gift is like a saddle. At first it is pleasant but soon it wears away the skin. Who will have a saddle that is tied on the back of a horse always?"

She laughed at the naive explanation.

"It kills the horse and the horse is worth more than the saddle. Also, I, Clung, have seen white women kill the spirits of their white masters. It was not good to see."

"You've never seen a happy married couple, Clung?"

"One pair. Marshal Clauson and his wife. But they have a great sorrow which keeps them together. They may have no children, and the grief for that is like a chain that holds them together."

"I can't understand you, Clung. Well, I'm glad of it. If I understood you, I suppose I never should have followed you."

He nodded.

"Yes. The book that I know by heart I put away on the shelf and the dust comes and covers it; but the book that I do not know is like the voice of a wise friend. I am always asking and it is always answering. And see: I have sat with you many times in the morning and in the midday and at evening, and each time the day was different. But after I left you the days ended. They have rolled all into one—one morning, one noon, and one night. It is very strange. But now you sit here again and time begins for me. I feel the ticking of the clock and every second has a new sound; I feel the beating of my heart, and every beat is happier. Is it not strange?"

"It is very strange," she nodded, and she leaned a little to peer at him, for he seemed to have been describing the very thing she felt. He laid down the pipe; his frail fingers interlocked; his smile no longer went far past her but dwelt on and around her like the warmth of a fire on a chilly night.

"You have made me rich with your coming," he said, "for night after night I shall sit here; I shall sip my tea and smoke my pipe and imagine you opposite me. It will be as clear as something that I touch with the tips of my fingers; it will be like something that I see with my eyes; it will be like the things I hear with my ears."

And she knew suddenly that this was love; she knew it not with revolt, but with a sharp and painful curiosity; there was fear somewhere in it. She stood up and found that her knees were not strong. And it seemed to her that the eyes of Clung, behind the veil of smoke, had grown all at once strangely glowing, like the eyes of a beast of prey, aggressive, reaching out for her. She felt that if she stared into them too long she would be helpless to leave.

"I must go," she said.

He rose; he bowed once more until the pig-tail slipped over his shoulder and tapped the floor.

"It is true."

"And I'm so happy, Clung, that we are friends."

"It is true."

"But may I never come again?"

"Clung does not know."

And an instinct made her know that he was fighting against a great hunger within him. She could not keep from tantalizing him.

"Do you wish me to come, Clung?"

"Clung cannot tell. He has learned one page of the book by heart."

"And the rest of the book?"

"What does it matter?" he said, and he smiled a little sadly, making a gesture of abandon, palms up. "All the days of Clung's life, if he were to turn a page every day, he could never learn them all. It is true!"

She stopped. She frowned high overhead, and her glance went inwards, examining her very soul.

"Do I dare come again?" she whispered to herself.

And aloud she said: "What is there to fear? I *shall* come again. Why not? I am never so happy as I am with you!"

And afterwards, Clung, from his open door, watched her go out to her horse and swing into the saddle. As she started down the road a large man on a tall horse came towards her. Clung saw the girl swerve her mount to one side and gallop off. The man followed, and Clung whipped out his revolver. But the distance was too great, the dark too blinding. He turned with a little moaning sound of anxiety and raced through his house to the stables where his horse stood ready saddled night and day. There, also, were riding clothes hanging ready and he literally jumped into them. An instant later his horse tore from the stable door and swept circling around into the streets of Kirby Creek in a pungent cloud of dust. It would need hard riding indeed to distance Clung tonight. But he had much ground to make up.

Chapter 25

When Kirk left their shanty, a little distance from the outskirts of Kirby Creek, he had ridden fiercely down the ravine towards the heart of the town. He had little hope of gaining upon Winifred; he was not even sure of her destination, but he felt reasonably certain that the same impulse which had taken him out of his bed was that which sent the girl on ahead of him. So he headed at a racing pace straight for Yo Chai's gambling house and pulled up before it with clattering hoofs. From the door he scanned the house swiftly but could not catch a glimpse of Winifred.

It seemed impossible that the girl could have gone to any other place, but nevertheless she was not in view. Wherever she had gone he had wasted too much time in the gaming house of Yo Chai to be able to trail her in a night such as this. He decided, finally, that she had followed some nervous, womanly impulse and ridden out into the night to find quiet. He did not understand her—he understood no woman, for that matter—and he readily dismissed the matter from his mind. There was little danger that she could come to any positive harm at the hands of these chivalrous Southwesterners.

Perhaps Kirk would have made a more extensive search, but it happened that as he completed his first round of the gaming house his eye caught on the whirling glitter of the roulette wheel and he stopped, fascinated. No one won; the man behind the wheel raked in several piles of money which lay stacked on the board before the wheel. Between the vast sombrero of a Mexican and the cap of a Portuguese laborer, he pushed his way to the roulette wheel and watched the next chance. The wheel stopped, and as if it were a plea for him to remain, the number was the red eleven. This time at least half the gamblers were playing the colors and a number of them cashed in on the red. Kirk watched them with keen interest.

The eyes of the little Portuguese bulged with a permanent excitement and he was continually moistening the palest lips Kirk had ever seen. As for the Mexican, he, also, kept an unchanging gaze fixed on the bright wheel, and his eyes glittered like a snake's. Yet he played with a sneer, as if he scorned to either win or lose. He was staking everything on one number, the black five, and his stake was invariably a five-dollar gold piece. He never won. That accounted for the steady sneer with which he played; it accounted also for the terrible glitter of his eyes. His money was nearly gone, yet he had carried to the gaming house that night all his own little fortune and the plunder of a robber and murdered comrade. Here the price of the murder was slipping from him. Even as Kirk stood there the Mexican fumbled in vain through his pockets, and at last produced a beautiful gold watch for which the man behind the wheel allowed him a hundred dollars. It was a last glorious stake. It went the way of the rest. The Mexican turned and stalked silently away; before morning another murder would lie to his credit; before twenty-four hours he would be swinging from a tree with a dozen men pulling on his rope.

Some sense of all this flashed through the mind of Kirk. Also a touch of scorn. He felt a supreme confidence that he would beat this game. He pulled two twenty-dollar gold pieces from his pocket and placed them on the red eleven. The wheel spun, whirred to a stop. It was on his number; and the man behind the wheel made a little pause while he counted out the win. A stake on a single number paid thirty-six to one. Nearly fifteen hundred dollars in gold was counted with lightning speed and shoved across the board to him. And Kirk, in his exultation, stared from face to face in a grinning search for envy or wonder. He found neither. One or two blank eyes glanced up to him, but no one acknowledged his luck; there was merely a general discontent that the game should have been delayed to pay this winning; someone suggested in a growl that there should be two payers on the wheel.

Kirk waited for four spins of the wheel. Then he laid a hundred dollars on the red eleven. Once more he won, and this time the house man glanced up sharply and considered the gambler with a moment's care before he paid. Slowly, this time—almost painfully. He passed thirty-six hundred dollars across the board to Kirk. And in the meantime every eye was upon him and there were no complaints for the waste of time. To have won once, no matter what amount, was nothing. Blind luck accounted for that, no doubt. But to win big twice in succession and on the same number—it bore a suggestion that something more than luck was involved—a system, the dream of the gambler's heart. The very possibility warmed everyone's heart. For every man's hand is against the house. The men nodded to William Kirk; they smiled; they bade him good evening as if they saw him for the first time.

And a tall, blond man, fully as large as Kirk, said: "A few more wins like that, my friend, and you'll have a little chat with Dave Spenser before you get home tonight."

A chuckle answered this sally.

"And who's Dave Spenser?" asked Kirk, carelessly.

"Why," said the blond man, who stood apart from the game rolling cigarette after cigarette and looking on at the losses and the winnings, "why, they say he's a chap about your size, and he seems to know all about who wins big money here at Yo Chai's. But haven't you heard of Dave Spenser?"

"I think I have," nodded Kirk, and as he spoke, with careless ostentation he piled a thousand dollars on the red to win. "Bandit sort of a chap, isn't he?"

"I'll tell a man," said the big blond fellow with a sort of dry enthusiasm. "I'll say he's a bandit, eh?"

A snarl answered him from the players. The snarl was cut short for William Kirk had won again; they looked at him now with a wonder half anxious and half joyfully expectant. As if with one accord everyone ceased laying wagers. Kirk had won three straight ventures.

"For that matter," said Kirk, thrilling to the sensation he

113

was causing, and allowing his original stake and his late winnings to lie still upon the red. "For that matter, sir, I'd rather like to meet this Dave Spenser. I think they call him the Night Hawk, also?"

"You'll know him when you see him," said the blond man coldly. "He rides a black horse—and I hope you'll be able to tell us what he looks like. Nobody's ever seen his face. I wouldn't be surprised," he added, for the wheel once more stopped on the red. "I wouldn't be surprised if you *do* meet the Night Hawk tonight. Every man who goes out of here with more than five thousand seems to be in danger. But of course you'll stay close about camp tonight?"

"Do you think so?" said Kirk scornfully, and without more than glancing down he raked up the gold of his winnings in handfuls. "I ride out of camp and up the ravine, and I do it tonight. What's more, my friend, I'll be taking about ten thousand with me."

"Well," said the big blond stranger, and he shrugged his shoulders carelessly, "I've warned you. The Night Hawk is fast with his gun."

"Perhaps," answered Kirk, "but he can't beat my luck tonight."

"I wonder if he couldn't?" said the other. "But I've a mind that Spenser would try his hand."

Kirk, for answer, chuckled scornfully and placed his next wager, a veritable little amount of gold. It was on the black, and the black won. By this time news of the big gaming had spread about in a whispering rumor and men stood in ranks six deep to watch Kirk rake in his winnings. The houseman was sweating with anxiety and he stared at the newcomers in a way half-baffled and half-defiant. Yet he kept his voice cheerful.

"Once more," he called, grinning at Kirk. "Let the coin lie, stranger, and try your chances once more. The wheel's with you tonight and you've got an even break."

"Not me," answered Kirk. "I've made a night of it."

He crammed the last of his winnings into his money belt.

"Besides," he continued, as he turned away, "I've got enough bait to make the Night Hawk bite, partners. So I'm off."

Chapter 26

He shouldered his way through the spectators, a murmur of applause following him, for they love nothing in the Southwest so much as a graceful winner, or vice versa; when an old beggar woman stretched out her hand to him at the door of the house, he brimmed it with gold, and it was as if he placed a crown on his own reputation. The applause behind him was almost a cheer.

It set a tingling in the ears of William Kirk to hear it; it made him square his massive shoulders and walk with something of a swagger; he would never have dreamed that the applause of these rough men could mean so much to him. But he was to make three steps backward toward the primitive and he had already taken the first step. After all, the need for careful English and proper clothes is a shallow necessity. He was breaking from the convention rapidly. Two great strides remained before him.

The thought of the Night Hawk was before him as he swung into his saddle, and he reined his mount to enjoy the elastic prancing of the steed. It was a fine animal, as fast and as durable as money could buy in Kirby Creek. He was about to touch his horse with the spurs and set out for home when the door of a house at the rear of the gaming establishment opened and the figure of a woman passed down the front step. Into the lighted square stepped the figure of Yo Chai, bowing until his long pig-tail swept towards the floor; and now the woman turned, the light struck her face in profile, and Kirk recognized Winifred.

If his heart went cold, its beat also quickened amazingly. It was beyond comprehension: why had she gone to talk with the squint-eyed Oriental? Then he knew. It was because of Clung. And it meant, moreover, that she wanted to see Yo Chai in secret; that she did not trust either her father or himself. At that William Kirk swore with a sudden violence and bared his teeth in the night. Winifred was in the saddle, waving back to the Chinese in the doorway, and Kirk spurred his horse alongside.

"What's the meaning of all this, Winifred?" he called angrily.

She jerked her head towards him with a cry of panic, then swerved her horse away and went racing through the dimly lighted street. He spurred after her, still cursing; a group of half-drunken men staggered out from the pavement; he thundered through them with loose rein, and they shrank from the horse with shrill shrieks of terror. But at the next corner a cart swung across the street, so suddenly that he had to pull his horse back on its haunches to avoid a ruinous crash. He loosed a triple-jointed invective at the head of the cart-driver and swerved around the wagon to follow his pursuit. But already Winifred was a dimly bobbing shape in the distance of the night, and as he followed her out of the town he was still growling. Perhaps she would be unsaddled and in her room before he got to the house, and in that case she might deny that she had been out that night at all. He could not accuse her if she wished to deny, and he felt, strangely enough, as if he were surrendering some sort of impalpable advantage over her.

It was because he rode so furiously, perhaps, with lowered head, that a horseman was able to ride out directly in his path. He was past the outskirts of Kirby Creek and already the shack was a black spot in the darkness ahead when a voice shouted at him. He looked up in time to catch the gleam of steel by the starlight, and threw his weight back against the reins. Yet in his blind irritation he had no thought of surrender. A black horse surmounted by a white-masked rider faced him.

"Hands up!" called the Night Hawk.

And Kirk whipped up his hands, but in one of them came his revolver and it exploded in exact unison with the gun of the bandit. A humming sprang into his face—his hat was whisked from his head—and he knew that the bullet had missed him by an inch. With a yell like a hunting Indian he spurred in at the Night Hawk, but the latter, without attempting a second shot, urged his horse to a gallop and passed directly by the side of Kirk. The maneuver was so sudden, so unexpected, that the second bullet of Kirk went wide. The snarl of the bandit was at his very ear as he whirled his horse and set out in pursuit.

A stern chase, on sea or land, is proverbially a long one. Yet Kirk might have overhauled the Night Hawk in the first half mile of the race if he had known the ground over which they galloped. But it was all new to him. The bandit seemed to know it as if a sun shone to guide him. He swirled here and there among the boulders of the valley and again, again and again, his course turned at sharp angles at the very moments when Kirk fired. Every shot must have gone wide by whole yards.

Now and again he used the spurs, but in spite of the speed of his willing horse he was losing ground, an inch at a time, and the figure of the Night Hawk faded more and more quickly into the darkness. There was a fierce happiness in Kirk. The winnings at the gaming house of Yo Chai were nothing. Mere gold which weighted his belt now and dulled his chances in the pursuit. How much greater this! to have conquered and put to flight the terror of Kirby Creek! His pulses sang. He wished that ten thousand people were watching that pursuit while he drove the bandit like a whipped cur before him.

It was strange that the Night Hawk did not attempt to fire back at him. He began to guess that the bandit had been wounded in that first exchange of shots. And the thought was a new triumph. He had beaten a great gunfighter of the Southwest with his own weapons, with the odds of a surprise attack against him; now he felt that there was not a single human being in the world whom he would not face with laughing confidence. And strangely enough the picture that rose before him of the most formidable man he could conceive was not of a big-shouldered fellow like himself, but of the slender grace of Clung and the lightning speed of his hands. To be frank, in the old days he had actually feared Clung ever since the moment when he saw the strange fellow whirl and drop from his seat with two guns in his hands as if they had been conjured out of thin air. Now he wished with all his soul that some test might come of their courage and their strength and their skill. He laughed fiercely, between his teeth, and buried the spurs in the flanks of his snorting horse.

They had passed, now, from the big, boulder-strewn ravine of Kirby Creek and entered the throat of a narrower valley. Here the ground was more nearly level and there was only a faint scattering of the big rocks. The effect of this new ground told almost at once. It was no longer necessary for Kirk to spur his horse. The animal seemed to lower towards the ground as it lengthened its stride, and its beating hoofs struck out sharp showers of sparks now and again from the rocks underfoot. The form of the Night Hawk, which had dwindled to a formless, shifting shadow in the night, now drew back rapidly to them, until Kirk could make out every detail of the man as he bent forward over his saddle-horn, apparently urging his flagging mount to greater efforts. The big man yelled with his triumph and poised his revolver for another shot—when suddenly the form of the Night Hawk, horse and man, vanished from sight as completely as if the ground had opened and swallowed them.

Chapter 27

With a chill of horror he pulled in his horse and swung him about in the opposite direction. There was no Night Hawk in sight; but far down the valley Kirk caught the clatter of flying hoofs, not departing, but approaching. Someone else had joined the pursuit, and a hot wave of anger touched the big man with the thought that someone else might share in the glory of the capture which was almost his.

The Night Hawk had vanished like a puff of smoke, yet it was perfectly impossible that he was gone. They had been riding close beside the wall of the valley, which at this point and for several hundred yards on either side was a sheer cliff of granite rising a full hundred feet from the floor of the ravine. Who could be absorbed into a block of solid granite? There was one possibility, a crevice in the face of the rock.

At the point where the Night Hawk had disappeared, the cliff jagged back at a perfect right angle. Along the face of the rock Kirk, dismounting, felt his way, and the horse followed at his heels like a dog, puffing on his back. The wall of rock was irregular, giving back here and there into small crevices, not sufficient to shelter even a dog. And so Kirk came to the point where the cliff turned back in its original direction. He turned back with a sigh of despair. And it was then that his foot struck a stone and he toppled sidewise against the cliff. His head struck heavily against the stone; but his fall continuing he found himself lying flat on the ground. Half dazed, he started up, and once more struck his head, more sharply this time. The meaning of it dawned on him.

On the way down the face of the cliff he had passed this crevice in the rock, because he had been feeling on the level with his own shoulder. It was, undoubtedly, the entrance to the retreat of the Night Hawk; this was how he had faded into the face of the cliff. As he stood there, setting his teeth for the adventure and gripping his revolver butt, he heard the clatter of hoofs sweep down the valley, past the mouth of the crevice. He had a mind, at first, to rush out and call after the stranger for help, for certainly it was work for the best two men who ever lived to beard the Night Hawk in his den; he would rather have invaded the cave of a mountain lion armed with a stick. For the spring of the mountain lion might not be fatal; but the stroke of the Night Hawk in that dark passage would be death.

Nevertheless it was this very greatness of danger which fascinated Kirk and drew him on now by its very terror. He began to feel his way down the passage.

Almost at once it increased in height, which explained how the horse had disappeared as well as the man; for it would be comparatively simple to teach a horse to creep through the low opening of the rock-tunnel—once inside the mouth, the animal could straighten to its feet.

He went on. The sand underfoot at first seemed to mask the sound of his progress, but in a little time the senses of Kirk began to grow attuned with the blanketing, horrible dark. His eyes saw odd imaginings in the blackness, glowing eyes winking at him a yard away; his ears caught a grim succession of sounds. The crunch of his feet in the dry sand which had drifted into the tunnel grew louder and louder until it seemed great enough to alarm a sleeping army. Other sounds besieged him; steps approached him and stopped at a little distance, and he could hear the heavy, guarded breath of the watcher.

A swift succession of fancies rose in his brain. Perhaps, after all, this was not the entrance to the cave of the Night Hawk, but was the lair of some mountain lion, a female with her hungry brood. Perhaps that was the heavy, guarded breath which he heard—the monster crouching and ready to spring. He stopped and listened. Not a sound except the wild thundering of his heart.

What had he to do in this dark tunnel in the desert? Well, there was nothing to make him pursue the search. He could turn and go back at any instant. It was that very fact which spurred him on, step after step.

Moreover, he thrilled with inconceivable delight at the thought of how he had met the redoubtable Night Hawk and worsted him in single combat. That brief meeting in the night was the second of the three steps which William Kirk was to take towards the primitive; and the third step was directly before him. Now, like the wolf which follows a wounded prey into the most dangerous covert, so Kirk with set teeth and thrilling nerves went down the passage step by step.

A long trip in the telling but a matter of seconds only until he saw before him a winking of light which at first was grimly like a glowing eye—so realistic that Kirk dropped to his knees and poised his revolver to fire. And it was then that he knew, in a burst of joyous certainty, that he was not afraid. He was excited, trembling with nervousness, but not afraid; rather the prospect of the battle was a glad thing.

In an instant he was sure that the light came from a point still further down the passage, and rising from his knees he ventured forward again. Now the tunnel widened constantly and finally made a sharp turn to the right—so sharp a change of direction that Kirk almost stumbled into full view of the

Night Hawk.

For it was he. He sat, apparently quite at ease in the security of his retreat, beside a small open fire. The burning stick lay between three rocks of considerable size, blackened by the soot of countless fires, and forming a resting-place for pots and pans of the rough cookery of the outlaw. As for him, he sat with his head bowed so low that Kirk could not make out his face, and he was busy wrapping a bandage around his right hand. It was now very plain what had happened in the encounter earlier that night. The bullet from Kirk's gun had ploughed a furrow across the back of the Night Hawk's hand; and it was this which had prevented the outlaw from opening fire on his pursuer.

Beyond the outlaw stood a black horse of matchless size and beauty. Certainly Kirk's mount could never have gained on such an animal as this had it not been that the outlaw's horse was weakened by long and continuous riding. The mark of the saddle was outlined by the grey salt of dried sweat along his sides and back; and his ribs still rose and fell from the exertion of the last burst of speed. There was a continual rustling and crunching as the stallion nosed among his forage.

All these things Kirk noted with the first glance, and still he delayed to make the capture. He let that easy task wait and rolled the taste of the pleasure of victory over his tongue. Still crouched in the throat of the passage he looked up by the firelight to the rocks on all sides. It was now perfectly plain how the refuge had been formed. A vast mass of rock—millions of tons—had tilted to one side and settled against its neighbor, crumbling close to it at the top, but leaving this narrow crevice at the bottom. A perfect retreat, for now Kirk heard what seemed several musical voices in distant conversation; listening more intently, he discovered the sound of running water. Here were all things necessary to the Night Hawk. The only inconvenience was the long tunnel through which he must drag all his supplies both for himself and his horse.

However, men and horses of the desert are trained to subsist on rations of small bulk. The safety of the place made up amply for every disadvantage. Here at the very doors of Kirby Creek the outlaw lived in security and preyed when and where he pleased.

The bandaging of his hand was now completed and after surveying the wounded hand for a moment and nodding as if with satisfaction, the Night Hawk lifted his head and William Kirk found himself staring into the face of the big blond man who had spoken with him in the gaming house of Yo Chai. A kindly face, now as then; though Kirk thought that he detected in it a glint of wildness, but perhaps that was the effect of imagination.

Still he delayed to jump out on the outlaw with his challenge and watched Dave Spenser rise from the fire, pick up two sticks of wood, ignite them over the flames and set them in turn in crevices on the sides of the rock-room. They had either been soaked in oil or they were extremely resinous, for they burned with a yellow and flaring light. By that illumination Kirk saw the strangest sight his eyes had ever dwelt upon.

Chapter 28

For the light of the first torch streamed down upon the most costly altar that had ever come into the dreams of William Kirk. A shelf of the natural rock was covered by a cloth of gold brocade, a treasure worth many thousands for the price of the materials alone, to say nothing of the art of the weavers. On either side of this cloth stood two golden candlesticks, each a full foot and a half in height and set with green and red points of light—emeralds and rubies worth in themselves a king's ransom. Above these and crowning the altar was a silver image of the Virgin with eyes of jewels, holding a golden Christ and crowned with a halo of solid gold, all cunningly worked. The robe of the Virgin was set with a border of diamonds, glittering against the dull silver of the image. It seemed to Kirk that he had never seen so priceless a relic.

Nor was this all, for the yellow light of the second torch flared down the wall of the cave and glimmered and lingered along a whole row of jewels. Chains of gold, necklaces of pearl and diamond, bracelets set with emeralds and amethyst and rubies—all these apparently hanging on little pegs affixed to the rock. The spoils of a thousand robberies lay within a second's sweep of the eye; and the bandit now unrolled a small rug of thick, soft weaving, and sitting upon it cross-legged leaned his back against the rock, filled and lighted a pipe, and between puffs of blue smoke rolled his eye contentedly from treasure to treasure along his walls. Turning at length, he dipped his hand into a small box at his side and raised it heaping with gold coins which he allowed to rain back into the treasure box—the sweetest of chiming to the ear of William Kirk.

Before that musical shower ceased he leveled his revolver and called: "Hands up!"

The bandaged hand of the outlaw raised instantly above his head; from the fingers of the other he allowed the last of the coins to fall into the box, and then the second hand went leisurely above his head.

"I was afraid," said the Night Hawk, "that you'd arrive before the place was lighted up."

And so saying he turned his face towards the mouth of the tunnel from which Kirk was now emerging with his leveled revolver. It seemed to Kirk that the teeth of the Night Hawk were set hard over his pipe and that his eyes glinted with a light as hard and brilliant as the sparkle of those jewels which took the place of eyes in the forehead of the silver Virgin. Yet if this expression were an actuality and not the effect of the shifting, swinging lights of the torches, it passed in an instant, and the face of Dave Spenser was as good-natured and careless as it had been when he warned Kirk in the gaming house of Yo Chai.

"But you took so long coming down the passage," said the Night Hawk, "that you gave me just time enough to get ready to receive you."

So saying, he smiled upon his visitor and Kirk looked curiously into the cold blue eyes of the bandit. There were many possibilities in them, from stupid good nature to wild, berserker rage and devilish cunning. The calm of the fellow alarmed him more than a leveled gun.

"Do you mean to tell me," he asked, "that you knew I was coming down the passage and yet you made no attempt to get me there in the dark?"

"In the meantime," said the Night Hawk, "my arms are growing a bit tired."

"Lower 'em," said Kirk, "but keep your hands quiet. I don't trust you, Spenser, and I'll blaze away at the first crooked move. Understand?"

"Perfectly," nodded the other, "besides, I've lived too long to be a fool."

And lowering his arms, he folded his hands on his knee.

"I won't tell you that you're a cool devil," said Kirk, "because you know that better than I; but why have you given up the game, my friend?"

The outlaw yawned leisurely and answered:

"Because in my profession"—here he smiled—"a man can only afford to lose once. After that he's done."

"I don't follow that."

"When a man's life is wanted by other men," explained Dave Spenser patiently, "and when he stakes his hand against the rest of the world, he loses a good many things—friends, companionship, comforts, and a long list of other things. He gets very few in return, but there *is* a compensation. For instance, before I turned the corner I was a poor gambler and a bad shot with any sort of a gun. But after I killed my first man all that was changed. Today it takes a pretty good man—somebody like Yo Chai, for instance—to beat me at the cards; and I never failed with my gun. I never failed because a single miss or a single slow draw meant death, nine chances out of ten. I killed the other man because I had to kill him and the possibility of missing him never entered my head."

Kirk had heard of this fatalism of the outlaw world; it interested him sharply to stand face to face with an exponent of the doctrine.

"Yet all the time," went on the bandit, "I knew that there was some man in the world who would finally beat me to the draw; and once beaten I knew I'd be no good. To tell you the truth I've been looking for that man for several years."

"Trying them out?" queried Kirk.

"Not a bit, but simply wandering about watching the faces of men. When you've gone wrong yourself it's pretty easy to read the faces of other men and tell a dangerous fellow when you sight him. That was why I talked with you in the house of Yo Chai. I knew you were a hard man—that you would give me a run for my money if I ever crossed you. And I wanted to keep away from you, but somehow or other I couldn't do it. It was like the temptation to jump when you're high in the air—the imp of the perverse. So I spoke to you at last and what you said filled all my expectations: you'd say that that should have been enough to keep me off your path, but it was the very thing which made me wait for you on the up trail. I couldn't resist the temptation of trying to learn whether or not you could beat me to the draw and wing me with your bullet. The rest of it's simple. You *did* beat me, and once beaten I knew I'd be good for nothing hereafter. My confidence would be gone; I'd pull my gun with shaking hand, and some drunken Mexican would down me, at last, in a saloon fight. Rather than that I decided to end the game tonight and lose all my cards to you. So I sat here and waited for you to come."

He puffed at his pipe with philosophic calm and let his eyes wander down the row of jewels on the wall.

"Of course," mused Kirk, "this is nine-tenths a lie, but I suppose there's a germ of truth somewhere in it."

"Naturally you're bound to use your reason and call it a lie, but in your heart, Kirk, you know it's the truth—all of it."

"What staggers me," said Kirk, "is that you can so calmly prepare to go back to town with me and be lynched—probably—by the crowd. For you know how badly they want your blood, Spenser."

"Go back to town?" queried the bandit, in some surprise. "I haven't the least notion of doing that."

"Want me to shoot you down here?" asked Kirk grimly. "Dead or alive, you go back to Kirby Creek with me, my friend."

"Well, well!" said the Night Hawk, "that's a fine little speech, Kirk, but it doesn't ring true."

"Why?"

"Too Sunday school. No, you won't take me back to Kirby Creek. Listen: why should we dodge the issue like a pair of four-flushers? Be frank with me, Kirk, and I'll be frank with you."

"I don't quite follow you; but it's getting late and there's a stiff ride before us. Stand up, Spenser, and turn your back to me. I'll have to tie your hands."

"By Jove," said the other with a sort of wondering admiration. "I almost believe you'd do it!"

And he nodded, smiling, showing not the slightest intention of obeying the order.

"Stand up!" commanded Kirk sharply.

"Come, come!" said Spenser, with much the same tone of weary patience one might use with a child. "Sit down and lay your cards on the table as I've done. There's no one here within earshot to repeat what you say."

"You're a devilish curious case, Spenser," said Kirk, smiling broadly. "Just what you have up your sleeve I can't tell, but I'm willing to listen. Why are you so sure that I won't take you back to Kirby Creek?"

"Because," said the Night Hawk, "you aren't the sort of crook who plays short on a pal even when he's in your line of business; you don't use the law for a friend."

Chapter 29

Understanding came to Kirk, and he laughed, softly and low. He sat down, still keeping the revolver vigilantly turned on the bandit.

"As they say in the Southwest, you've followed a cold trail, my friend. I'm not in your line of business, Spenser."

He chuckled again at the thought.

"In fact, I'm only down here on a little vacation. My business lies up north—and it's a good-sized business at that, Spenser, and brings me in even more than your night-riding has brought you. Why, Spenser, do I look like a night-rider? Do I talk like one?"

And he smiled with whimsical good nature on the outlaw.

"Well," responded the Night Hawk, "do *I* look like a

night-rider? Do I talk like one?"

It silenced Kirk as effectually as a gag; he could only stare.

"My dear fellow," said the Night Hawk, "I don't mean that you are actually in my line of business now; but before long you will be."

"But why in the name of heaven," said Kirk sharply, his amusement passing and irritation taking its place, "should I pass into outlawry? Do I need money? Have I injured any man illegally? Do I fear the law?"

"For none of those reasons," answered the Night Hawk, "but for the same reasons that I started and stay in the game."

He waved his hand toward his treasures.

"Don't you suppose that I could sell a tithe of these things and retire? Why, sir, I have enough gold cash to settle down with a gentleman's competence, and these odds and ends of trinkets could be all velvet, Mr. Kirk. For that matter, I wasn't poor when I started this game."

"You mean to say it was deliberate choice—this trade of robbery and murder?"

"Is it deliberate choice," answered the Night Hawk with his first show of irritation, "that makes the drunkard drink? Don't talk to me of choice! But the hunger for adventure—the love of chance—the game of life and death —the ridings in the night—the glory of fighting against the hand of every man—the thrill of the secrecy. These are my treasures. I sit and gloat over them at night like a miser. Not because they are valuable, but because I've risked my life and taken lives for almost every one of them."

He leaned forward and stretched his bandaged hand towards Kirk.

"What! Kirk, haven't you felt the same thing? Nonsense! Of course you have! I read it in your face when I saw you in the house of Yo Chai. The same wildness that's in mine, no matter how we mask it. I saw it and understood, perhaps even more clearly than you understand yourself. The jaw and the eye of the man-killer, Kirk. I saw it in you!"

And Kirk, staring at the outlaw, felt like a child who hears a strange prophecy from a mysterious soothsayer.

"Yes," nodded the Night Hawk, "you're afraid. Of what? Of yourself, Mr. Kirk. No, you won't take me back to Kirby Creek!"

"By God!" exclaimed Kirk, "I don't believe I can! Spenser, I feel as if I were being hypnotized!"

"When a man sees the inside of himself," answered the other, "it often makes him feel that way. But the strangeness of it will pass; take a moment and think."

In fact, Kirk needed time for thought. The world spun before his eyes. He remembered the strange urge which had been in him ever since he started on the trail of Clung, freshening when he entered wild Kirby Creek, and when he beat the roulette wheel in Yo Chai's gaming house, and coming like thunder on his ears when he beat the Night Hawk in single encounter. And now this seemed the logical end of the trail—outlawry, battle against other men, the tricky balance of chance wavering this way and that. He felt as if he were being tempted and was about to fall. Something like hate for the Night Hawk rose in him. Common sense, in a cold wave, brought him back to reason; but at the same time it took a fierce and happy thrill from his blood. He shrugged his shoulders and scowled at the Night Hawk.

"You think you've got back to reason," nodded the outlaw, "but you haven't, Kirk. You'll probably leave the cave tonight and go back to Kirby Creek, but when you're safe in your house you'll remember the secrecy of this place and the ease with which you could play a double part and live two lives, one by day and one by night. You'll remember that I'm out here waiting for you to come back—and you'll come eventually."

"Are you sure?" asked Kirk, with an attempt at a mocking smile.

"Listen!" said the Night Hawk sharply, like one who wished to brush away a veil of deceit with a single phrase. "Have you never done wrong to another man? Think!"

The suddenness of the question wrenched at Kirk's inner self, and the answer burst forth involuntarily: "Clung!"

It was the turn of the Night Hawk to start, and he stirred so violently that Kirk wondered.

"What of Clung?" he asked.

"I wronged him," muttered Kirk, "but he drew it on himself."

The Night Hawk drew a long breath.

"I'd rather see the devil than hear the name of Clung," he said. "Queer thing, Kirk, but the only two men I've ever dodged have been two Chinks: Clung and that dark-eyed fiend Yo Chai. I've never seen Clung but I've heard of his work; I *have* seen Yo Chai and I'd rather throw my money away than play against him."

"I beat his wheel," said Kirk, with a rather boyish triumph.

"But not Yo Chai," said the other, unmoved.

"However, I'll try him later on."

The outlaw shrugged his shoulders.

"You're too rare a fellow to turn over to the law, Spenser," went on Kirk, "and I suppose I *will* leave you here. But I'll never come back."

"Why?"

"Because if I can't face temptation I can at least run away from it."

The Night Hawk smiled sourly.

"Try it and see. No, Kirk, you'll be back. This is the beginning of a partnership."

"Perhaps," grinned Kirk, "and if it is, here's my hand on it."

The outlaw held out his left hand and they shook, clumsily.

"I wonder if there's a meaning in that left-handed shake?"

said Kirk, half in suspicion, half whimsically.

"You see the other's wounded?"

"Let it go, but to continue our charming frankness, Spenser, I've an idea that if I turned my back you'd as soon knife me as light your pipe."

"Before you're through," said the bandit, "you'll understand me better than this."

"Perhaps. In the meantime let's hear some of the stories of your night-riding."

"Is this your turning your back on temptation?"

"The devil take temptation. That silver Virgin, Spenser?"

The eye of the Night Hawk passed like a caress over the bright image.

"That," he said, "was the beginning."

He unbuckled his gun belt and tossed it across to Kirk.

"The first four notches are charged to the silver Virgin, Mr. Kirk."

Kirk drew out the long, shining revolver and balanced it easily in his hand. The weight was perfect; it seemed impossible that a man could miss his shot with such a weapon. He spun the cylinder; the action was perfect.

"I thought the same thing," said the Night Hawk, "when I first put my hand on that gun."

And Kirk, glancing up sharply, frowned. It was not the first time that his mind had been read that night. Yet he said nothing and examined the butt of the revolver. There were no notches there.

"Under the barrel," suggested the Night Hawk.

Kirk obediently ran his forefinger under the barrel of the weapon and found a row of little notches filed slightly into the steel. They came in swift succession and he numbered them with a growing feeling which was neither horror nor awe. Once more he glanced up at the outlaw, but those cold blue eyes were raised to the roof of the cave in pleasant meditation.

Chapter 30

"When the Aztecs were in their prime," began the narrator, "you know that they used to make their gods out of precious metals, and when the Spaniards gave them a new creed they retained their old habit wherever the conquerors left them enough riches for the purpose. There was one of these native metal workers who possessed such rare talents that his Spanish master sent him to Spain when he was still a boy to study his craft there. He came back with a high reputation and was almost immediately engaged by an Indian prince of enormous wealth and a new convert to the faith. His work was the silver Virgin you see there. Yet the wealth of his master was not sufficient for the completion of the Indian's design. It furnished the precious metals but not all the jewels for the border of the robe and left the eyes of the Virgin blank hollows. Each of them, you see, is filled with an enormous black diamond.

"For half a dozen generations various pious men and women of wealth gave great sums of money for the completion of the image, and finally the eyes were placed in the forehead and the border design of jewels was completed. For a long time it was the admiration of a million pilgrims until finally the church of Guadalupe, in which it was placed, was destroyed by an explosion of gunpowder placed there during a revolution. The silver Virgin was lost hopelessly in the ruins and it was not until a very few years ago that a man of wealth conducted a careful search for the lost and almost forgotten treasure. It was found after weeks of excavation; and it was discovered in the miraculous state of preservation in which you now see it.

"The party of the excavation started back from the ruins but the fame of the discovery was already noised abroad and before they had journeyed many miles towards the City of Mexico, they were waylaid by half a dozen bandits who attacked the caravan in the middle of the day and through their boldness escaped with the silver Virgin and the loss of only two of their number.

"If you had been in the City of Mexico at that time you would have heard of the daring robbery. Among others, it came to the ear of a young Englishman. He had recently arrived in Mexico on his way from India back to England, for he was completing his Oxford education through traveling. He was naturally of an adventurous disposition and he decided to strike out boldly through the mountains in search of the bandits. He figured that they would never fear the approach of one man and for that very reason he might be able to take them by surprise. It turned out exactly as he had hoped. He came on the band and knew them by the description which had been published broadcast. He took them by surprise, shot down two in the first attack, and forced the remaining two to surrender.

"With that he bound them securely hand and foot and examined the treasure. It was—but you see it before you, sir; and much as you may admire it, the Englishman admired it still more, for he was by nature a lover of the beautiful. He knew that he could never part with the silver Virgin.

"So he went to the two bandits who remained alive and he killed them both while they slept. Then he took two of their horses, one a sturdy brute which could bear the weight of the silver Virgin, and the other the finest specimen of horseflesh he had ever seen—that black stallion, sir, which stands yonder!"

"Ah," said Kirk, "and you met the Englishman, and—"

"And I am the Englishman," finished the Night Hawk. "For after I had my feet well started on the way I could not draw back—as you will find."

The emotion which was neither horror nor awe rose again in William Kirk. He found it to be envy—a great and soul-filling envy. As if to flee from that feeling he rose hastily as if to stretch his cramped legs.

"Any other tales to match that one?" he asked, and all the time he kept the revolver automatically directed towards the outlaw.

"A thousand," said the Night Hawk. "I could keep you amused for a month. That little iron box over there—it is filled with nuggets and dust and a dozen men have helped to fill it. This case here at my left—yes, you'll be interested in this. On the whole, I think it's a greater treasure than the silver Virgin—so great a treasure that I always keep it covered."

And so saying, he raised from the little case the most marvelous knife which the eyes of Kirk had ever rested upon. It was a poniard with a guard, a sort of stiletto except that the blade was triangular and grooved deeply. The blade itself was about eight inches in length and the handle scarcely two and a half. And such a handle! The knob on the end which gave it weight and balance was an enormous ruby; four great diamonds, each worthy of being a pendant at the throat of a queen, faced the four sides where the hilt joined the top of the blade.

"A dainty little weapon, eh?" smiled the Night Hawk, and he balanced the poniard deftly, resting the point on the nail of his thumb. That point was drawn to a needle fineness and Kirk guessed that the slightest jar would send the deadly little blade through the thumb-nail and through the flesh of the finger below.

"A toy for a king," continued the Night Hawk, and he narrowed his eyes like a connoisseur to regard the poniard, "with a story, moreover, attached to it. Among the followers of Cortez was Piombotti, a one-armed Italian. He had been in his time a great warrior and had distinguished himself in a dozen pitched battles until in the last of these he was literally cut to pieces and left for dead on the field of battle. Afterwards, however, he recovered. His right arm had to be cut off at the shoulder and the left arm was badly torn with wounds. So badly, that it was only possible for him to use one violent motion, an overhand motion like a pitcher throwing a baseball in your country, Mr. Kirk. Piombotti labored for hours every day taking a knife by the point and throwing it. He used a round-bladed poniard, so that he could hold it without danger of cutting his fingers when he threw.

"Finally he took a ship to Spain, won the sympathy of Cortez for his singular accomplishment and sailed with the conqueror to Mexico. There he fought through the wild battles which ended with the destruction of Montezuma and his empire. In every conflict Piombotti exposed himself recklessly, and every time he threw his poniard it brought down a man. A hundred times, I suppose, blood has spurted over the length of this poniard, sir.

"And Piombotti came to have an almost superstitious regard for the weapon. Cortez rewarded his followers for their deeds, and Piombotti came in for a large share of these rewards. For every fresh exploit lands and treasure were showered upon him, and each time he added something to the adornment of his poniard. Every one of these emeralds—see!—means at least one death; a score of lives, perhaps, went to the purchase of this big ruby, red, you see, as blood. Until half the wealth of Piombotti was lodged in his poniard.

"When I got the poniard I was more interested in the story of Piombotti, I think, than I was in the jewels. I used to practice as he must have practiced with it, throwing it at a slab of soft wood; and though I never attained a tithe of his expertness, still the poniard became in my hands a pretty sure weapon. Yes, many an hour I've sat much like this, and taken the poniard, much like this, between my thumb and my forefinger—using the left hand, you see, as Piombotti did—and I have spent the hours tilting it slowly back over my shoulder in this manner and fixing my eyes on the mark—"

Chapter 31

William Kirk, his mind following in careless interest every motion of the outlaw, watched the dagger sway back over the shoulder of the Night Hawk, the point held firmly between the thumb and forefinger of the bandit. And then, with the last words of the man, he saw a glint of diamond brilliancy come in the eyes of Spenser and knew that he was the mark—that the poniard was about to fly on a deadly errand at his throat.

Only that hint of a suspicion saved him. At the very moment that he threw himself to the side the poniard twitched over the shoulder of the Englishman and whirled in a glittering circle towards his throat. It brushed past his ear; his movement had been too sudden to allow the Night Hawk to change his aim. The gun barked from the hand of Kirk, and Spenser settled back slowly against the rock wall.

The slayer rose to his feet, stupefied by the suddenness of the thing. There was, for the moment, no change in the expression of Spenser. Then his lower jaw sagged. He seemed to be laughing silently, with expressionless, cold, blue eyes.

"You treacherous hound," cried Kirk, "I ought to murder you in cold blood for that little trick, but—"

And then he saw that the outlaw was dead, and that it was a dead laughter which transformed the face of the Night Hawk.

The idea of death stopped his thoughts as a finger may stop the telling pendulum of a clock and still the voice of its ticking. His wits wandering, he turned, and saw the gleam of the poniard like a red eye against the wall. He plucked it out. The blade had lodged in a bit of soft rock and the perfectly tempered point was not broken by the impact of the blow. Still half sleeping, his eyes wandered from jewel to jewel; he turned again and stared full in the face of the dead man. These were the jewels; there was the price.

Then his pulse began with a fresh and quickening momentum; the horror left him. In his hand he held the price of a hundred deaths; it was his by right of conquest, won in open fight. Matched against the Night Hawk, victor in so many battles, his eye had proved the quicker, his hand more sure. A hot exultation went thrilling through him. He strode to the bandit and grasped the man's shoulder. It was limp, which had once been so powerful; the nameless feeling of dead flesh tingled in his finger tips. And suddenly Kirk felt like rushing from the cave and galloping to Kirby Creek and shouting, not: "The Night Hawk is dead!" but simply "I have killed a man!"

Yes, that was the important fact. He had killed a man. An instinct as old as the days when man first fought for meat or for a mate was satisfied in him. He had killed a man; he had justified his existence.

And by the right of conquest all that had belonged to Spenser was now the possession of Kirk. His eyes went proudly from the silver Virgin to the row of jewels along the wall. For the moment he revelled only in the gorgeous property which he had achieved with a single shot. He stepped to the black stallion and patted the smooth, shining shoulder. The horse lifted its head with a wisp of the hay still bristling in its mouth, turned, and nuzzled the shoulder of the new master in complete acceptance.

All was his—all! Of course, eventually, he would bring the officers of the law to the cave and show them what he had done and turn over to them all the treasure. But why turn it over immediately? There was no hurry. The law had waited a long while for its victim. It could wait still longer. In the meantime for a few days he could ride out here often at night and take care of the black charger. He could sit in the evening against the rock where the dead Night Hawk now lay and survey the jewels of the silver Virgin, and the poniard of Piombotti. He could retell the stories of Dave Spenser; he could imagine other tales to fit each of the possessions. Yes, decidedly the law must wait.

In the meantime, the body of the bandit must be disposed of. He heaved the inert bulk over his shoulder and strode with his burden further down the passage. The glimmer of the torches faintly illumined his way. In passing he raised one from its crevice and went on, bearing the light high above his head. Almost at once he passed a pool of water, looking as black as ink by the torchlight. On the other side of it the passage descended; dropping more and more swiftly, until the water from the spring, which ebbed over the edges of the pool, trickled with increasing sound from ledge to ledge of the tunnel.

At a considerable distance, his foot rolled on a pebble and flung him to his knees; he dropped the torch in his fall and stretched out his left hand to break the descent, but the hand plunged into a vacuum and he crashed down on his breast, his head overhanging nothingness.

The torch was now spluttering out, but he raised and twirled it until it flamed brightly again; then he extended it over the ledge. Below him stretched a narrow pit walled by jagged rock. He could not see to the bottom of the pit, but he heard the far-off tinkling of water as the little stream splashed in the pool at the bottom. The stumble had saved him. Another step would have precipitated him into the abyss. The thought made his knees buckle beneath him and he sat down until the blood once more circulated freely. At least, this was a ready-made grave for the Night Hawk. He rose again, dragged the body of Spenser to the edge, and sent it toppling down into the blackness. There was an appallingly long pause, then the loud, distant splash of the heavy form into the waters of the pool below.

With a certain giddiness making his head spin, he stumbled back up the tunnel to the wider space which the outlaw had used as his cave. Compared with the rough passage and the pit which ended it, everything in the cave was like a welcoming, familiar face to Kirk. It was a homecoming.

By this time the greater part of the night was gone, and he prepared to start back to Kirby Creek. It was not easy to leave the riches of the cave. He decided to take what he could conveniently dispose about him, and he selected the rich poniard of Piombotti, the revolver of the Night Hawk with its tell-tale notches, and a handful of broad gold pieces from the box beneath the figure of the silver Virgin. He came within an ace of prying from their setting some of the larger jewels with which the Virgin was bedecked, but he shrank from this at the last moment as from a sacrilege.

Laden with his spoil he started down the passage. The black stallion whinnied after him and he called back in a low voice, "Adieu!"

At the mouth of the tunnel he found his horse standing with head high facing the east, for the dawn had made its first faint beginning. Once in the saddle he set a brisk pace back through the crisp, cool air of the morning. Not that he was hurried; he would reach the cabin long before Sampson and Winifred were awake, but his present mood brooked no slowness of action.

Certainly he was happier than he had ever been in his life. He felt like a man who has spent many days climbing a range of mountains until at last he stands on the summit. And as the man on the great mountain feels that he can survey half the world at a glance, so William Kirk felt that life lay at his feet.

It was still semi-dark when he entered the mining district of the lower ravine, but already the miners were up. A hundred camp-fires showed dull red along the slopes; he caught the voices of men hallooing to each other. Now and again he caught the clangor of picks being sharpened; the world was awakening to the business of the day. He heard that growing sound with the ear of a master. All this valley had paid regular tribute to the Night Hawk, and now, perhaps—

Here he stopped his thoughts abruptly and spurred his horse viciously. Nevertheless the thrill of the uncompleted surmise remained with him. He was the heir of all the Night Hawk's wealth. Why not the heir of his tribute also? These were the laborers of the day. He was the lord of the night and could harvest what others sowed with pain. After all, was not might right? From the beginning of time it had been so; to the end of time it should continue: he began to sing softly. He had made the third step back into the primitive.

Chapter 32

The minutes rolled on into hours, and still there was no movement in the room save the occasional slow lifting of the slender hand of Clung and the sound of the crisp rustling of the falling leaf. It was a very ancient Chinese volume, the characters large and exceedingly black in neat columns, and the parchment leaves turning a delightful yellow at the edges. So Clung read on, and at every lifting of his hand the loose silken sleeve fell back and exposed the girlish frailty of his wrist and forearm.

At length the door gong sounded, and Clung lifted his head slowly. From behind the screen stepped the vast bulk of his Mongol servant.

"It is a white man," he said in Chinese, "who says that his name is Marshal Clauson, and he will not go from the door but says that he will break the head of Yo Chai's servant if he is not let in."

Clung rose and slipped his thin hands into the sleeves of his robe.

"Yo Chai's servant is a pig and the son of a pig," he said calmly. "His brain is full of fat and he cannot think. He should know that Marshal Clauson is the father of Yo Chai. And who is the son who will not receive his father?"

The servant vanished with a grunt of haste and in a moment Marshal Clauson stood at the opening of the screen. There was a succession of faint clicks behind him.

"What the hell's the idea?" exploded the Marshal. "Is that squint-eyed Oriental locking me in?"

"My servant," said Clung, "is closing all the doors so that Yo Chai may be alone with his white father."

"H-m-m!" rumbled the Marshal. "If you wasn't my friend, Clung, I'd raid this joint. It looks spookey to me; listens like a hop-joint."

He sank on to a divan so low that his legs thrust out far before him and accentuated the size of his stomach. In this position he pushed his hat far back from his forehead and wiped off the sweat, for it was a hot night.

He looked leisurely around the apartment. His eyes gleamed with approbation.

"When a Chink puts on style," he said, "he don't spare the coin. There ain't no way of doubting that. Why, Clung, if you had a decent chair to sit on, and a table to eat off that a man could put his legs under, and a calendar or two hangin' on the wall, I wouldn't mind stablin' here myself."

"I shall bring you everything you wish," said Clung, and with that he tapped a number of times on his gong, in a sort of telegraphic code.

The sound scarcely died away before a withered little Chinese entered at a sort of dog-trot and arranged on an ebony table at the side of Marshal Clauson a tall bottle of rye whiskey flanked with seltzer water and glasses

"If I drink some of this," grinned the Marshal, "I won't be thinkin' of your furniture, Clung?"

"It is red magic," said Clung, pouring a drink and holding it for the Marshal.

The latter tasted it, sighed deeply, and then swallowed the glassful.

"And how," he queried, wiping his lips, "how in the name of sixteen saints did liquor like that come to Kirby Creek?"

Clung filled his visitor's second glass.

"Clung brought it," he said, "for he hoped that Marshal Clauson would visit him."

"Clung," grinned the Marshal, "I like to hear you talk even when I know you're lyin'. Here's kind regards!"

And he downed the formidable drink at a gulp.

"How's business? Robbing the miners, Clung?"

"At first," said Clung, "I made much money, but now for four days—five days—I have lost steadily and much. There is one man who wins it all at roulette. His name is William Kirk."

"Him!" grunted Clauson. "That swine still around?"

"He always wins," said Clung unemotionally. "The gods must love him."

"Then," said the Marshal, "they love a skunk. I tell you what, Clung, a man that'd do what he done to you is a coyote in a man's skin."

"It was only one thing," said Clung, deprecatory.

The Marshal raised an argumentative forefinger.

"It don't take more'n one thing to show the color of a feller's insides. You can lay to that. And now this swine is up here breakin' your game, Clung?"

"Clung has very little left, but he waits."

"For what?"

The head of Clung tilted back and he smiled.

"Clung waits until William Kirk leaves the roulette wheel and comes to play at Clung's table."

The Marshal grunted his admiration.

"And then?" he asked.

Clung waved his almost transparently frail hand.

"It will be very pleasant," he said, and smiled again.

"Pleasant?" bellowed the Marshal with great enthusiasm. "It'll be a slaughter, lad, and I'd give an eye to see you trim him."

He grew more sober.

"But I got to get down to business, Clung. First, have you got time to help me out on a deal?"

"The time of Clung is the time of his father."

"That sounds good to me. Now, Clung, you've heard a pile about the Night Hawk, which some thinks is a gent named Dave Spenser, without anybody having seen his face?"

"Clung has heard."

"Kirby Creek is in my district and I've got to stop the Night Hawk or I'm through. That's straight. Clung, you're handy to this spot. All I ask is for you to keep them eyes of yours open and when you get any dope, slip it on to me. I'll come up from Mortimer and try my hand with the Night Hawk. When the shooting party comes maybe you'd trot along with me. I'd rather have you than any man that ever packed a six-gun."

"Clung will be all eyes. A little time ago he followed a man he thinks was the Night Hawk, and the man disappeared in a ravine. Clung will follow him again."

"That," sighed the Marshal, "is simple and to the point and I wouldn't be in the Night Hawk's boots for all the gold in Kirby Creek. One more little talk with your red magic, Clung"—here he poured and swallowed a prodigious drink —"and I'm on my way."

He puffed out his whiskers like a panting walrus.

"I'll be thinkin' of you often, Clung, and I'll dream of your liquor. S'long."

"Good-bye," said Clung, and he attended his guest to the door.

"Ch'u men chien hsi," he said.

"Whatever that means," grinned the Marshal from the door-step, "the same to you, and a million dollars in luck, my lad."

"And is there any trail of the Night Hawk to follow?" asked Clung.

"Only two things we know. One is that he packs a gun with notches filed on the under side of the barrel. The other is that he lifted about a thousand dollars in twenties from Buck Lawson, and old Buck had marked every one of the coins with a little knife cut on the tail side of the coin. If one of them marked coins comes across your table, Clung, you can know that it comes straight from the Night Hawk."

And he vanished into the night.

Chapter 33

"Listen," said John Sampson, and held up a warning forefinger.

From the next room came a thrilling voice:

> "What made the ball so fine?
>   Robin Adair;
> What made the assembly shine?
>   Robin Adair!"

"She's up at last," commented Kirk. "Well, isn't it time? Near noon, Sampson."

"Time!" grunted the financier, disgusted. "Kirk, there isn't an eye left to you, no, nor an ear! D'you ever hear of a girl waking up at noon and starting to sing?"

"Why," said Kirk, "Winifred always had a cheerful disposition."

"Until she started on the trail of Clung," corrected her father.

"I don't follow you."

"Kirk, you're a total loss. You go about with your head in the air and fire in your eyes like a man about to make a million dollars. What do you do with yourself? Still spending your time in Yo Chai's house?"

"Part of it," said Kirk, noncommittally.

"In fact," said the gloomy millionaire, "you act so much like Winifred that sometimes I think there's a secret between you. Out with it, Kirk! What's the secret?"

The big man started and eyed the other carefully for a moment. Then, convinced that there was no covert suggestion in the remark, he answered: "No secret. None between us, at least. You've grown suspicious, Sampson. This Clung business is getting on your nerves."

"I've lost twenty pounds," groaned Sampson, "because of that damned man-killer. You came down here to help me. Why the devil don't you do it?"

"Tell me where to start," suggested Kirk.

"If I knew where to start for him," responded the other, "I'd send a posse and not one man."

His manner changed; the father came into his voice as he laid a hand on the shoulder of Kirk and went on: "As a matter of fact, I'm seriously worried, Kirk, and I need your help."

"You can count on me to the limit."

"I know I can, I know I can, my lad, and there's a lot of comfort in the thought. I always prized you, Kirk—in a good many ways—but since you've come South this time, you seem much more of a prize than before. You seem more alert—

stronger—keener—more of a man; you seem, in a word, to have come into your own!"

"I think," said Kirk softly, and his eyes smiled rather grimly into the distance, "that you're right."

"Enough of that," went on Sampson, "my trouble just now is less with Clung than with Winifred herself. You know how little she's said about Clung the last few days—ever since we reached Kirby Creek, in fact?"

"Yes. But she's found something else to think about."

"You don't know her, lad. She's a veritable bulldog for hanging on to an idea. Nothing but death will part her from something she wants. Haven't I raised her, confound it? Well, Kirk, I've wondered at the way she allowed Clung to lapse, and I've watched her closely for the last few days, and last night, after she'd gone to bed, I sat up for a time thinking. Finally I decided to go to her pointblank with a question. I went to her door and knocked. Gad, man, what do you think happened?"

"There was no answer," nodded Kirk

Sampson started violently.

"By the Lord," he cried, "you and she are playing some sort of a midnight game together! You're right, there was no answer, and when I opened her door and went in I found the room empty and there was no sign of Winifred. The bed had not been touched. Kirk, what's the meaning of this?"

"I think I can tell you—in a way."

"What do you mean? 'In a way!' "

"Just this. The first night we came here you remember we came back pretty late after going down to Yo Chai's gaming house and seeing the shooting."

"Exactly. The same night you went back and played the wheel. That's what started you on this infernal gambling, Kirk."

"I wasn't the only one who went back to Kirby Creek that night."

"Winifred!" gasped Sampson.

"Exactly. She left the house just before I did. I saw her horse disappear; before I could get mine out and follow her she had disappeared towards the town. I rode hard for Yo Chai's place but she wasn't there. I stayed a while to play the wheel, you know, and on my way back I saw Winifred come out of a house and climb on her horse."

"Come out of a house?" repeated Sampson, white of face.

"Exactly! I rode up to her. But she turned her horse and galloped like mad up the valley. She beat me home."

"And you said nothing about it to me?" asked Sampson hoarsely.

"If she had wished you to know it she would have told you," said Kirk coldly. "I waited for her to speak."

"God!" breathed the elder man, and straightened to his feet with his hands clenched at his sides.

"You think——" he whispered.

"I think nothing," said Kirk, and shrugged his shoulders. "But the house she came out of that night was Yo Chai's. Perhaps Clung was inside it."

"It must be right," groaned Sampson, "and now she knows everything about Clung—knows he's white—knows——" He stopped and blinked his eyes. "Kirk, I'm in hell!"

"Nonsense," said the younger man, and he frowned. "I'd trust Winifred to the end of the earth. If I thought——"

"If you thought Clung was in Yo Chai's house," suggested Sampson dryly, "you'd go there with a gun to find him, and be shot from behind a door, eh? I suppose you would, Kirk. That's your way. But I know that Winifred has been at Yo Chai's house every night for this week or more and she's been seeing someone there who——"

He looked at Kirk for help, but the other was blank.

"Don't you see?" suggested Kirk. "She likes to do strange things. She's gone secretly to see Clung because he's an out of the way sort? That's all there is to it and she doesn't dream that he's white. If she did, don't you suppose that she'd run to you to tell it? What keeps her from speaking to you now is because she knows you're only interested on the surface in a half-breed outlaw."

"I'll follow her tonight," said Sampson, hurriedly, "I'll follow her tonight, if she goes out, and if she goes into the house of Yo Chai—"

"Bah!" snorted Kirk, and he rose as if this conversation wearied him. "In the meantime I'm going to find out all about Clung—if Yo Chai really has him in shelter."

"How?"

"Well, you know that I've been playing the machines in Yo Chai's place?"

"Yes, and beating them with fool, blind luck."

"And tonight I'm going down with a mule load of gold to play old Yo Chai himself. I'm going to break him, and after he's broke, I'll offer him all his money back if he'll tell me what he knows of Clung."

"And *if* he tells you?"

"I'll take Clung and serve him a handsome horsewhipping and send him out of the country. The puppy needs a lesson for playing about with Winifred in this manner."

The elder man searched the face of Kirk with the beginning of a sarcastic smile which gradually died away.

"By Gad, Kirk," he muttered at length, "I almost believe that you're man enough to do it. And then Winifred? You're my last hope with her, Billy!"

"When the time comes," said Kirk calmly, "I'll go to her and take her."

"Take—Winifred?" gasped the financier, his emphasis rising.

"Once," said Kirk harshly, "she promised to marry me. It's a bond on her still. She's my woman!"

"Are you drunk, Billy?" asked the other anxiously.

"Drunk?" thundered Kirk suddenly. "Yes, I'm drunk!"

He threw his great arms above his head in a gesture of exultation.

"Drunk with life, Sampson, and drunk with living. I've crept out of the little rat-hole I used to call the world, and now I'm seeing things as they really are. Drunk? If this is drunkenness I hope to God I'm never sober. Winifred? Bah! What is she but a woman—a pretty girl. When I want her, Sampson, I'll come and take her!"

"There will be a fine little war over this," answered Sampson. "I suppose I ought to be irritated to hear you talk of my daughter like this, but I'm not. It rather pleases me in a way to think of the little tyrant finding a master. But Gad, Kirk, what a war there'll be when you come to her like this!"

He chuckled at the thought.

"D'you think so?" said Kirk carelessly. "Not a bit, sir, not a bit. We've handled our women too gently. What they need is a master who'll show 'em their right place—and that place is at the foot of the table. S'long."

"Wait!" called Sampson, and he trotted up to the side of the big man. "I've got a dozen things to ask you."

"*Manana!*" snarled Kirk. "Today I'm busy. I'm going down now to break Yo Chai!"

Chapter 34

His broad shoulders bulked in the door, blocking it from side to side, and then he swung down the path to the stable. In a few moments he was trotting down the road to Kirby Creek, leading a pack mule behind him. It was a small pack, but a weighty one, for it contained in gold all the tens of thousands of dollars which Kirk had won from the gaming house of Yo Chai.

In the street of the mining town many men knew him, for he had grown the most conspicuous figure in the gaming house of Yo Chai. They shouted their salutations and he waved a hand back at them. A tipsy miner stopped him and proffered a drink from a flask. Kirk accepted and half drained the flask at a single swallow.

"Where you bound?" asked the miner, who was too drunk to recognize the lucky gambler.

"Bound for Yo Chai's," said Kirk, "with a mule load of gold. I'm going to break him."

It was too spectacular an announcement to be overlooked. Rumor took up the tale with her thousand tongues, and the tongues of Rumor in Kirby Creek did not whisper. They shouted aloud and men heard the announcement with a joyous cheer. This was better than gold-digging. They swarmed across the street in front of William Kirk like the vanguard of an advancing army. And Kirk, his flannel shirt open at the throat, his face darkened with the unshaven growth of two days, cheered them on, and they cheered him to the echo in return.

Into the doors of Yo Chai's place the host poured. Kirk dismounted at the entrance, tethered his horse, and strode on through the doors, leading the pack-mule straight to the center of the gaming house. The place was in riotous tumult. From every table the players had arisen, staring at the strange host of invaders, and finally joining their voices to the clamor. The drunken miner who had stopped Kirk in the street now went forward like a herald. Instead of a baton he carried his nearly empty whiskey flask. Climbing on to the dais at which Yo Chai sat, he flourished the flask around his head and brought it down on the table; it crashed in a million splinters of shivering glass, and the gamblers shrank back from the deadly shower.

"Get up!" yelled the drunkard. "Get up and let a gen'lmun with a mule-load of gold play agin the damn Chink!"

They rose willingly enough and turned to gape at Kirk who stood with his mule behind him wagging its long ears. Clung rose also.

The hubbub rose to an inferno. Through it the voice of Clung cut like a knife, not loudly, but with a sharp, metallic sound distinct from the hoarse roaring of many throats.

"Silence!" he called.

He repeated it once more and the confusion died away, falling to a hum in the farther corners.

"Yo Chai," said Clung, turning his smile upon Kirk, "has been waiting for you. Name your game."

Kirk stepped on to the dais, laughing.

"For a game chap," he said to Yo Chai, "you rank with the best, and I hate to do it. But a gambler takes his chances. And because of that I'm going to break you, Yo."

"This," said Clung, "is pleasant talk to Yo Chai. What is the game?"

"Something quick," answered Kirk. "Stud poker, eh?"

"You can pick your dealer," said Clung and waved towards the crowd.

Kirk chose at random from the faces nearest him, and he selected a small man with white hair and beard and wrinkling eyes that shone with honesty. They settled at once around the table. So the game began.

As for the rest of the house, there was not a single table in action. Everyone stood up and waited. A self-elected talesman mounted the dais where he could command a view of the game and proceeded to enlighten the listening crowd in a voice of thunder: "Ace to Yo Chai, seven of spades to Kirk; jack of hearts to Yo, king of clubs to Kirk," etc.

And people cheered when Kirk won and groaned when he lost.

Which was not often. He won the first three hands in a row and the table in front of him was piled high with chips, for the betting ran a hundred dollars at a chip. It was worthy of Monte Carlo at its reckless best. The fourth hand Yo Chai won. The fifth hand Kirk wagered a thousand on a pair of sevens, was called by Yo Chai, and won over a pair of fours. The whole house went wild.

Manifestly there was little skill in this. It seemed the point of honor for each man to take the bet of the other, no matter how high the bet might be placed. It was gambling raised to the n-th power; it satisfied even the hardened heart of the Southwest.

The spectators began to pool their money and gamble recklessly on the side, for the high stakes of the central table set the pace. Gold gleamed and rang on all sides, and changed hands as the voice of the stentorian announcer boomed out the results. The gold on the back of Kirk's mule had not been touched, and the chips before him were stacked high.

Already the spectators were beginning to imagine what the place would be in the hands of the new owner. He would be hard to beat, they all agreed. And they waited breathlessly for the time when Yo Chai should rise with his head tilting back and his lazy smile in the way they had all come to know, and announce: "Gentlemen, the bank is broke!"

A red-letter day even among the sensations of Kirby Creek. Something to be remembered. A dozen men lined the bar drinking the luck and health of Kirk. Every man's voice and hand was against the "damn Chink."

But the certainty with which he had entered the house was rapidly leaving the heart of Kirk. It was the unshakable calm of Yo Chai which daunted him. It was the very size of his own winnings which unnerved him. First it began to seem to him that Yo Chai had resources which even his greatest winning could never drain. Then, again, he felt that the half-smile on the lips of the seeming Oriental was a continual mockery.

Perhaps Yo Chai had a reason for consenting to this game. He wondered if all his successes had been purposely planned so that he would be led on and on until he began to lose, and then he would give doubly all that he had taken.

Surely there must be some trickery in the business, hidden from sight. How else could any mortal man, Occidental or Oriental, sit there so calmly and see good dollars depart by the thousands. He began to hate Yo Chai; he began to wait for the turning of the game.

Then he wished that he had not chosen this day for the game. Then that he had not brought so much money to wager. Then that he had not brought more. He decided to cash in the chips that were before him, and was on the very point of doing it and turning away, when he remembered the breathless crowd which waited for his victory. He could not leave. He turned in his chair and saw on every side scores of burning eyes fastened upon him, waiting, waiting. They burned their way into his brain. He called for a drink.

"It is waiting beside you," said Yo Chai.

"You knew I'd drink?" thundered Kirk, suddenly and unreasonably angered. "You Chink devil, d'you think you can beat me, drunk or sober? T'hell with you and your crooked plans!"

He raised the glass from the tray which the patient Chinese servant held, tossed off his drink and turned to wager a thousand on the hand. He lost.

The chill of that loss counterbalanced the flushing heat of the whiskey. He decided to play cautiously. With care he could so husband his chips that when the house closed that night he would still have a comfortable margin.

From now on he would not wager high on anything lower than three of a kind.

But once more he remembered the hungry, waiting eyes of the crowd. He dared not start a conservative game after that wild, spectacular opening. From the tray beside him he raised another glass.

After that there came a time when he played automatically, scarcely knowing what he did, until he finally caught his voice saying: "Call a hundred, raise a hundred."

And the soft rejoinder of Clung: "With what, sir?"

He looked up with a start from his trance. The chips had disappeared in front of him. They were piled now before Yo Chai.

"Lead up the mule!" he shouted to the crowd.

And when the mule was led up he wrenched open one of the hampers and dragged out a canvas sack, ponderous, chiming as he jounced it down on the table. The whole house rang with the cheer of the crowd.

And as if that cheer had brought him luck, he began to win again until half the pile of chips had drifted back to his side of the table. He drank again and ordered drinks for every one in the house. And there were hundreds.

Another cheer for Kirk, but this time he lost.

Lost three heavy wagers in a row.

A heavy, sullen anger possessed him, and with it a certainty that he would lose. He felt, also, that if he could break away from the table only for a moment he would change the luck of the game. Now he knew that it was the eye of Yo Chai, steady, gentle, inflexible, which was breaking his spirit and making him play stupidly

"I'm cramped from sitting down so long," he said, "and besides, I'm hungry. I'm going over to the bar to eat."

"It is good," nodded Yo Chai, and smiled encouragement.

He wanted to take that yellow throat and crush it. It would not be hard to do: hardly the work of a moment.

Chapter 35

When he turned from the dais and glanced over the heads of the crowd towards the doors he was astonished to see that it was already dark; yet the crowd still hung about the place, waiting. Assuredly they wished him well, but it seemed as if his mind was breaking under the burden of their anxiety. There was a dull ache above his eyes as he turned towards the bar.

They accepted the recess in the game with approbation and fresh rounds of drinks. They literally fought their way to get close to the gambler as he walked towards the bar, and he had to lean forward and shoulder his way through them in a manner that reminded him of his football days. A thousand good wishes rang at his ear, but he said: "Give me room, boys, and a chance at a sandwich. I'm starved."

A dozen hands reached to supply his wants and there were clamors to learn how much he had lost. He did not know that himself, and he shrugged the questions away with carefully assumed indifference and set himself to eating. Seeing that he would not respond they turned to other topics; moreover, the game had proceeded so long that some of its interest was now worn away. Finally he heard a voice near him, at the bar, lowered in a way that proclaims something of vital interest.

And another man said in surprise: "That little old chap?"

And he pointed.

Kirk turned his head in the direction of the pointed arm and made out a withered fellow of about fifty, evidently as hard as tanned leather. He made his way unobtrusively through the crowd, which gave way before him.

"Yep," said the first speaker beside Kirk, "that's Charlie Morgan himself."

"Speakin' personal," mused the other of the two, "he don't look much to me."

"He don't," agreed the first man, "but I've seen him fan his gun and knock over a rabbit at twenty yards. That's straight. They's a lot of talk about these fast gun-fighters that fan a gun, but outside of Charlie Morgan I ain't never seen it done."

"And him you've seen do it once?" suggested the other, scornfully.

"A dozen times, I tell you. I was out with him trappin'. Maybe there's some that's faster on the draw than old Charlie, but there ain't none surer, and I bet twice on the sure shooter for once on the feller that makes a snappy draw and can't hit the side of a barn when he gets his iron out."

"So he's going out after the Night Hawk?" queried the other.

"You don't have to talk low. Charlie wants the whole of Kirby Creek to know it. He's going right down the ravine to-night with his pack-mule and he's going to have a bit of dust in the pack. He *wants* the Night Hawk to know he's coming, and he swears he'll get Dave Spenser's hide tonight. You see, Happy Lynch was Charlie's partner, and when Charlie heard that Happy'd been bumped off by Spenser it made him so riled he couldn't sleep of nights. So he come up here to bag the Night Hawk."

"Here's wishin' him luck," said the other, "but I got my doubts."

"I ain't," said the first speaker. "Of course the Night Hawk might down him from behind, but that ain't the Night Hawk's way. He tackles his meat from the front. And give 'em a square break like that and I bet on old Charlie Morgan."

"What time's he go up the valley? I'd like to see him start."

"Says he's going at moonrise. I dunno jest when that'll be."

"Seems to me," said a dry voice near Kirk, "that Yo Chai has about used up his patience waitin' for you, partner."

He turned and went back to the table. The mouthful of food had strengthened him; the drink seemed to have cleared his brain, and as he settled into his chair at the table it seemed to him that he could break Yo Chai through the sheer force of physical strength and superior size.

He started again with the old recklessness, but it was as if his brief absence had broken his power over the cards. He was losing now two hands out of three. He emptied one of the mule's hampers. He began on the other.

In spite of himself the mental stupor returned, the feeling that he was being hypnotized into stupidity, and with it rose the sullen anger—the desire to kill. The occasional drinks he took instead of clearing his brain were like oil on the fire. Half the time he sat with his attention fixed on the loose sleeves of Yo Chai, waiting for the appearance of one of the cards which he was sure must be buried up the sleeve of the Chinaman. But there was never the least flickering of cardboard there to give an excuse for the gunplay. He lifted the last sack of gold from the hamper; it followed the course of the rest; he was broke. And all that he had won from Yo Chai had flowed back to the gaming house. He rose, forcing himself to smile, for one must lose at cards gracefully in the Southwest.

"Yo Chai," he said, "there's some golden lining for you. And here's thanking you for a pleasant evening."

There was a little hum of approval, almost stern, from the bystanders. Clung rose and bowed deeply.

"It is true," he said, "but it is not the last."

"No?" asked Kirk sharply.

"You will come again to Yo Chai," said Clung, "for the luck may run another way. It is like water. It cannot always run uphill."

And he made a little smiling gesture to indicate the inferiority of his height.

"You will come," said Clung, smiling still, and nodding, "again and again, and still again. Tonight there was a time when Yo Chai had only ten chips—ten pieces of gold—one hundred dollars—that was all."

"By God," groaned Kirk, "did I come as close as that?"

"Ah," smiled Clung, "the heart of Yo Chai was cold many times tonight."

"I believe," frowned Kirk, "that you're mocking me, you old scoundrel, but I *am* coming back, Yo Chai, and I'll bring more money the next time—a check book, Yo."

"It is very good," sighed Clung, "your paper is better to Yo Chai than another man's gold. It is true."

"There's a double meaning in you," mused Kirk, "but I'll think it out some other time. Adios."

He turned and strode from the room. There were men who stopped him, who clapped him on the shoulder, and every touch went through his heart like a bullet. He had been beaten, and the thought kept him writhing. Kept the automatic smile steadily for his well-wishers, and buried the murder in the shadow of his heart. In the dim shade of the door, away from the crowd, he looked back and let his hatred twist his face. Already they were flowing back to the games around the tables. He saw Yo Chai standing at the central table welcoming a group of players in the usual draw-poker. He had been the sensation of half a day and already he was forgotten.

Grinding his teeth, he swung on to his horse and spurred him savagely up the valley towards the shanty where they lived. He was hardly past the outskirts of the town when a growing light to the east drew his head to the side. It was the rising moon.

Chapter 36

And though the valley in the daytime swarmed with a thousand laborers, in the moonlight it showed only a blank and sandy waste. The little huts scattered everywhere showed not at all, or only as blacker spots against the grey background; the hum and faint clangor of iron against rock had died away, the silence of night was complete. And by that night all things were magnified. The mountains grew taller, rougher, blacker. So black that by contrast with them the dull sky overhead took on a shade of mysterious blue.

This in turn changed, for as the moon rose the stars went out by hosts and myriads, like camp-fires of a great army, extinguished at a signal. The dull sky was now a metallic grey and from the mountains thick shadows swung out and across the ravines.

Even at night there was no peace among those mountains. The eye of William Kirk swept up their jagged summits or plunged down dizzy heights to the floor of the valleys in swift change. Those crests lunged against the sky like spearpoints. They were a revolt against eternal order; they nodded their heads against the sky like a menace, and they roused a fellow-feeling in the heart of Kirk.

He, also, needed action, sudden and strong and terrible, to pacify the sullen fire within him. He wanted to destroy, overthrow. For he stood at the end of his third stride in the primitive. That night he had been baffled and beaten in the gaming house of Yo Chai, and since he could not wreak his hate on the gambler he cast about for another object which he could seize and crumble. It was the rising of the yellow moon as it rolled like a wheel up the steep side of an eastern mountain, that gave the hint to him, for he remembered then Charlie Morgan, who by this time must be riding with his pack mule up the valley. A challenge to the Night Hawk!

And in a sudden outburst of exultation and rage, Kirk threw back his head and shouted. The sound was muffled behind his clenched teeth and came like the roar of a beast. It would have frightened Kirk in any other humor to feel this madness rising in him. Now it stimulated him to a sort of hysteria of joy. He whirled his horse, plunged the spurs deep and galloped at full speed down the valley, fast, fast, and faster. He took off his sombrero and brandished it against the stars, and yelled drunkenly; and the thunder of his heart kept pace with the clangor of the hoofs of his racing horse against the rocks of the ravine.

Out of the upper ravine he turned into the lower, with no more boulders to dodge and a straight path for the cave of the Night Hawk. In a moment he was there, swung from the saddle, and stumbled down the passage.

It was strange how easily he entered it now. He knew by instinct every turning of the rough rock walls. In the apartment within he found at once the matches, kindled his tinder, and flung the saddle upon the back of the black stallion. And the horse turned his head to watch the process, and as the light shone full in his fine face, his eyes seemed to glow yellow in fierce anticipation of the coming battle. He whinnied; he caught the shirt of Kirk at the shoulder with his teeth and pulled at it softly as if to urge his flying hands to a still greater speed.

There was no need to lead the charger out of the tunnel. He had been many days standing without exercise, and now he followed at the heels of Kirk like a trained dog. His forehoofs rapped many times against the hurrying heels of Kirk; his hot breath whistled down the back of the man.

At the entrance, the stallion crouched and crawled through

the low hole with uncanny agility. Once outside Kirk vaulted into the saddle, and the black reared straight up and struck at the air with fighting forehoofs.

There followed a wild burst of pitching here and there. Not the stiff-legged bucking of a horse which strives to throw its rider, but rather the overflow of joyous energy. And Kirk laughed and shouted encouragement, and struck his hat across the eyes of the black, and enjoyed the wild sport to the tips of his toes.

Then he realized that it was time for action, for by this hour Charlie Morgan, if he had made good his boast and his challenge to the Night Hawk, would be far up the lower ravine, and making good time on the level going. He called in a stern voice to the black, and the horse, as if it realized that the hour for playfulness had passed, stood instantly still—an image—a horse carved of shining black rock in the moonlight. His head was high—his ears flat back on his neck. It needed only a slight loosening of the reins and he was off at once down the canyon with a gait as swift and easy as the dipping flight of a sea-gull.

Moreover, the stallion seemed to know every foot of the way and chose a path where the sand was hard and smooth, fit for rapid travel. That long, elastic stride, also, muffled the beat of the hoofs, and, comparatively speaking, they moved down the valley as silently as a great black shadow, rider and horse one creature bent on destruction.

The impulse which had made Kirk wave his hat and shout to the stars was still hot in him, but now it kept him silent. He held the spirit in behind his teeth until it gave a cold purposefulness to him; his eyes swept the valley before him. He seemed to have gained the power, in that brief ride, to pierce the darkness of the night and search out the objects of his prey with the eyes of a wolf.

How else could he have seen, so far away, the small shape which moved up the ravine, close to the wall, under the very shadow of the eastern rock? But he saw it, and knew at once that it was Charlie Morgan, already past him and heading at a dog-trot up the ravine. His hurry seemed to tell William Kirk that the old gun-fighter somewhat regretted the vaunt he had made in the town of Kirby Creek that day. To be true he was making his boast good, but the touch of haste showed something of uneasiness.

The upper lip of Kirk writhed back in a grin of malicious joy. He had no more thought of failure than the mountain lion has when it scents a solitary calf, lagging far behind the driven herd in the night—a calf not large enough to race away, just large enough to flesh the teeth of the lion.

Kirk swung his horse around and galloped to the western wall of the ravine. Once in the shadow he urged the stallion again to full speed, and the fine animal, as if it guessed the purpose of the master, hugged the course of the rock wall closely, and never once went half a dozen yards from the edge. Still Kirk could make out across the narrow floor of the valley the moving shadow of Charlie Morgan and his horse and pack-mule. He himself might be more easily visible, for he had no shadow over him to shelter him from the keen and experienced eye of the trapper. But he trusted with absolute certainty that even at this distance his shape would be blent with the wall of the valley and he would escape notice. He felt the superiority, indeed, of the night hawk which sees unseen.

The point he made for was a narrowing of the ravine some distance ahead. Here, among a cluster of mesquite he left the horse, and slipped on foot to a point of vantage among the shrubbery. His hand struck one of the sharp thorns, but he felt the little warm trickle of the blood with not a vestige of pain.

Then came a crunching sound of the jogging animals, the creak of saddle leather, the grunt of the horse as the rider swung it sharply back and forth through the sharp-thorned bushes, the low voice of Charlie Morgan cursing at the lagging mule behind. A low voice—almost trembling—as if the man hated the mule for the noise which it forced him to make. And Kirk knew that he was the cause of this fear—the heart and center of it. It was a reversion of all the course of his life. He remembered with chilly distinctness the times in his boyhood when he had lain awake at night listening—all ears—to the creaks of the stairs, regular, approaching sounds so distinct that he could even visualize the form of the night-walker, could see the size of his bony hand on the banister, the mask across his eyes. But now he was himself the walker of the night and the terror which he had felt in those old days had fallen upon other men, upon Charlie Morgan, hunter and trapper and familiar of the wilds.

Out from a dense growth of mesquite came the trapper; his quirt cracked loudly on the side of the horse, which broke into a canter and passed Kirk in his hiding-place so close that he could have reached out his hand and touched the flank of the animal, or seized Charlie Morgan by the leg and dragged him from the saddle. A maddening temptation came to do the thing; and then another temptation to yell aloud in exultation for the danger which was coming.

That temptation also he restrained as he stepped boldly out into the narrow path which Morgan was following.

"Charlie Morgan!" he called, "I'm here!"

And he waited with his revolver poised.

All at once he knew that he could not fire on the fellow first. He would wait until Morgan had drawn and blazed away. And a perfect certainty came to him that Morgan would miss. Then he would shoot—and he could not fail.

At his shout Morgan whirled in the saddle; his steel gleamed very brightly in the moon, and by the same light Kirk glimpsed the teeth of the man. His lips were twitched back in a hideous grimace of terror.

"Who?" shouted the trapper, and his voice was a scream of

harsh uncertainty and the will to kill.

"The Night Hawk!" answered Kirk, and still he stood with his revolver poised.

It seemed that there were minutes between everything that happened—the curse of Morgan—the leveling of the revolver—the spurt of flame from the mouth of the gun—the hum of a bullet beside his arm—giving the cloth a little tug.

There were other minutes of pause while his own gun descended, while his finger pressed on the trigger, and then the bark of the bullet, kicking up the muzzle of the gun. Charlie Morgan threw up his arms. His revolver dropped through the moonlight like a bit of fire from the hand of the trapper. Then Morgan leaned forward, struck the pommel of the saddle with a grunt of suddenly expired wind, and flopped heavily on the ground.

Kirk twirled his gun. His first emotion was merely joy in the easy action of the weapon. No wonder that the Night Hawk had killed many with such a gun. He shoved it leisurely back into the holster, and went humming to examine his work of the night. The horse sidled uneasily away and stood snorting and sniffing at the figure fallen in the path. There was gold in the pack of the mule, but Kirk had no desire for it. His purpose in coming out there that night had merely been to uphold the honor, in a way, of dead Dave Spenser. He kicked the saddle-horse brutally in the stomach and the poor brute lashed out once with its heels and then started off at a broken gallop, tugging the pack-mule after it. All at once a panic seemed to seize on the two animals. They burst into a racing pace and fled crashing through the shrubbery. Kirk watched them with a grin and then leaned down over the fallen body.

It lay on its face. He turned it. There, exactly where he had intended, was the red mark of the bullet. It had passed through the chest, directly in the center, or a little to the left. If he had located the spot with a line and compass he could not have planted the shot more carefully.

"A bull's-eye," grinned Kirk, and with his toe caught under the shoulder of Morgan he slopped the body back upon its face.

"And so," finished Kirk, "exit Charlie Morgan."

A soft whinny came to him through the night.

"And so," he muttered to himself thoughtfully, "re-enter the Night Hawk?"

He shrugged his broad shoulders and the burden of the murder before him slipped off his conscience.

"After all," he said, "perhaps the Englishman was right."

And he went back to the black stallion.

Chapter 37

All that afternoon there had hung before the mind's eye of John Sampson a problem like a problem in geometry, one of those perplexing things in which the lines and circles are simple enough, but in which the axioms of explanation refuse to come to mind. The problem was a certain relationship between Clung and Yo Chai. It had dwelt in his memory since the evening when Yo Chai shot down the two Mexicans and thereby gained a proud name in Kirby Creek, that there was some connection between the gambler and the outlawed man-killer.

Ever since that time he had turned and twisted the thing back and forth in his mind, but it had never become an object of vital interest until today, when he learned that Winifred had been going regularly at night to the house of the gambler. Now he sat for hours with his head dropped between his hands and tried to work out the puzzle. It was like the man who sat in the robbers' cave and strove to think of the magic name which would open the door, but all that he remembered was that the name was that of some grain, so he sat calling: "Open, barley, open, wheat, open, oats"—but he could not think of the right one—the "Open Sesame." So he remained perforce in the cave until the robbers returned and cut him to pieces with their sabres.

In such a quandary was John Sampson. He could not find the little watchword which would admit him to the secret. All that he knew was that the relation between Clung and Yo Chai, if he could call it to mind, would prove the undoing of Yo; and with a lever to work on the Chinaman he could gain the reason of Winifred's comings and goings to the house of Yo Chai in the night.

Evening came, but still the key to the locked room was not his. He and Winifred ate supper in silence, gloomy on his part and gay on the part of the girl. Now and again her eyes went through the window to dwell on the rapidly dimming outlines of the hills. There was complacency in her gaze, and a certain expectation which stopped the heart of John Sampson in mid-beat.

It was some time after supper before his sharpened ear heard a stir in the room of Winifred, to which she had retired under the pretext of a headache. A headache! she who had never known a sick day!

A stir and then a sound suspiciously like the creak of a slowly raised window. Still he waited. Far off he caught the snort and stamp of a horse from the barn. A little later, listening with the front door a little ajar, he caught the hoofs of a horse crunching faintly upon soft sand. That was all.

The weight of fear turned to a burden of despair in the heart of John Sampson. He felt helpless, disarmed; and this in conjunction with a wild hatred of all the world, and particularly of the patient half-smile of Yo Chai. Finally he could stand it no longer, and went out of doors. Before him, further down the hill and the side of the ravine, glimmered the thousand evil lights of Kirby Creek. For a time he walked up and down in front of the house. Then he started down the ravine. Not with any purpose, but because he could not bear to be too close to the lonely little shack from which Winifred had stolen away.

His hands were clasped behind him and his head bent sadly as he entered the first street of the village. It led, like all the streets of the town, to the gaming house of Yo Chai, and down that street John Sampson strolled. He was quite heedless of all around him, yet every picture that he saw this night was imprinted for ever, indelibly, in his subconscious brain. In the door of one hut stood a very tall woman, her figure swaying out in front, her arms akimbo. One lock of hair straggled down her cheek, plastered against it with sweat. She chuckled at the sight of a little boy rolling and wrestling with a big shaggy dog in the center of the street, and her laughter was like a succession of grunts, a struggle between weariness and mirth. Further on a group of youngsters, having found a streak of clayey ground which would hold the peg, were playing mumble-the-peg, and their faces were besmeared with mud. The heart of John Sampson ached in envy of the parents who had these thoughtless youngsters for their own. At least they were too mindless to lock secrets inside their hearts.

A crowd had gathered before the jeweller's window. And in front of the window was a large group. They were all talking at the same time; they were picking out the stones they would buy on the morrow, or when they made their big strike. They were all happy, and Sampson hurried past. Happiness in others was painful to him this night.

Now the distant roar of the gaming house reached him plainly, like the sound of distant surf. Straight to the door of the house he went and looked in towards the central table with a malevolent eye. But Yo Chai was not there. That was the meaning, then, of the early hour at which Winifred had left the house.

A man pointed out Yo Chai's private dwelling behind the gaming house, and in front of it, across the street, he stood for a long time purposeless, helpless, meaningless. And still the problem surged through his brain, maddening him. The relation between Yo Chai and Clung—what could it be? What was the one word—the "Open Sesame!"

Yet he could not be absolutely sure that Winifred was in his house. Certainly Kirk said that he had seen her come out of the house on one night, but that was not a sufficient proof to his aching heart. He decided to sit down on a rickety box nearby and wait for a time to see if Winifred would come out of the house. Yes, and if he confronted her suddenly was there not a possibility that she would tell him everything—all the reasons which made her come to the house of Yo Chai— whether or not Clung was actually concealed there?

The thought made John Sampson almost happy. He sat down on the box and composed himself for a long wait, for hours, if necessary.

Yet to his mind, busied as it was every moment by the problem, it was not a very long time before the door of the house opened. At the entrance stood a tall, bulky Chinese with his hands stuffed in the alternate sleeves. He looked slowly up and down the street, and then, as if satisfied that there was no one else in plain sight, he stepped back through the door.

Almost at once a woman slipped out upon the steps, and turned back towards the door. Her face was away from him, and the light which fell upon her was very dim, but he knew with strange certainty that this was Winifred who stood there, poised on the steps of the Chinaman's house. He started up from the box and made a step across the street when another form appeared in the door and he stopped his progress.

It was Yo Chai. The light at the entrance fell plainly across his face, showing with distinctness even the sparse black moustaches of the Oriental. And he stood with his head tilting back, smiling down upon the girl. She waved her hand. A hand, thin to frailty, appeared from the loose sleeve of Yo Chai and waved adieu in response. Winifred turned and passed down the street; the door closed upon Yo Chai.

Yet Sampson made no effort to turn down the street and intercept his daughter. His mind was filled with an image which had started out suddenly upon it, of Yo Chai, pushing back his chair in the gaming house on that now distant night, and smiling. The clue to the problem was upon him with a rush. It was in the smile of Yo Chai and the smile of Clung. One smile and one man. Clung and Yo Chai—they were one and the same. And Sampson shook his clenched fist above his head and then started almost at a run for the door of Yo Chai.

Chapter 38

The door was opened to him by the bulky Chinaman he had first seen there, and in his excitement he would have pushed past the fellow had not a vast arm shot out and blocked the way as effectively as a stanchion of wood.

"Go tell Cl—, go tell Yo Chai that John Sampson will speak with him—at once," commanded the financier.

The big Oriental turned his head leisurely and spoke in a tremendous guttural, changing to a whine of question ridiculously thin and high at the end. From the interior of the house a soft voice, which Sampson could barely hear, made answer, and then the bulky arm was withdrawn and he stepped into the little box-like hall of Yo Chai. The servant pointed to a screened doorway at one side of the hall and, stepping past this, Sampson found himself in front of Yo Chai, who sat among a heap of cushions reading from a large book of Chinese characters. Sampson found himself at once perfectly at ease. It was rare, indeed, that he was embarrassed in an interview. It was his stock-in-trade. He measured the lean face of the other with a critical eye.

"I suppose," he said with a half smile, "that you won't pretend that you don't know me?"

"No," said the other, rising, "Yo Chai remembers when you sat at his table and played a little game."

And he bowed very low to John Sampson.

"Just now," said the business man, "I don't give a damn what Yo Chai remembers. I'm more interested in what Clung has to say."

The bow of Clung was still under way, and he remained a moment with partially bent head. When he raised his face it was expressionless.

"When I look into your face," said Sampson, with some admiration, "I'm almost puzzled again to know you, and I've seen through the riddle, my friend, and it can never puzzle me again."

Clung was silent. He pointed to the low divan.

"Thanks," said Sampson, and he seated himself with a sigh of comfort.

Manifestly he was complete master of the situation.

"I was perfectly certain," he went on, smiling upon Clung, "that the age of disguises was past. But I see that you've resurrected it again. And very well done, Clung, very well done indeed."

Clung bowed as profoundly as before, and remained standing, his eyes going past Sampson and apparently focussing on the screen behind him, as if at that moment another person were entering the room.

"To put you entirely at your ease," went on Sampson, "I'll tell you that it's unnecessary to be quite so Oriental before me. I know you're a white man, Clung."

And still the eyes of Clung remained immovably fixed upon the wall behind his visitor. Sampson shifted in his chair a bit uneasily and flashed a glance behind him. There was only the barren wall. However, the bullets in Sampson's armory were almost inexhaustible. He was confident that at his will he could break through the calm of Clung.

"There is a certain advantage in method," he began again, "so we may as well start by admitting that there is a disadvantage in your present position, my friend. The disadvantage is that if the crowd of Kirby Creek knew that you were Clung they would promptly send a posse to nab you."

Clung smiled gently upon John Sampson.

"See," he said, and he waved his hand to the four corners of the room. "There are many doors, and there are many roads from Kirby Creek."

"Cool devil, aren't you," said Sampson, "but you'll admit that it might be rather a close call, even for an artist like yourself?"

"Only a pig," said Clung, clinging to his picturesque metaphors, "loves safety—and a sty!"

"Good again," grunted John Sampson, "but granting that you'd like to have the boys give you a run after a while, it would be rather inconvenient to leave all your coin behind you."

"What is money?" said Clung contemptuously. "It is lead around the neck. It sinks the man who swims. Clung will not sink."

"You'd cut and leave all your loot behind?" queried John Sampson with wide eyes. "Gad, boy, I almost believe you would!"

"Not all," said Clung, with another of his gentle smiles, and from one of his loose sleeves he produced at once a little box no larger than the palm of his hand, and square. It opened with a snap, and John Sampson glimpsed a flare of colorful jewels before the box was closed and restored to the sleeve.

"Guarded on all sides, eh?" he remarked scowling a little now, "and I see that you have the true gambler's spirit, Clung. Perhaps you're not in such a good position as you claim; however, I've not come here to do you any injury or to make any threats—unless I'm forced to it. And I won't be forced. You must be a man of *some* reason, Clung, or you wouldn't have lived as long as you have and done the things you have done. They still talk of the way you slipped away from under the nose of Marshal Clauson."

He chuckled, and so doing he failed to see the little flush which showed through even the yellow stain on Clung's face, nor the lowering of the other's eyes.

"We'll get down to business at once," said Sampson. "I've come for this reason: I want to know why my daughter— Winifred—" he choked a little over the name—"has been coming to see you so often in the night."

For the first time the equanimity of Clung was disturbed ever so slightly. His eyebrows rose a trifle.

"No," explained Sampson quickly. "Don't trouble yourself on that score. But I've been missing her, and tonight I saw her come out of your house. Clung, why has she been coming?"

He barked out the last words and leaned forward with jutting lower jaw. He was like a bulldog in more ways than one. Many a Wall Street power would have shuddered to see that expression on the face of John Sampson; but Clung merely smiled and a glint of study came in his eyes.

"Clung has heard," he said, "that in the old days when books were rare, they were often chained to the walls in libraries. And students came and read the books in the libraries and could not take them home to read them when and where they pleased. Your daughter—Winifred—" he paused before and after the name, so that it stood musically by itself—"has found Clung a book which she could not take from the wall and carry home to read when and where she pleased. So she has come to Clung's house, and there she opens the book whenever she pleases and reads in it, and closes the book, and goes home, and forgets Clung."

There was a long pause.

"Well," said Sampson slowly, drawing out every word, "damn my eternal eyes!"

"That would be a great sorrow," said Clung.

"Are you mocking me?" barked the financier.

Clung waved a slim, deprecatory hand.

"Don't put me aside with any asinine trivialities like this. I haven't come to listen to poetry. I want some hard facts. Clung, why does the girl come here?"

And like the hard facts which Sampson commanded, the face of Clung grew stern and expressionless.

"Listen to me," said the older man with a sudden change of tactics. "I am her father, Clung. Haven't I the right to know?"

It was like the melting of ice in Spring—so swift was the change of Clung's eyes. He bowed once more, and then stood erect, his eyes at the feet of Sampson.

"Clung had forgotten," he said softly, "but now he will make himself open. You can read in me."

Chapter 39

"Lad," answered Sampson more gently, "I see you are white—in more ways than one. Now tell me frankly. Why does my girl come to you?"

"To talk to Clung."

"Come, come! What do you mean by that one word?"

"To talk to Clung," said the other, with a certain contemptuous emphasis, "Clung, a dog of a Chinaman!"

The eyes of Sampson widened marvelously.

"You mean to say that you haven't told her that you are white?"

"If she knew that Clung was white," he answered, with a touch of sadness, "she would come no longer."

The mind of Sampson whirled; and there was an infinite relief which struck him like a cool breeze on a very hot day.

"I think I understand, but make it clearer. I must know exactly what you mean to her."

Clung waited, searching for the clue.

"A horse you know," he said at last, "you have no pleasure in riding. He is yours. He will run straight. He will not buck or shy or balk. There is no pleasure in riding him. Is it not true?"

"Ah! I begin to see. Go on!"

"A man you know, he may be your friend, but you will not go a great distance to see him or to hear him talk. But a man you do not know; you may not like him, you may hate him, you may be afraid of him, but you will go a great way to see him and to hear him talk. Is it not true?"

"Exactly!"

"Your daughter—Winifred—she finds me a strange book—because I am written in Chinese! But if she knew Clung to be a white man she would shrug her shoulders—so!—and never come again."

"I wonder," said the other, thoughtfully, and then he shook his head. "Clung, I'm afraid that you're not altogether right."

He smiled with a sharp interest at the younger man.

"I wish I could believe it, but I can't—altogether. I'm afraid there may be—something else."

"What?" asked Clung, with a ring in his voice.

But Sampson shrugged his shoulders.

"I am going to ask you to stop her from coming here, Clung."

The other straightened, his lips drawing to a thin line.

"Give her up?" he repeated in a dull voice that alarmed Sampson. "Suppose a woman has one child—would you ask her to give the child up? Suppose a painter has one great picture—would you ask him to give it up? Could you borrow or beg or buy the picture from him?"

"If it was for the betterment of the child," said the other anxiously, "the woman would give up the child."

The pause came again.

"It is true," said Clung in a faint voice.

Then his eyes rose and met the gaze of Sampson with such intensity that it was like the shock of a physical force.

"Why must Clung give up seeing her?"

"Because it is bad for her."

"Is there poison in this air? Is Clung a dog who bites? Answer!" and the ring in his voice, though it was not loud, shook Sampson tremendously.

"For the oldest reason in the world," he answered, "and for one which you have already named yourself. Her way of life is not your way of life. How would people speak of her if they knew she stole out by night to visit—a Chinaman!"

He brought out the word with brutal force.

"Then I shall no longer be a Chinaman. I shall be Clung, a white man!"

"Clung, a hunted outlaw, reputed a half-breed. Her friends would turn her from their doors."

There was that solemn pause again, and then the bitter voice of Clung: "It is true, and the opinions of other people are very loud in the ears of women. My father, Li Clung, has said it."

"Then—?" queried Sampson, with something of pity softening his voice.

"I shall tell her tonight that I am white," said Clung simply.

"No, no, no!" cried Sampson. "Not that, Clung, in the name of heaven!"

"And why?"

"For many reasons."

He stopped, stammering. It was hard and shameful for him to speak the fear which was in him.

"Speak quickly," said Clung, "and tell Clung what he must do. Every minute is like a whip on a raw place; Clung is very tired!"

"I will be as brief as I may," said the other, "and I expect you to keep on meeting me half way, as you've done so far. In the first place, she has been very often to see you, has she not?"

"It is true."

"And she is glad to be with you?"

The head of Clung tilted—the familiar musing smile touched his lips.

"She seems very glad," he murmured.

"Gad," said Sampson, half to himself, "what a rotten mess it all is—for all of us."

He said aloud, gruffly: "I'm going to ask you to have a woman in here with you the next time Winifred comes. And when Winifred sees you with a woman I'll guarantee that she'll never come back."

"A woman?" said Clung blankly, and then he started: "A concubine?"

"Not a bit, not a bit!" said the other, reddening furiously, "but only a girl—a Chinese girl (there are plenty of them around the town) who will *seem* to be—er—familiar with you. You get my point, Clung?"

"It would be a lie," said Clung hoarsely.

"Sometimes a lie is excusable. Besides, my dear boy, you've certainly told little lies before."

"I have never told a lie," said Clung quietly, "except to say once that my name was John Ring, and once again that my name was Yo Chai."

It was so naive that Sampson had to bite his lip to keep from smiling.

"Is it the only way to drive her away?" said Clung.

"It is the only sure way," answered Sampson.

Clung stiffened, and his hands straightened at his sides; he stood like a soldier at attention.

"If it drives her away," he said, "it will mean that she thinks of me now—as a white woman might think of a white man!"

"I don't mean that she thinks of you in that way," answered Sampson with a hurried anxiety. "God forbid! I'm merely telling you the sure way of sending her back to me and away from you. And you admit that that is a good thing."

"It is true," said Clung, panting, after another of those deadly pauses.

And he added: "But it will prove—if she goes when she sees the Chinese girl—that she has thought of me—as a white girl thinks of a white man!"

"I'm not denying that!"

"And at the very time when I know it," whispered Clung, "I shall kill that thought in her!"

"I suppose so," admitted Sampson miserably, "and yet not altogether. Mere disgust would send her away."

"And her thoughts of Clung afterwards would be ugly thoughts—pah!—unclean thoughts, like a disease!"

Sampson could not speak.

"Then to the house of what white man would you let her go?" asked Clung in the same faint voice.

"To one of her equals—a man who moves in her own social circles," said Sampson carefully. "Well, to a man like William Kirk, for instance."

He was sorry he had used that illustration, for a fire came in the eyes of Clung.

"Is Kirk a clean man in your eyes?" he asked scornfully.

"I admit," said Sampson hastily, "that he did one rather rotten thing—with you. It was a slip such as any one in Winifred's circle would understand. She, herself, has forgiven him for it."

"Is it true?"

"It is true," answered Sampson, falling into Clung's own manner of speech.

"And if Clung were a man like William Kirk?" asked the younger man.

"Then," said Sampson, "I assure you I would not have a word to say. She could come to see you every day—and at night also."

He smiled genially on Clung.

"Clung does not understand," said Clung. "He will not try to understand; he is sick and cold inside."

"And the girl?" asked Sampson, as gently as he could.

"I know no woman," said Clung.

Sampson stared.

"You can hire her to come in and stay about your house for one evening, surely."

"There is no other way?"

"If there were, I'd accept it with open arms, upon my word of honor."

"Then Clung will do it."

It was said with such simplicity that Sampson could hardly believe what he heard.

"Then, by God, Clung, you're a gentleman, and as such I'd like to have the privilege of shaking your hand before I go!"

But the hands of Clung were once more thrust into his sleeves, and Sampson was suddenly aware that during the entire interview his host had never once sat down.

"Clung had rather," said Clung, and his head went back

with that familiar, musing smile, "Clung had rather remain a dog of a Chinaman than be such a gentleman."

The teeth of John Sampson clicked with his anger, and then, grown suddenly hot about the face, he turned and stumbled out of the room and into the street. It was a warm night but the air felt strangely cool to his forehead.

Chapter 40

Something above the door of Yo Chai's house stopped Winifred at the very moment when her hand was on the knocker the next night. She bent her head back and peered anxiously up through the bloom, and then she made out that there were wreaths of flowers overhanging the doorway; the sweet breath of them was sharp and pleasant. Strange flowers such as she had never smelled before, and she wondered how they had been brought to the desolation of Kirby Creek. But then Clung was a man of mysteries, and as such capable of anything.

When the door opened to her she was smiling in anticipation, and her expectations were correct, for in the little hall she found at either side tall vases filled with flowering shrubs, and the scrolls above the table were almost covered with festoons of greenery. A festival occasion, this night of her coming, and guessing at the pretty tribute, a flush went up from her throat to her cheeks and stayed there as she entered the inner room.

But Clung was not there, and she had been on the divan for several moments before he appeared, hastily, and bowed before her. He relaxed on his usual pile of cushions and sat with folded arms staring straight before him; and he made her think of a pleased child which waits to be questioned about the meaning of a surprise. Everywhere about the room were the flowers, the green things which seemed so priceless in the middle of the desert; they must have been conjured into existence; they could not have grown. And the very dress of Clung showed that it was an extraordinary occasion. His robe was a rich brocade rustling so stiffly that it almost crackled when he moved. At length she could keep in her questions no longer.

"What is it, Clung?" she asked impetuously. "Is all this in honor of my coming? Tell me?"

"When one of my fathers took a woman into his house," said Clung, and for the first time his eyes rose from the floor and rested gravely upon her, "he always made the place pleasant for her coming. Clung, also, has done this."

"Take a woman in your house?" she queried, with sudden alarm, and rising, she noted again that the doors behind her, as usual, were locked. "What do you mean, Clung?"

"Only what Clung says, that tonight he takes a woman into his house."

The eyes were very blank as they rested upon her, but old tales of the treachery of the Oriental swarmed back upon her mind and made her blood cold.

"Clung, have you dared—" she began, until her voice grew weak and she stopped perforce.

Every door was locked behind her. What could she do?

"Have you dared to think of keeping me here?" she asked at length, with as much grief as fear in her voice.

"You?" queried Clung in gentle surprise, and he tapped softly once on the gong beside him.

The answer was a little Chinese girl who came slowly through the doorway—slowly, for her feet were painfully small. Her trousers and all her dress were of the rarest of fine silk, and they, like the robes of Clung, were everywhere broidered with rich thread of gold. A necklace of jade, earrings of pearl, bracelets of woven gold set with little emeralds in the design of a tiny dragon—she had never seen so rich a costume. The face was round and the features diminutive, but not unpleasant, and there was about her that air of infinite refinement, millenniums of culture, which the Chinese sometimes bear about them.

And still Winifred could not or would not quite understand.

"Who," she asked sharply, "is this?"

And Clung made answer carelessly, making the girl sit down beside him in obedience to his gesture: "This is a woman of the house of Clung."

"A woman?" repeated Winifred slowly. "A woman?"

And then, after a breathing space: "I never dreamed that you were married, Clung!"

"Married?" he repeated, and his eyebrows arched a little. "No no! Why should Clung take a wife, a burden upon his shoulders? This is only a woman, a handmaid for Clung; he has often been lonely."

"A woman!" whispered Winifred, and her eyes dwelt on the face of the girl, pale for one of her race, with a tint like peach-bloom in her cheeks, slanting dark eyes, and little white teeth.

"But let us talk," said Clung. "You may talk very freely before the girl. She will understand no more than the image of the Greatest!"

He rose and bowed to the hideous, grinning idol and sat down again.

"Or if you wish," went on Clung amiably, "Clung will send the girl away. She is here to come and go at the will of Clung. Is it not true?"

He turned to the girl and spoke sharply to her in Chinese, and she nodded slowly—slowly and very low, and all the while her eyes were fixed in mute submission upon the face of the master.

Winifred rose, and she had to remain standing a moment gripping the back of the divan and squinting her eyes tight while her senses cleared.

The voice of Clung, concerned, eagerly inquiring, broke in upon her.

"There is a sickness upon you," he said. "You are faint? Is it true? The sight of the girl sickens you? Clung will send her away!"

She forced her eyes open, at that, and it seemed to her that the face of Clung had changed, grown grim, and all the features were more sharply defined, as though a pain were etching them more deeply.

"No," she managed to say at length, "keep the girl, keep her by you always, in case you should grow lonely again."

"But," said Clung, stepping beside her as she went feebly towards the door, feeling her way, "but you do not go so soon from Clung? He has many things to say!"

Her strength returned with a sudden outburst; she whirled on him.

"I've heard the last of your talk," she said fiercely. "I shall never see you again."

And she walked quickly to the door and out of the house, but as the door slammed it seemed to Clung that he heard something like a sob. Or was it only a natural sound of the night, for the wind was rising?

He remained where he had been standing, his hand stretched out after the girl, but his arm fell almost at once to his side, and his head lifted. He saw the little Chinese girl staring at him with wide eyes.

He drew his purse from the loose sleeve, a purse of wire net worked with the figure of the dragon, and from it he shook gold pieces and placed them in the small palm of the girl.

"You are paid," said Clung. "Go!"

Still she hesitated, her eyes large and fixed steadily upon him; her lips moved, but no words came. Then she bowed to the floor and, turning, went with her small, painful steps from the room. She stopped at a table of ebony and on it she laid the gold which Clung had given her. When she went on, her head was bowed, and Clung, standing with his head back, and that half smile upon his lips, heard the beginning of a sob as the door whisked to behind her. He laughed softly.

"Clung also," he said, "Clung also; the sound of it is growing big in his throat. But why should he be a woman?"

He gathered himself and pulled the robe tightly about his breast. He rose almost on tiptoe and cast out his hand, palm up, to the mocking face of the idol.

"I am Clung," he said defiantly, "Clung, the son of Li Clung. It is true!"

And he sat down in the divan and produced his long-stemmed pipe, placed a pinch of tobacco in the bowl, lighted it, puffed twice or thrice deeply; knocked out the ashes and refilled the miniature bowl, and so on and on, smoking until a blue haze formed in front of him and rose like heavy incense and drifted across the face of the idol until it obscured the grin and left only the bright, beady eyes staring down through the smoke.

Chapter 41

The voice of William Kirk went before him through the night, a great and ringing voice which the steep sides of the ravine caught and flung down again in sharp echoes, so that it was hard to tell from what direction the singing came; it seemed to be showering out of the sky. He galloped his horse straight through the door of the stable and brought him to a long sliding halt on the boards within, a thunderous proceeding; and when he had torn off the saddle he went on into the house, singing again.

He found John Sampson, in a state of great agitation, walking up and down, up and down the room. There was a cigar in his mouth, unlighted, but chewed to the edge of the wrapper.

"Shut up!" commanded Sampson. "I can't think with this infernal minstrel show of yours going on!"

"And why think?" asked Kirk in his big voice. "Why think, Sampson? Do something better."

"Such as what?" said the smaller man, and he halted with his arms aggressively akimbo.

"Why," answered Kirk carelessly. "Eat, and sleep, and eat again. They're both better things than thinking. Thinking, Sampson, has worn the hair off your head. And look at my shock?"

He ran his fingers through it so that it stood up on end, burst into a thunderous laugh, and began a song again:

> "Old Thompson, he had an old grey mule,
>   And he drove him around in a cart.
> He loved that mule and the mule loved him
>   With all his mulish heart!"

"Kirk!" shouted Sampson. "In the name of God, stop that damned racket!"

"What's the matter, man? Winifred still?"

"Winifred always," moaned the miserable millionaire.

And he literally collapsed into a chair and mopped his forehead. Kirk grinned broadly upon him. Sampson sat up with a jerk that threw the purple blood into his forehead and shook his fist at the younger man.

"When," he thundered, "when are you going to do what you promised—take the girl in hand?"

"When I get tired of Kirby Creek," answered the other coolly, "and at present I find it interesting—very!"

"Where've you been for the last forty-eight hours?" asked Sampson, warily shrugging away the thought of his last question, and then his eyes sharpened to a rather malicious light.

"I suppose," he said, "you've been off by yourself trying to forget what happened in the house of Yo Chai the other day? Ha, ha, ha, ha! Well, lad, those who won't take advice have to learn by experience. *I* knew what would happen when you sat down opposite Yo Chai—the old Oriental magician! A mule load of gold lost—thrown away—ha, ha, ha! I'll tell this when we get north!"

"Don't hurry with your story," said Kirk with twisting lip and a pale face. "Wait till you see what happens with the second load of gold."

"Gad!" breathed Sampson, sitting bolt upright and grasping either arm of his chair. "Lad, you aren't fool enough to go back and try the same route? The first money you lost was what you'd already won. This next bunch will be your own coin!"

"Perhaps," said Kirk, and smiled mysteriously, for he was thinking again of the boxes of gold and dust which he had taken from the cave of the Night Hawk and poured into his saddle-bags that night. All the readily convertible coin of the bandit was in his load, and it made a less bulky but a richer cargo than that which he had borne into the house of Yo Chai on the back of his mule the day before.

He changed the subject.

"And where is Winifred now?"

"She started from the house an hour ago," said Sampson.

"Then," answered Kirk, "we might as well go to bed now. It'll be close on midnight before she returns."

"Other nights, yes," answered Sampson, "but tonight, I think—God knows how I hope it!—will be her last trip to Yo Chai!"

He rose and resumed his hurried pacing of the floor.

"Talk of something else," he commanded. "I'll go mad if I

let my mind dwell on that girl of mine!"

"What shall we chatter about?" said Kirk, and he yawned.

"Anything—what the whole town is talking about."

"What's that?"

"The murder of Charlie Morgan."

"Eh?" queried Kirk sharply, for somehow that brief and brutal word shocked him. "Murder?" he repeated.

"Murder!" nodded Sampson. "Damnable, cold-blooded murder! The Night Hawk again. Strange how long they let that fellow roam around!"

"Strange indeed," said Kirk, and smiled carelessly.

"Haven't you heard about the murder?"

"Not a word."

"Where've you been? This Morgan seems to have been a harmless old trapper—a good shot, they say, in his younger days. The other day he made some drunken boast about leaving the town with a pack of gold dust and going straight through the Night Hawk's territory. Well, he started, and that devil met him and shot him down in cold blood. Didn't even take the poor devil's money. They found it all in the mule pack, shortly after they located the body today. Think of it, Kirk, think of the cold-souled fiend who would shoot down an old man like that!"

"Rotten," said Kirk, with dry throat.

"The town is wild about it," said Sampson. "Even the Chinaman—your friend Yo Chai—is up in arms and has offered a reward for the apprehension of the Night Hawk. Seems that Yo Chai had befriended old Morgan and staked him with grub and supplies when he started on his trip the time before last. Now he wants the blood of the Night Hawk, but I suppose even the Chinaman's money can't get that."

"Neither his money nor his luck," said Kirk.

Sampson turned swiftly on him.

"You say that in an odd way," he murmured thoughtfully.

Kirk frowned.

187

"Don't look at me like that, Sampson," he said coldly.

"In what way?"

"By God, I won't stand for it!" thundered Kirk, with a sudden mad rage. "Sampson, I swear there's an accusation in your eye!"

"Good Gad, Kirk," gasped the old man, starting back from the other. "Are you mad, boy? What do you mean? Accusation of what?"

Kirk set his fists in tight knots and forced the fire out of his eye.

"Nothing," he said in a strangled voice. "The fact is, Sampson, my nerves haven't been of the best ever since that demon Yo Chai got the money from me yesterday."

"Let it go at that," muttered Sampson, and then he looked partly with awe and partly with curiosity at Kirk. "Why, man," he said softly. "There was murder in your eye a minute ago. *Murder!*"

"Nonsense," said Kirk, and he waved the thought away with a flourish of his ponderous hand. "Utter nonsense, Sampson. But what's that?"

The front door opened, and Winifred stood in the opening. Her expression was so strange that Sampson jumped to his feet and fairly ran to her.

"Why, Winifred," he called, "what's the matter, girl?"

"Nothing—everything!" she answered in a dull voice, and crossed the room to her door. She paused there with her hand on the knob and turned towards them.

"Dad," she said, "we leave here tomorrow. I can't stay another day. I'm tired of the place. *Sick* of it!"

And she vanished into the room. Sampson caught Kirk by the shoulders and shook him joyously.

"Did you hear, lad?" he cried softly. "Did you hear?"

"What the devil has happened?"

"Tomorrow we start."

"Tomorrow evening, then. I take my last whirl at Yo Chai

tomorrow afternoon. But what *has* happened?"

"Yo Chai—"

"Damn him! I've stood enough from him. I'll—"

"Hush, lad! Neither of us is worthy of kissing the shoes of that—Chinaman!"

Chapter 42

There are some places where two make a crowd, in spite of the old saying, and certainly in no place could it have been truer than in those early days in Kirby Creek; for on one day William Kirk rode into town and led a mule load of gold to gamble away in an effort to break the bank of Yo Chai's gambling house, and to see him the whole town turned out and stayed hour by hour watching the historic game. Yet, only two days later, when he went under identical circumstances with a far larger sum to wager, men hardly turned their heads to watch him pass. It was an old, old story. Had it not been seen before? And were they the men to care for a twice-told tale?

To be sure, there were a few who had not seen the proceedings of the day before, and though they had been told of them they would hardly believe. Now they formed a comparatively large crowd watching around the central table at which William Kirk played against Yo Chai. But there was no stentorian announcement following the dealing of every card, and in a deadly silence they played. It was stud poker again, but this time, as though luck itself had wearied of the persistence of William Kirk, it held steadily against him. His gold coin passed across the table, and after that the gold dust was weighed and followed the coin duly, and then the nuggets, and last a considerable stock of jewels and still the river of misfortune caught up the chips of William Kirk and carried them away to the side of Yo Chai.

There was no mental stupor to which Kirk could attribute his defeat this day. He touched no liquor and there was no spell cast over him by the steady eye of the gambler, and still he lost. His wits were sharper than they had ever been before in his life, and in spite of himself there was forced upon his brain the consciousness that he was struggling against a force which in some mysterious way was greater than his own. He laughed at the idea, he sneered it away, but it persisted.

And he commenced to study the face of Yo Chai between hands. He sat, as usual, with his head rather far back, and his shoulders bowed forward in the stoop of middle-age. Yet there was a change somewhere in him from the Yo Chai against whom Kirk had played only a few days before. The features were more sharply drawn. The purple shadows about the eyes, making them seem deeply sunken, were as they always had been, and there was no palpable weakening of the eye. It was as bright and steady as ever. Yet in some manner Kirk gained the impression that the Chinaman was weary, weary to death. It was like playing against a machine. Half the glamour was taken from the cards.

Half the sting was taken from defeat, also. It was not like being beaten by a machine. It was like witnessing the triumph of an automaton. But as the game progressed it exercised a clarifying power over the mind of Kirk. It convinced him gradually that the West was no place for him. This machine-like loss of his money made him yearn to be back again in the north, among his fellows, among men where reason counted, where he would be valued for other reasons than the quickness of his hand or his luck as a gambler.

What did it mean in the life of Kirk? Was it the end of his descent into the primitive? Was it the beginning of his turn towards culture again? The time came when he had no more money, but he was anxious now to rid himself of every cent he had taken from the Night Hawk. It was like the act of washing his hands of the past. He hunted through his pockets and finally found a small sack of canvas which had been in the largest money box of the Night Hawk, though why it had not been turned in with the other contents of the box he could not tell. Perhaps it had been the last haul of the outlaw and he had kept it still in the small bag for that reason. This canvas bag he drew now from his hip pocket and tossed down upon the table. It was in itself a large stake—fifty twenty-dollar gold pieces, all freshly minted.

"My last stake, Yo Chai," he said carelessly, "the last coin I toss across this table. Tomorrow I leave the town. A quick chance for this thousand, Yo Chai. What say? Flip a coin heads or tails for the stake?"

"It is good," said the mechanical voice of Yo Chai. "Throw your coin."

Kirk pulled out a half dollar and juggled it a moment in the palm of his hand.

"I'm going to lose," he said nonchalantly, "I know it beforehand, perfectly well. But though I've lost a lot of money to you tonight, Yo Chai, I've gained something in return that's worth a lot more than any coin. Here goes. Heads for me!"

The half dollar flicked in the air and rang on the table—tails!

"I knew, you see," smiled Kirk, and he bowed to the proprietor, "and if you want to play with me again, Yo Chai, you will have to follow me. Quite a long way, I hope!"

And laughing, he turned from the dais and walked towards the door. The dull eye of Yo Chai turned after him. He was a rich man from the work of the last three days, but no starving beggar could have looked after the portly form of Kirk with such bitter envy as showed in the face of Clung the moment the back of the big man was turned. He watched it through the door and then he began to gather in the coins mechanically. But as he did so, something stopped him. He turned one of the coins so the light struck full across it.

Then, with greater haste, he picked them up one after another and examined them with painful care, as if he were doubtful of their value. The usual group of five was settling around the table for their session of draw poker and one of them asked: "What is it, Yo Chai, counterfeit? Counterfeit money, Yo Chai?"

Clung stood with a coin held to the bright light. It was like all the others: there was a small line cut with a sharp knife across the tail-side of the twenty-dollar gold piece. He tossed the last coin into the drawer.

Then he laughed a long time, softly, his head back and a marvelously evil light in his eyes.

"Counterfeit money?" he said at last in his gentle voice. "No, but a counterfeit man! A counterfeit man! Ha, ha, ha!"

He broke off and said gravely to the men: "Gentlemen, Yo Chai plays no more."

"Tired, Yo?" asked one of them. "No more play tonight?"

"No more play for ever," said Clung, and turned from the dais.

And from that moment the middle-age stoop was gone from his shoulders, he walked straight with the elastic, quick, soft step which had been his of old. And his lips moved slightly as he said to himself: "If you were a man like William Kirk you could come both day and night. If you were a man like William Kirk!"

Just that phrase repeated over and over again. He went straight to his assistant who sat behind the desk in the little corner office of the house.

"Let the house be closed," he said abruptly at the door of the office.

"But for what reason? The players are just arriving. For what reason? The night is hardly begun!"

"It has to be purified," said Clung, and with that enigmatic reply he turned on his heel and went straight to his house.

The door-keeper, as usual, bowed to the very floor before the master.

"Call the servants," said Clung in Chinese, "call them at once and say that Yo Chai will speak with them in his hall."

He went to his divan and sat among the cushions cross-legged.

Almost at once the servants came hurrying, and they were marshalled before him in single line by the door-keeper. Besides him there were four, for the house of Yo Chai was exceedingly well served.

He said: "You have served Yo Chai."

They bowed as if at a given signal, and all equally low. Rising, their pig-tails soared in unison and slapped against their backs.

He said: "Yo Chai has eaten well, he has lived in a clean house, he has slept in a quiet bed."

Once more they bowed and once more, rising, their pig-tails slapped against their backs.

He said: "This is the last day of your service with Yo Chai."

They bowed again, but this time the big door-keeper uttered a little whining cry oddly out of keeping with his bulk.

"If there is one among us," he said, fixing a vicious little eye upon the smallest, oldest, and most withered of them all. "If there is one among us who has not pleased Yo Chai, if there is one among us like a chattering monkey who talk-talks all day and does nothing, let the master say the word and we will beat him much with sticks. Also, we will throw him afterwards out upon the street. But do not let the master send the rest of us away. He is our father. We are his children. We sleep when he sleeps, we watch when he wakes; if a sorrow should come upon him we would not eat for seven days."

And then the little man said: "It is now clear in my eyes.

Word has come to us that the master has played for much money in the gaming house. He has lost his money. He is poor. See! we will serve for nothing for many days."

"It is true," said the chorus.

"Yo Chai is pleased," said Clung gravely.

They grinned in unison and bowed again.

"But nevertheless you must go."

Like automatons that could not do otherwise, they bowed again, but their faces were woeful.

"Not one of you has offended Yo Chai. You are his children. But you must go. Find other masters. Yo Chai shall need no more servants. This is his last day."

A wail rose from them, shrill, whining.

"The master is about to die!"

"No," said Clung, and he smiled on them, "Yo Chai is about to be purified and to pass into another life. He will lose all that is his, even his name. And therefore his children must leave him. Yo Chai will sit here and wait. His children will hasten and prepare the things that are theirs. Also, if they see other things about the house which they can carry and which they cherish, they are welcome to those also."

They bowed again and were gone like leaves before the wind. Thereafter, for the next few minutes, figures scurried soft-footed into the room and went out again more slowly, and things disappeared as sand melts under a heavy rain. They were taking the word of their "father" at its most extreme value. Finally when he struck his gong at the end of an hour they came with their bundles.

"Yo Chai will pay you."

"We have been paid," they protested, "ten times the value of our wretched lives. We have been many times paid."

"Nevertheless," said Yo Chai, still smiling, "you shall be paid again."

And he pulled from one of those capacious sleeves his purse of wire-net engraved with the form of the dragon. From this he took out a little handful of gold for each of them, emptying the purse. They bowed; they almost beat their foreheads on the floor at his feet. They called the blessings of a thousand gods upon him, and Clung sat all the time with his head tilting back and that musing smile touching the corners of his lips. Then they were gone.

But before he had a chance to rise the door opened again and the big Mongol stood once more before him. He prostrated himself almost at full length, and Clung knew with a sudden thrill that this was the prostration of a man who knew the ways of the Imperial Court of China.

"Rise, my son," said Clung.

The big Chinaman stood erect.

"These," he said, and his contemptuous thumb indicated the other servants who had already passed through the door, "are not worthy, but Gee Wing has seen many times and great masters. There is danger coming to his master. Gee Wing will come also."

"Would you follow Yo Chai, Gee Wing?" asked Clung softly.

"Around the edge of the world," said the big Mongol

"But I go North into a cold country," said Clung.

"Gee Wing laughs at the cold."

"It cannot be," said Clung. "Yo Chai is going where no other Chinamen that ever lived could follow."

And he smiled strangely.

Gee Wing prostrated himself again. Then he rose.

"There is only one door at which Gee Wing cannot stand guard for Yo Chai," he said sadly. "Farewell."

And he also was gone, and the door banged heavily behind his hurrying feet and the long echo went mourning through the house.

Chapter 43

But there was no mourning in the manner of Clung as soon as Gee Wing disappeared. Rather there was something approaching a quiet happiness, and a phrase came over and over again on his soundless lips.

He went directly to his wash room, filled a tub with steaming water, threw off his Chinese robes, and stepped in. The change was almost instantaneous, and when he stepped out his lean, muscular body was a pure white. For the long wearing of the yellow stain and the life indoors day and night had removed the last vestige of the tan from the skin of Clung. He removed the long pig-tail; his black hair was cropped short.

Then from the closet of his own room he brought out hidden clothes, the common wear of a cowpuncher. About his waist he buckled a belt of cartridges with a heavy forty-five swinging low in its holster. He drew the gun and spun the cylinder, and as he did so his head went back once more and the familiar musing smile was again on his lips.

The moment the gun was back in its holster the attitude of Clung changed sharply. He stood with his feet close together and his eyes glancing restlessly about so that he gave the impression of one who had stolen into a house where he had no place. Finally he left the house by the back door and in the stables he saddled a grey horse—a beautiful animal whose slender limbs would scarcely have supported for a single mile the bulk, say, of William Kirk; but the weight of Clung would rest easily even on that delicately-rounded back. This horse Clung saddled with painful care. Then he walked swiftly to the rear of the gaming house. He found some brush and tore it up. Lighting it, he held the flames here and there against the tinder-dry walls of the frame buildings. When the wood started to burn, he went quickly back to the stable for his horse.

Soon a yellow arm was reaching up into the heart of the sky. At that danger signal yells of excitement and alarm sounded and a throng poured into the streets in the space of a few seconds.

Two deputy sheriffs appeared and took command. They divided the crowd into gangs. Part of them formed lines with buckets and began to wash down the roofs and sides of neighboring buildings so that they might not kindle from the heat of the gaming house. Three other bucket lines attacked the gaming house itself by as many doors, battering down partitions with axes to get at the flames more freely. Another bucket line beat in the front part of the flimsy wall of Yo Chai's house and attacked the flames there.

But plainly it was a hopeless struggle to beat down the fires. They were too carefully started, and the frame buildings went up with a puff and a roar like so many piles of tinder. Still the bucket lines persisted in their labors for an obvious reason. Yo Chai's chief clerk was among them, running here and there, wringing his long-nailed fingers and shrieking out directions, pleas, offers of reward to the rescuers. Twenty dollars for every man who helped quench the flames; fifty dollars for every man who put in an hour's work. A hundred dollars for every man on the spot when the flames were quenched. That offer called other bucket lines which were pouring streams of water steadily over the roofs and walls of the near-by houses. Moreover, it was plainly seen that on that windless night there was no danger that the fires would jump from the big gaming hall to the neighboring dwellings.

So peaceful was the air that the four yellow and red stained columns of flame over the gaming house and the dwelling of Yo Chai rose in steady towers, leaping higher now and again as if they were trying to kindle the stars above them.

Inside the gaming house, in spite of the steady streams of water from the buckets, the flames had swept across the floors in yellow tides of fearful heat. The faces of the foremost fire-fighters were blistered and seared raw. They staggered back in groups, blind, reeling, and collapsed on the street. Yet others rushed up against the flames to take the place of the men who were exhausted.

Suddenly Clung saw his five servants. They stood in a line, one behind the other, each with his hands thrust into alternate sleeves, and they looked upon the conflagration with calm, unmoved faces. One of the deputy sheriffs rushed up to them and required them with curses to aid in the rescue work, but they shrugged their shoulders and remained impassive witnesses. Clung worked his horse a little closer to them, curiously. The flames belched more wildly above the buildings and cast a bright light over the group of Chinese. Something was wet and gleaming on the face of the big Mongol who had kept the door of Yo Chai. And as if inspired by the coming of Clung, the others lifted their heads together and gave voice to a wild, discordant wail, repeated monotonously over and over again, a lament for the dead. This, then, was their understanding of how Yo Chai, their father, had purified himself for another life into which no Chinese that had ever lived could follow him.

There was a roar of descending timbers, ending in a boom and crash, and a vast shower of sparks darted up into the night and went out. That flare of light picked the whole town out of the heart of the night and gave it back to the day for an instant.

Women screamed, and began shouting encouragement to the workers; but obviously the end was near. The house of Yo Chai was now a roaring bonfire, and the flames swept up the outside of the walls, vomiting through the windows in steady columns. The two deputy sheriffs ran to the chief clerk of Yo Chai.

He spoke to them, shaking his head, and when they turned away he flung the edge of his mantle over his face and turned away into the crowd. Then the deputies went among the crowd and ordered that the useless fight be given over. The majority obeyed willingly enough, but a few, either too strongly tempted by the offers of reward, or else carried away by the hysteria of excitement, had to be torn from their places and carried forcibly back beyond reach of the flames.

Then a horror caught the minds of men away from the actual fire for a moment. A horseman who had recently ridden into the crowd was observed to be fighting with his horse. The brute was pitching madly in an effort to shake the rider off and get closer to the flames. Half a dozen leaped forward to catch the reins of the frantic animal but at the same instant it worked the bit into its teeth, straightened its head with a jerk that tore the reins from the hands of its rider, and galloped straight for the inferno of fire.

The man tossed up his arms with a yell of despair. The yellow flare of fire framed him, his hat off, his hair blown back, and his cry was drowned by the roar of the men of the crowd and the shriek of the women. At the very edge of the wall of flame the rider flung himself from the saddle and struck the ground; the horse sprang on into the flames.

Striking the wall, everywhere undermined by the fury of the flames, a whole section of it gave way and crashed down before the wild horse. Its neigh of agony rang back; it echoed shrill over the sudden silence of the crowd, and then the poor beast was seen, galloping still further into the heart of the wilderness of flames. Yellow hands of fire reached from every side against the animal, and it swerved here and there like a dodging polo pony through the mass of red and yellow flames. Straight on it held towards one of those three piles of steadier

fire from which the conflagration had started, and into this
with a great leap the horse flung itself.

Apparently it struck with its whole weight the central pillar of the hall, already mostly eaten through by the fire, and
now the pillar of wood buckled before this blow, and the roof
directly above came lunging down with a gigantic flurry and
outward puff of flames.

There was a yell, human in its piercing pain, superhuman
in its terrible volume; and then only the roar of the fire, and
Clung saw men who had witnessed, perhaps, a score of gun-
fights cover their eyes with their hands.

He turned his grey horse, which was trembling with excitement, and wove his way through the dense crowd and out on
to an open lane. He rode with his face towards the purity of
the stars. He stretched up his empty hands.

"Out of fire," said Clung, "and into a new life!"

He urged the grey to a gallop and went swiftly up the ravine.

Chapter 44

Two things drew Kirk back to the cave of the Night
Hawk when he left the house of Yo Chai that night. The first
was a desire for a final sight of the silver Virgin; but this was
not so strong an impulse as the wish to look once more on the
strength and wild beauty of the black stallion. His reason
convinced him that he must never go near the place again,
but the emotion was greater than the reason. He had no wish
to take the silver Virgin away with him. The image was in itself a great treasure, no doubt, but it seemed to Kirk that it
was the baleful influence of those diamond eyes which had in-

duced him to step out of the lawful path just as it had once tempted Spenser years before.

That whole grim altar and all the jewels of the cave should stay where they were. But he could not bear the thought of leaving the black stallion to die of starvation in the cave. Already the fine animal had gone twenty-four hours without water. It would be a short and simple act of charity to send a bullet through the brain of the horse.

So he urged his horse to a steady canter and arrived quickly at the mouth of the tunnel. While he was still in the passage, and while the sound of his footsteps in the sand surely could not have reached into the main part of the cave, he heard the snort and then the shrill whinny of the stallion; and the sudden sound stopped his heart with a strange misgiving. It seemed to Kirk that there was a note of anger as well as triumph in the neigh. For be it remembered that he was at the end of his third step back into the primitive and his mind was open to more elemental influences and moved in almost childlike veins of superstition now and then.

So it was that when he had lighted the torch in the cave he held it high above his head and approached the stallion with rather cautious steps. The large brute lifted its fine head and turned towards him with distended nostrils. In his very ear it trumpeted a greeting, a challenge, perhaps. For there was little of welcome in its aspect. The small ears were flat back on the neck and the big eyes gave back the light of the torch with a greenish-yellow gleam. Perhaps it was the lack of water which had maddened the horse.

But when Kirk came closer, the stallion bared its teeth and lunged at him like a biting dog. He shouted and jumped back. The display of temper did not irritate him; rather it roused in him a fierce desire to master the brute and a feeling of joy in the combat. He drew his revolver and poised it for the shot, aiming squarely between the eyes of the horse. Yet his hand lowered. For a picture came to him of how he had ridden on the black down the canyon on that night when he had met and slain Charlie Morgan, and how the stallion had galloped like a swift and noiseless shadow. Also, the anger of the dumb brute was like the anger of a man who knows that he is about to be shot down for no crime. It became as difficult for Kirk to press the trigger as it would have been for him to murder a defenseless human being.

He cursed, and raised the revolver again, but once more his hand faltered and fell. He thought now of riding the stallion down one of the riding-paths in the Park, and how all eyes would go over to him. There was not a mount in the Riding Academy to compare with this one! To be sure, there was some danger of appearing near Kirby Creek with a black stallion, for the Night Hawk was known to have ridden a mount such as this. But he could prove with a thousand alibis that he was not the Night Hawk. He had been still in the far north in the very height of the outlaw's career. He made a sudden resolution to take the black away with him. The silver Virgin and all the jewels of plunder could remain here in the eternal night of the cave, but he would carry away the gun, the horse, and the poniard of Spenser.

Having made up his mind to the thing, he set about leading the stallion to water. It was no easy task, for the horse still acted as if in a frenzy. He had to take a half hitch with a rope around the nose of the brute, and when the horse reared and struck at him with its forefeet, he bore down heavily on the rope, shutting off the stallion's wind and nearly choking it. He kept up the pressure until the stallion staggered with glazing eyes. Then he released the grip of the rope a little and led the horse to the pool of water.

Yet all the way he had to keep half turned towards the animal, for the minute his back was turned he felt that the ears of the stallion would lower and the fire come back in its eyes. At the pool the black plunged its nose whole inches into the water and drank, but before it had finished the draught Kirk pulled up its head again. There was another furious display of temper, but Kirk knew too much about horses to let the half-famished brute take its fill of water. He pulled the stallion back into the cave, tied its head short to the stall, and taking off his saddle from his horse at the mouth of the tunnel, he carried it back and placed it on the black.

Then he placed the torch in a crevice of the rock near the silver Virgin and looked his last upon the image, and as he led the horse into the mouth of the passage it seemed to Kirk that the black diamond eyes of the Virgin turned and followed his leaving.

It was no easy task to lead the big horse down the tunnel, and again and again the stallion lunged forward against the rope in its desire to reach the man. He choked the black down, and kept him a safe distance until they reached the mouth. There, as before, the stallion crouched like a dog and wriggled its way out to the open. Kirk put his other horse on a rope and started back up the ravine.

It was a difficult progress. When his own horse approached too close, the black lashed out with vicious heels and even when the led horse lagged behind to the end of the rope the stallion kept sidling and flashing grim glances back to the other animal, as if it waited for the opportunity to jerk away from the controlling hand of the master and make an attack. Kirk enjoyed the very ferocity of the animal. It filled him with a rather foolish pride to think that this wild charger was his, submissive perforce to his superior strength and cunning; and in the strong, supple movement of the animal beneath him, the elastic and easy spring of the legs, he felt that he had at his command a speed which no other beast on the Southwestern desert could rival.

Prancing and side-stepping like a dancer the black made its way up the ravine, and in front of their cabin Kirk hallooed. The voice of Sampson answered faintly from within, and then the financier appeared in the doorway.

"Bring out a lantern and take a look at a piece of real horse-flesh," suggested Kirk, and when Sampson came out again carrying a lantern, Kirk tossed him the rope of the led horse and put the black through a few paces, making him rear and plunge, and finally sidling him up to Sampson with high, prancing steps. He had to twist the head of the black clear to its shoulder before he could bring him to stand before the financier. Sampson grunted his admiration.

"A horse that is," he agreed, and he stepped about to view the stallion from every angle with a horse-lover's appreciative eye. "I'd pay you a cool couple of thousand for that horse—if I could ride him; but taking all things into consideration, I think you'd better take out a heavy life insurance if you intend to keep the brute."

"That," said Kirk, "is the reason I want him. When we're up in the peaceful north, Sampson, the black will give me a touch of Southwestern excitement now and then."

"Southwestern devilry," added Sampson. "But where did you pick him up?"

"From a poor devil who was broke and drunk. He would have sold the black for the price of a drink just then, but I paid him five hundred and he nearly wept for joy. They'll stare when they see this horse in the Park, Sampson."

"They will, and they'll also run to get out of the way. Look out, there! He'll have a piece out of your knee in a moment!"

"Not a bit," grinned Kirk. "I can read his mind. I tell you; this horse is after my own heart."

"After your new heart, perhaps," said Sampson, "but in the old days, Kirk, you'd have rather signed your death-warrant than climb into that saddle on that horse. I wish the air of Kirby Creek affected me in this way, Kirk," he added a bit wistfully, "and I'd think I'd found the fountain of youth. Put up your nag and let's go in and talk to Winifred. She's in a bad humor, Kirk, and sits there daring me with her eyes to ask questions about what happened to her last night."

"And what *did* happen?" asked Kirk.

"The devil!" broke out Sampson, and pointed down the ravine.

A tongue of yellow flame like a waving hand of fire soared above the roofs of Kirby Creek.

Chapter 45

"Winifred!" he called. "Fire in Kirby Creek!"

She came to the door at once. And the three stood watching in wonder the growing flare of light. It mounted higher until all of Kirby Creek was bathed in yellow light.

"Shall we ride down?" suggested Kirk.

"What about it, Winifred?"

"The fire's already dying down," she said, "and it will be almost out by the time we arrive. Besides, it's not spreading."

"What's the matter, Winifred?" asked Kirk maliciously. "You're not keen for anything these days."

"For nothing except to leave this dropping off point of the world," she answered wearily.

And as she was turning back into the house her father said in a low voice: "Gad, I think it's the place of Cl—of Yo Chai!"

Winifred stopped short at the door.

"The place of Yo Chai?" she echoed sharply.

"Look!" answered John Sampson.

Their place on the side of the ravine was at a considerable elevation above the town of Kirby Creek, and as the fire lighted the roofs of the town they were able to see with perfect distinctness that it was from the broad roof of the gambling house that the fire was belching.

"Poor devil!" muttered Sampson. "Poor Yo Chai!"

"What difference does it make?" said the girl coldly. "Perhaps he's in the flames—he probably is to save his gold. But what difference does it make?"

"But burned to death!" said Sampson. "Gad, how horrible!"

"Bah!" snorted Kirk, "let him go. After all, a gambler takes his chances even with fire! Let him go!"

"Burned to death!" repeated the girl, and she turned with a muffled cry and ran into the house.

"What's up with her?" asked Kirk suspiciously.

"Someday I'll tell you, lad," said Sampson, deeply moved. "But now let's go in to her."

They found her huddled on her bed weeping hysterically. And when her father tried to comfort her she fought him away.

"Keep your head high, Winifred!" he pleaded. "There's not one chance in twenty that he's caught in the fire!"

"You don't know!" she said, and suddenly she was clinging to her father, still weeping. "You don't know, but I do! I can almost see him start that fire with his own hand. Oh, Dad, oh, Dad!"

"Hush!" he said, patting her back with clumsy tenderness. "Hush, my dear, for it will all turn out all right in the end!"

"How can it for him?" she said almost fiercely. "I tell you, it's the end of—of Yo Chai! Dad, yellow or white, there's not his like left in the world. And I'm alone, oh God, how utterly alone, Dad!"

"Hush," he said again with a shaking voice, "or Kirk will hear!"

"Yes, Kirk!" she sat bolt upright, the tears gone. "If it had not been for Kirk—"

"Well?"

"I hate the ground he walks!"

"Do you still hold that old slip against him?"

"Dad," she said suddenly, "what a fool, what a weak and cruel and selfish fool a woman can be!"

She broke away from Sampson and stood erect.

"We leave in the morning," she said, "and we have to get our things together."

He said, alarmed: "But wait till you've quieted down, Winifred. You're half hysterical now."

And she laughed in such a way as he had never heard before.

"Do you think that anything matters now?" she said. "I was never calmer in my life!"

She proved it, it seemed, by the absolute quiet in which she set about packing the few belongings which they had taken into the mining camp and Kirk and Sampson sat in utter silence watching her with a sort of awe. Through the window they saw the fire had passed its height and now the flames fell, and there was only a red glow over the town and a faint red spot in the sky of the night above Kirby Creek, like a grim sign.

And while that red sign of wrath was still plainly visible in the sky above the town, a voice called from the night, "William Kirk!"

They were silent in the room; the girl turned strange eyes upon the door.

"William Kirk!" called the voice again, not loud but with peculiar carrying power.

And Winifred sank into a chair and cowered.

"Clung!" she said in a faint voice. "The ghost of Clung!"

"Clung?" cried Kirk, and he sprang up, his face terrible. "Who said Clung?"

"William Kirk!" called the voice again.

"My God!" said the big man, "it *is* Clung!"

"For God's sake, Kirk!" pleaded Sampson, "don't go out! It's murder if you do!"

"Murder?" growled Kirk, and he flung Sampson away with

the slightest motion of his hand. "What does an old fool like you know about murder?"

"William Kirk!" called the voice.

"Don't go!"

"Damnation!" thundered Kirk. "Am I to stay here like a whipped puppy because a dog of a half-breed Chink yells outside the door? I'm coming!"

And following the roar of his voice, he threw open the door. In the night he made out a slender figure on a grey horse, holding the black stallion by the reins.

"Who's there?" he shouted.

"Clung. Your horse is ready. Are *you* ready, Kirk?"

"Damn you, yes! Ready for anything! What d'ye want?"

"To ride with you, Kirk."

"Where?"

"A long distance for one of us and a short time to ride it in!"

And Kirk, bareheaded as he was, strode through the door. He was trembling, but it was the hunting dog's tremble of eagerness.

"Close the door!" said Clung.

And Kirk obeyed automatically; he wondered why he obeyed, and also he wondered why he hated that quiet voice so profoundly.

Now, outside the house, away from the glare of the lamps within, the light of the newly-risen moon was sufficiently clear for him to make out distinctly the face of him he had known as Clung. Thinner, perhaps, and marvelously pale; a single glance, even by that dim light, was sufficient to show that there was no trace of Chinese blood in this man. For his face seemed to actually shine, so profound was its pallor. Kirk halted.

"Why do you want me?" he asked again, to make sure.

And he found himself looking into the muzzle of a revolver which had been conjured out of thin air, and behind it was

208

the well-known, musing smile of Clung.

"I have the horse of the Night Hawk," said Clung, "and now I want to see his gun!"

"Damn you!" said Kirk, after a little pause.

"Move slowly," said Clung calmly, "and pull out the gun with the butt towards me. That is good."

He took the revolver and slipped his forefinger under the barrel. Then he turned to Kirk again, and with a smile of positively womanly brightness.

"It is true," said Clung. "Now take your horse and ride on with me—ahead. I will give you your gun when the time comes!"

And he slipped the weapon into the holster on the side of his saddle.

Chapter 46

"Which way?" said Kirk shortly, as he obediently reined the black stallion in front.

"It makes no difference," said Clung calmly. "No matter what way you go, the end is the same."

And Kirk understood. As soon as they reached some deserted place in the ravine Clung would restore the weapon to him and they would fight it out on equal grounds. That was good. One last battle before he left the Southwest and returned to the chained life of the north. And in that battle he could wipe out the one spot against him, remove the one thing he had feared—Clung!

He cursed with a savage satisfaction and urged the stallion to a gallop; but with the first few swinging strides a change came over him; his heart grew light, his brain half dizzy. He glanced back over his shoulder to make sure that Clung was not even then growing larger in his saddle. No, he was at a little distance and still as small as before. Yet the dizziness persisted, and Kirk knew that he was afraid. If it had not been that he was galloping in front, he kept saying to himself, all would have been well, but now he seemed to be fleeing, and the very act of flight filled him with a foolish panic.

Moreover, he was beginning to think. He hated Clung for the very sufficient reason that he had once wronged him. And he dreaded Clung for many other reasons. He remembered how Clung had dropped out of that chair and had suddenly had two revolvers leveled upon him. He remembered with surpassing vividness how Marshal Clauson, famous gun-fighter though he was, had approached the disarmed Clung with caution and manifest fear, even at a time when Clung was surrounded by enemies with leveled guns. If Clauson feared, there must be some superhuman power about the fellow.

Clung! The very sound of the name was like a promise of death. It went through him like a knife. Clung!

And now the speed of the black stallion was bearing him swiftly and smoothly to his death. It suddenly came to him that he might use that speed for another purpose—escape! Certainly the grey of Clung would never be able to catch them. From that instant he bided his time. Finally, as they reached a boulder-strewn portion of the valley, he began to pick an extremely zig-zag course, twisting here and there among the monstrous rocks.

And Clung, at times, fell out of sight. The third time that happened, seeing a clear lane between the rocks ahead of him, Kirk buried his spurs in the flanks of the stallion. The startled animal sprang ahead at racing speed. Instantly behind him came the halloo of Clung, but he leaned over the saddle-bow and plied the spurs again and again. There came no following shot, but a louder rattle of hoofs behind him. He looked back and made out in the clear moonlight that Clung was losing ground at every jump. At that distance there was hardly a chance of one in ten that even as great a magician with the gun as Clung could strike him with a bullet by that uncertain light and from a racing horse.

So he spurred the black stallion again and yelled back his defiance at Clung; in the space of a few minutes the outlines of Clung were blurred to indistinctness behind him.

And it was then that he noted a change in the gait of the black. His stride began to grow less smoothly elastic. It jolted and jarred the rider. And now the big stallion tossed his head high and to one side and neighed as if to give direction to the pursuer. Kirk cursed and struck the horse between the ears with his closed fist.

In response, the stallion reared at a full halt, and came down bucking. By the time Kirk could straighten him out and start him running again, Clung was once more upon him, and now gaining. He spurred the black again and again, but still the stallion journeyed at a labored pace, coming down hard. And his ears were flattening against his neck. The spirit of an obstinate devil seemed to be in the animal. And now the distance between them grew perilously short, and shorter. The stallion was traveling at hardly more than a hard gallop. Kirk accepted the inevitable. His rage at the horse had raised his courage again, or something to take the place of courage. He pulled the willing horse to a stop and swung from the saddle; Clung was on the ground at the same instant and only a few paces away. He tossed the gun to Kirk and it flashed in the moonlight and then rattled on the rocks at his feet.

"Pick it up," said Clung, his voice shaken a bit from the wildness of that night gallop. "Pick it up, Kirk, and begin. Clung will wait!"

Clung will wait! And Kirk remembered how not long before he also had waited—waited with an absolute certainty that Charlie Morgan would miss his shots. He knew what was passing now in the mind of Clung—what fierce and subdued exultation that made him tilt his head in the old way so that Kirk could guess at his smile. And Clung was right. Kirk knew it perfectly; his hand was shaking like a leaf!

"Shoot and be damned!" said Kirk in a sudden frenzy, and he threw his arms high above his head.

The cold voice of Clung cut through him. "You murdering dog," said the voice. "You murdering cur!"

And then the revolver was tossed to the rocks from the hand of Clung.

"Your big hand against my hand, Kirk. Will you fight that way?"

"What way?" repeated Kirk, incredulous.

And then he made a cautious step nearer. Still Clung made no effort to recover his revolver. In fact, it now lay an impossible distance away.

"God!" whispered Kirk, and his fierce joy nearly choked him and cast a haze before his eyes. "God!"

And he raised his big hands and slowly clenched them; the sense of physical superiority.

"You crazy—Chink!" he said at last, and laughed, bending back his head. "You suicidal fool! Ha, ha ha!"

And in the middle of his laugh the slender man leaped into action. At his forward spring the broad-brimmed hat was blown from his head. Kirk glimpsed a lean, marvelously pallid face, and then the grip of a thin hand tore like a hot iron at his throat.

He beat the hand away and smashed at the white face. His hand lunged through empty air, and a bony fist crashed twice against his face. He turned, grappled, lifted the slender body above his head with absurd ease, and dashed it on the ground; but the body twisted, cat-like, in the air, landed on hands and feet, and recoiled like a bounding spring in the face of the big man. Once more those bony hands tore at his throat like the talons of a bird, and when Kirk, gasping, tore that murderous grip away, skin came with it.

Clung, whining softly like a fighting dog in his eagerness, leaped in again. Again Kirk struck, and again his fist missed that swerving figure. The constricting fingers were at his throat. With a yell he clubbed his huge fist and beat it down on the head of Clung.

The very weight of the blow drove the other away, staggering, but as Kirk rushed in pursuit, again the two bony fists crashed against his face with audible impacts, cutting the skin like knives.

"Charlie Morgan!" said Clung, as he slipped away and circled, ready for another leap in. "Think of Charlie Morgan, Kirk!"

"Damn you and him!" cried Kirk and rushed again with swinging arms.

The agile form, as if the wind of the blows beat it away from the path of the burly fists, ducked under the swinging arms; the grip was at his throat. And at that moment the foot of Kirk rolled on a pebble and he dropped to his knees. There, a little to the right, he saw the gleam of the revolver which Clung had thrown away the moment before. He lunged with his whole weight forwards and down and managed to lock his fingers around the barrel of the gun. No time to reverse his grip and take the weapon by the butt. For the fingers at his throat were working towards the windpipe, and once they seized it—Kirk raised the revolver and smashed it down on the head of Clung.

He flattened on his back—limply. And Kirk rose and stared at the helpless form. Then he laughed, like thunder, and the side of the steep ravine caught up the sound and rolled it back on him with inhuman force. He dropped to his knees beside the figure which lay with arms thrown out, crow-wise; he set his hands on the slender throat; how slender it was!—one grip would crush it to the neck-bone!—and he shook the prostrate form furiously. He would bring the fellow back to consciousness before he throttled him, make him look his death in the face before he went to it.

And he succeeded in bringing back Clung to life. His eyes opened and he groaned.

"Look up!" said Kirk. "Look up at your master and beg, you swine, beg for your life!"

But the fingers of Clung, as his arms lay extended, had closed around a stone—a stone which fitted comfortably into the palm of his hand—a stone with rough edges.

"How shall I beg?" he gasped, and drew in the hand, bearing the stone, to his shoulder.

"Offer money!" snarled Kirk, "or offer service all the days of your life. Offer, and see what Kirk will do!"

"Good!" said Clung, and he smote with the stone between the eyes of Kirk.

A weight of suffocating hugeness dropped upon him, almost strangled him, and blood ran hot across his face. He managed to wriggle out from beneath. Kirk lay prone upon his face, and Clung leaned over him and listened with an ear pressed against the back for a heart-beat. He caught no sound. So he straightened and stood up, wiping the blood from his face.

"It is good," whispered Clung again, "it is very good."

The black stallion, which had stood with pricking ears and head high during the combat, now approached cautiously, sniffed at the fallen figure, and then with flattened ears pawed at Kirk's body. That alone was a sufficient proof, to Clung, that the man was dead.

Clung swung into his saddle and headed north up the ravine—and never once turned his head back towards the body of Kirk nor to the right towards Kirby Creek.

Chapter 47

Yet Kirk was not dead. The blow had not fractured the skull as Clung hastily concluded, but had merely stunned the giant. He lay for some time longer, prostrate; it was a sharp blow on the shoulder which roused him to sensibility—a blow so painful that he twitched his head to one side in a daze and saw the great black stallion with forefoot raised to strike again, and ears flattened back like a demoniac. Fear brought complete sensibility back to Kirk. He rolled swiftly from beneath the impending stroke and started to his feet, but the horse was upon him with a leap, reared and struck furiously.

But the rage of defeat and the torment of the pain in his head gave Kirk the strength and agility of a madman. He leaped in and to one side, grasping at the reins and jerking them down with a force that pulled the stallion down upon all four feet. Before he could rear again and strike Kirk had planted one foot in the stirrup and was swinging into the saddle. His other foot, however, in that awkward effort to mount, was passing over the back of the animal, heel down, and the whirling rowel caught and slashed the hide of the stallion from the hip down towards the flank. The big black leaped forward, throwing Kirk off his balance. He strove frantically to regain his position, gripping with both legs, and in so doing driving the unstirruped right foot, with its spur, deeply into the flank of the horse. The stallion, snorting with pain and fear, leapt up into the air and came down stiff-legged. The jar shook Kirk completely from his seat and he floundered to the earth, falling towards his left side, and back, while the stallion, at the same instant, lunged forward at a racing speed, and the left foot of Kirk, twisting in the stirrup, was firmly jammed.

He was jerked forward and through the air, landing several yards away with a terrific crash that deprived him of his senses. The stallion, frantic with fear of the weight which flew behind it, lashed out with both heels. They landed; the man screamed. Again the stallion raced on through the rocks, and now the weight behind him dashed continually from rock to rock, crashing and rebounding. Straight up the ravine and towards the cave of the Night Hawk the stallion raced, crept through the mouth of the tunnel and into the dark recess where the silver Virgin reigned by the flicker of a dying torch. Here he drew up at last and stood still and turned his small, fine head, and stared with yellow eyes at the formless thing which still dragged behind him.

And it was at about this time that John Sampson and Winifred, sitting in tearful silence in the shanty, heard the clatter of a galloping horse stop before the house, heard steps mount the front steps, saw the door swing open, and in the lighted rectangle stood a slender man with a very white face, doubly white because of the red smear across the forehead. His eyes were fixed steadily upon the girl.

She rose, her lips parted and her eyes staring with a wide and bright fascination.

"Winifred!" called John Sampson.

The steady eyes of Clung turned upon her for a single instant and he could not speak again; the words were frozen in his throat. The girl crossed the floor, and passed through the door, and the door closed behind her. Instantly the gallop of a horse began, and rattled away over the rocks. Then life returned to John Sampson.

He rushed to the door, threw it wide, and running out into the moonlight he cried at the top of his voice: "Winifred!"

There was nothing in sight but the shadows of the rocky

walls; and all he heard was the far, departing rattle of hoofs upon rocks.

"Winifred!" he called again.

The side of the ravine gave back the word like a mocking whisper close to his ear.

Max Brand® is the best-known pen name of Frederick Faust, creator of Dr Kildare™, Destry, and many other fictional characters popular with readers and viewers worldwide. Faust wrote for a variety of audiences in many genres. His enormous output totalling approximately thirty million words or the equivalent of 530 ordinary books, covered nearly every field: crime, fantasy, historical romance, espionage, Westerns, science fiction, adventure, animal stories, love, war, and fashionable society, big business and big medicine. Eighty motion pictures have been based on his work along with many radio and television programs. For good measure he also published four volumes of poetry. Perhaps no other author has reached more people in more different ways.

Born in Seattle in 1892, orphaned early, Faust grew up in the rural San Joaquin Valley of California. At Berkeley he became a student rebel and one-man literary movement, contributing prodigiously to all campus publications. Denied a degree because of unconventional conduct, he embarked on a series of adventures culminating in New York City where, after a period of near starvation, he received simultaneous recognition as a serious poet and successful popular-prose writer. Later, he traveled widely, making his home in New York, then in Florence, and finally in Los Angeles.

Once the United States entered the Second World War, Faust abandoned his lucrative writing career and his work as a screenwriter to serve as a war correspondent with the infantry in Italy, despite his fifty-one years and a bad heart. He was killed during a night attack on a hilltop village held by the German army. New books based on magazine serials or unpublished manuscripts continue to appear. Alive and dead he has averaged a new one every four months for seventy-five years. In the U.S. alone nine publishers issue his work, plus many more in foreign countries. Yet, only recently have the full dimensions of this extraordinarily versatile and prolific writer come to be recognized and his stature as a protean literary figure in the 20th Century acknowledged. His popularity continues to grow throughout the world.